The Inca Code

Colin T. Nelson

Rumpole Press of Minneapolis, MN

Copyright @ 2017 by Colin T. Nelson

ISBN: 978-0-692-85847-9

First Edition: April 2017

Rumpole Press of Minneapolis, MN

Dedication

To my *wonderful wife, Pamela.*

Together, we'll celebrate our new chapter!

Also by Colin Nelson

Reprisal
Flashover
Fallout
The Amygdala Hijack
Up Like Thunder

Short Stories

Taste of Temptation

Acknowledgments

The writing of any book is really the result of many people contributing besides the author. In my case, the following people were of immense help: Marilyn Curtis, Reid Nelson, and Pam Nelson, who all took their time to critique the rough manuscript and give invaluable advice; the cover art design from *Divine*; and my long-time editor, Jennifer Adkins, who is so good and generous with her help.

At his best, man is the noblest of all animals; separated from law and justice, he is at his worst.

—Aristotle

The Inca Code

Chapter One

How odd to receive a paper letter in the digital age, Pete Chandler thought as he opened the envelope. There wasn't any return address. A card fell out, heavy stock with a rough texture. Handwritten in loopy letters, it read:

Leftenant—

I'm outside the wire down here and Ali Baba's off the perimeter send reinforcements!! u helped last time

— Dow

Pete's stomach twitched, and the chair he sat in hardened against his back. The card was from an old friend that Pete hadn't seen in years —Judd Crowe. Although they both worked for the US Export/Import Bank, Pete was posted in Minneapolis, and Judd had gone somewhere in South America years ago.

Leaving his cubicle office at the bank, Pete hurried to an open area. He looked out the sixth floor window. Below him the Nicollet Mall vegetable stands sprouted along the sidewalks. The sellers hid from the hot sun in the shadows of their tarps. Suffocating humidity still clung to the city—odd for this late in the summer. Customers on the street looked like hummingbirds darting from one stall to another before they hurried back to air-conditioned offices. Although Pete wore a cotton golf shirt, dampness still spread over his chest. He looked at the card. What really punched him in the gut were the words, "u helped last time."

Judd had been Pete's commanding officer in the Iraq war when they were assigned to the Army Criminal Investigation Command. More importantly, Judd had saved them from disastrous trouble—but at a steep price.

Pete thought of him: short but solid as concrete, fearless and crazy. About fifty years old by now, and probably still married to Deborah. Pete had been the best man at their wedding. If Judd needed Pete's help, it would be something serious.

He headed back to his cubicle. Tan sheetrock walls at shoulder height gave him a little privacy. Pete had worked at the bank since leaving a disastrous investigative position in Washington, DC. Next to him the other investigator for the bank, Kendra Cooper, had a similar cubicle. Through the outside wall of his office, Pete heard people moving through the skyways that linked the buildings together with air-conditioned tubes of glass and steel. His boss, Martin Graves, had shoved the offices in a deserted corner of the floor. It was like an imaginary island in a sea of open space, and Pete liked it.

Kendra stepped around the edge of the wall and rested her arm on the top. She wore yellow glasses that contrasted with her dark skin. "How's Ace Ventura, Pet Detective today?" she kidded him.

"Worried." He told her about the card.

"Crowe?" She cocked her hip to the left. "I met him once at a conference in Miami. Wicked smart, I thought."

Pete looked past her into open space. "Wonder what happened in South America?"

"Look him up. It's on the GF-OP 2000 site."

Pete leaned forward in his chair and stretched his arms. He was thin and in good shape, thanks to the tae kwon do training he practiced. "Great idea, but at my pay grade, I don't have clearance."

A smile crossed Kendra's face. "You can't do it, but maybe I can. I've got a contact at human resources in Washington. She owes me a favor."

Pete laughed. "After all, you're an investigator. I'd hate to be on the wrong side of you."

"Talk to my ex-husband. I took him down for max child support. Isn't hard if you know where to look for information—and dirt." She straightened. Her lower half had filled out, but she always said her new man liked his women full figured. Checking her iPhone, Kendra said, "Still got time. I can catch her now. Be right back." She turned and looped out of the cubicle.

In ten minutes, Kendra returned. "Here's the info on the dude." She set a tablet in front of Pete and pointed at the screen. Gold rings clustered between her knuckles, several on each finger. "I had my friend send it to my personal tablet so it would be harder to trace if anyone got nosy."

"So much for tight government security. No wonder the Chinese can get access." Pete read the data on the screen to Kendra. "He's been posted to the Ex/Im Bank office in Quito, Ecuador, for eight years. Looks like he asked for the location specifically."

"That's unusual."

"Oh?"

"Well, the Ecuador/Peru office is only a tiny market for the bank. We've placed ten times more loans in Africa and India. Lot more action there." Kendra hummed a song as she sat in the only chair that could fit into the cubicle space. "What was Judd's assignment?"

Pete continued to read. "He worked in IT. Looks like he was in charge of everything. I remember he loved cyberspace better than he liked the real space he lived in. Which makes me even more suspicious. Why would a digital guy use something as ancient as a letter?"

"Especially if he's in trouble. Why the slo-mo?"

"I remember he was desperate to get out of the Army and make some money. Big money." Pete ran his hand over his head as if to flatten his already combed hair. Black and still thick, it had receded up his forehead a few inches.

"Not going to happen at the Export/Import Bank. Thank God for our pensions." She leaned forward and pulled Judd's card from behind Pete's computer. "What's this mean?"

"I was a lieutenant, but he always called me 'Leftenant' as a joke between us. 'Ali Babas' was a term over there for the bad guys."

"And 'Dow'?"

Pete grinned for a moment. "Came from college, I guess. Judd took so many drugs that his friends called him 'Dow,' like the Dow Chemical Company." When Kendra frowned, Pete continued, "By the time I knew him, he was totally straight. After all, he got us out of, uh, a situation." He dropped the grin.

Images of South America entered Pete's mind. Mountains, people wrapped in colorful blankets instead of coats, horses and guitars. Women with red lipstick leaning over iron balconies. And the sun glittering across the dusty domes of colonial churches. What could possibly have threatened Judd there?

"Gonna go?" Kendra's voice interrupted his thoughts.

"I should."

"The bank's got some problems down there."

"Oh?"

"We're in a battle with the Chinese. The Ecuadorian and Peruvian governments are allies to the US, but lately they've hedged their bets and have actively sought Chinese financing for new projects."

"Maybe that's why Judd needs my help."

"Good luck, dude." Kendra grunted as she stood. "Not that you're asking, but if it were up to me, I'd go."

"The boss is tight with the funds."

"You could remind him you're an investigator for possible problems at the bank—even problems in South America." She left a faint whiff of her musky perfume behind her.

Pete decided to heat some water for the instant coffee he always drank. He pulled out a packet of Starbucks dried coffee and ripped it open. Drinking instant coffee was a habit he must have gotten from his father, who had drunk it all his life. Not that Pete wanted to be like him. In fact, he tried in most ways to be opposite. The relationship between them had been rocky, to say the least, until the day of the old man's death.

Even more frustrating was that Pete had vowed to be a better parent than his father, but the relationship with Pete's daughter, Karen, was also rocky. He was failing as a father just like his own parent had fallen short.

When the water boiled, Pete poured it into the cup. The water flushed black without hesitation. At least it smelled like real coffee.

Judd had never asked for Pete's help since they'd been discharged from the Army. Why now? Pete decided to talk with the director of the office, Martin Graves.

On the tenth floor, Pete said hello to Graves' secretary. Graves had sufficiently high rank in the bank to qualify for a human secretary, called an operational adjutant. Pete stepped past the oak door and into the office. Because of the air conditioning budget cuts from Washington, the office was warm and sticky.

Graves looked up and waved Pete toward the circular table in the corner. Graves had pink skin and an expanding middle. He owed his position as the director of the bank to his unique ability to memorize government procedures and negotiate the Byzantine hallways of Washington. "What's wrong?"

"It shows, huh?" Pete sat at the table and crossed his arms over his chest.

"What is it?"

Although Pete trusted Graves, he was hesitant to tell him about the cryptic message in the letter. Graves didn't like to spend money on trips outside the bank's jurisdiction. "How are the kids?"

Graves sighed. "Soccer practice started up again. Well, it never really ended. And with this heat, it's tough on the kids. Besides, you can't believe the forms. They've got more than we do."

"That's bad. Too bad you can't put gin and tonic into a Super-America coffee cup and sneak it onto the sidelines."

"Impossible. After months of games, we've become close to all the other families. They'd catch me." Graves led Pete to the table and pushed aside a half-eaten Egg McMuffin nestled among wrinkled paper on the table as if he were trying to hide it. It smelled of warm cheese. Graves shifted in the chair, and the springs squeaked. "So, why are you really here?"

Pete watched the glow of sunlight streaming through the window. Outside, it rolled in from across the plains and heated the streets like a frying pan. Without looking at his boss, he asked, "Don't you have oversight for the Latin American offices?"

"Some of them." Graves nodded. "The western regions. Now that Colombia has stabilized, it's coming on as a new market for our lending."

"How about Ecuador and Peru?"

"Yes, those are also under my jurisdiction."

"Do you know the personnel down there?"

"Oswald Lempke is the director. Good man, smart, spent some time in our office here years ago."

Pete cleared his throat. From his back pocket, he removed the card from Judd Crowe and handed it to Graves. Pete said, "I want to go down there."

5

"With your history, I can't believe you'd ever want to go overseas again."

"I know, but look at that."

Graves read it. Pete interpreted the words for him. Graves remained motionless, shoulders hunched forward. His head bobbed up. "Wait a minute. I just got an e-mail from that office two days ago. Haven't opened it yet."

Graves squeezed out of his chair and walked behind his desk. He tapped on the keyboard of his laptop. Without moving his head, he lifted his eyes over the top of the screen to look at Pete. In a scratchy voice, he said, "You better read this."

Pete hurried to Graves' desk and peered over his shoulder at the screen. Pete fell back a step, and his chest tightened.

The e-mail from the office in Quito read:

Memo: U.S. Ex/Im Bank, Quito, Ecuador, Avenida Cristobal Colon
From: Director Oswald Lempke
To: All personnel in grades E-3 and above
Message: It is with great sorrow that I inform you of the accidental death of our esteemed colleague, Judd Crowe. Judd was tasked with our IT for years and was a genius at his work. He will be missed by his wife, Deborah, and by all of his friends and colleagues here in Ecuador. More details to follow.

The room was close and hot. Pete straightened from leaning over the monitor and headed for the door. He took the space in a few steps but paused before leaving. "Get me a flight down there."

Graves called after him, "Don't forget to fill out form INT 989 before you go. It's my ass if you forget."

Chapter Two

By late afternoon, the Human Resources department at the Export/ Import Bank had tentatively booked his flight through Miami and on to Quito, Ecuador. If the last-minute connections worked out, he'd leave tomorrow. People complained about "lazy government bureaucrats," but Pete found the people at the bank to be committed and hardworking. The bank had been authorized by Congress during the Great Depression. Its mission was to lend in risky business situations in order to provide markets for American import and export opportunities.

On his way to Graves' office to check on the latest information, Pete's cell phone vibrated, and he read the text from his daughter, Karen. She would meet him at his place after dinner. His stomach tightened. He hoped it wouldn't lead to another fight. They'd made so much progress in their relationship up to now, and he wanted it to keep improving.

Pete found Graves reading his laptop. He curled his hand toward Pete to bring him closer. Graves stopped and said, "Well, the reports make his death tragic. Judd was on a tourist ride in a metal basket on steel cables over a river when he fell out of it." A smile squirreled across his mouth. "Of course, considering what I've heard about Judd's personality, I bet some exasperated tourist guide pushed him out." Graves stopped chuckling. "I'm sorry, Pete. I know he was your friend."

Pete raised his voice. "We have a history that I can't ignore. And he was a great athlete. I'm surprised he fell out of anything."

"Okay. Problem is, no one actually saw him fall. The first thing anybody knew, a body was seen far below on the river bank. And his wife, Deborah, has already shipped his remains home."

Pete stepped around Graves' desk and read a summary of information from the Quito office. The more he learned, the more he wanted to go to Ecuador. He read out loud. "No autopsy done, cremated within twenty-four hours of death, local police aren't doing any more investigation, and Deborah has already been to Judd's office to remove his personal things."

"That's fast."

"Too fast." Pete read more. "The ride was about seventy miles south of Quito."

"But no one saw him fall? Wouldn't you think he'd scream and draw attention?"

"Right. How could anyone miss that? Judd was wide as a brick." He continued to read. "Local police went down to recover the body. The body was moved to Quito immediately." Pete ran his hand backward over his hair.

"When one of my employees dies, I want some answers," Graves demanded.

"I'm going to get them," Pete said and hurried out of the office.

He rode down the elevator and stepped onto the Nicollet Mall. The sun sliced between the high-rise office buildings. The heat hit him as he came through the revolving doors. The air smelled wet, and he started across the street, closed to all traffic except buses. He felt like he was swimming through an aquarium that left a greasy coating on his skin.

As he headed for the parking lot where his car baked in the sun, he passed the old *Star Tribune* newspaper headquarters. Like so much of the media, it had changed, and now the office and printing plant crumbled before the wrecking crews.

The shell of the building still held broken floors and walls. Tangled steel rods twisted away from the wreckage. Two yellow excavators with levered necks had buckets at the end that resembled open mouths. They poked among the wreckage like two T-rex dinosaurs browsing for food. When they found something worth eating, the jaws of the buckets darted forward, clamping down on broken sheetrock and cement, and tore off a big bite. Then, with a loud crash, they coughed their load into dump trucks that shuddered with the weight of the refuse. The remains of the western wall blocked the sun and cast the work space in shadows.

Pete skirted past the site, but it left him with a sad feeling. His own life had pockets of wreckage in it. After the mother of Pete's daughter— they'd never married—had left him, he thought it was simply loneliness that shadowed him. It was, but there was more.

He'd been trying for years to improve the relationship with Karen. Things were getting better, but the gaps between them yawned open like the bucket heads on the excavators he'd just watched. Why couldn't she understand him?

He reached his car and got in to start it. He drove an old BMW convertible. Karen always kidded him that only old white guys drove those, but Pete didn't care. He loved the feel of driving with the top down.

Pete slalomed through the typical Minnesota drivers, "speeding" along at forty-five miles an hour. He headed south. After reaching Highway 62, he looped off it to cross the Mississippi River by Fort Snelling and merged onto Shepard Road, which hugged the edge of a bluff above another section of the Mississippi. The river cut a gash in the flat plains as it churned south to New Orleans until the river itself flattened out in a broad, damp delta.

After Pete had returned from Southeast Asia on a bank investigation, he had only wanted solitude and peace. He'd almost been killed there trying to rescue someone. To beat the stress, he'd bought a houseboat that was moored in the Watergate Marina on the river. For several miles, the banks of the Mississippi had been allowed to return to their natural state—much as they had probably looked hundreds of years earlier. It became his refuge and meditation.

He reached the turnoff for the marina and waited while two bikers in bright red outfits pedaled by on the bike path that, like the river, ran into St. Paul. He turned and dropped down through the green tunnel that led to the water and the marina. The Crosby Farm Regional Park surrounded him with thick stands of oak trees that made Pete feel secure and sheltered in his houseboat at the marina.

He wanted some time to prepare for Karen's visit.

Her fiancé, Tim, had worked as a sous chef in a new restaurant called Ticket to Ride. Things had gone well for him. Karen and Tim had approached Pete shortly after he had returned from Myanmar. They wanted to buy into the restaurant. Pete was hesitant but agreed to fund part of the down payment. Business continued to grow, as did his relationship with his daughter. Pete had hoped this would continue. Then the problems started. Their best chef quit, suppliers couldn't get enough organic chicken, and the cash flow dried up. Pete had a pretty good idea why

Karen wanted to meet with him tonight. The thought made his stomach rumble again.

He parked on the gravel bank above the marina, closed the top, and walked around a box of wilted marigolds at the head of the gangplank that led down to the docks. Pete could smell the fresh water as it lapped against the boats. Down here, it even felt cooler. His houseboat was halfway out in the harbor at slip F-18.

He had electric and fresh water hook-ups like an umbilical cord to keep him connected with civilization. Beyond that, when he shut the door of his boat, Pete was all alone, floating like an island on the flat water.

His houseboat was a Sumerset, and at forty-two feet, it was one of the smaller ones in the marina. Pete had sold his suburban home and bought the boat a year ago. He could stay there all year in spite of the water freezing because his boat had an aluminum hull strengthened with steel braces inside, designed to withstand the crush of ice.

Unlike older houseboats that looked like a boxy house set on a hull, his boat was designed to expose maximum open space. Each deck was positioned just ahead of the one below it, which made his boat look as if it were straining to go forward at high speed—something that was impossible for a houseboat. And it was up to date with every gadget. He had navigation equipment that would enable him to cruise the Mississippi River as far as he wanted. A microwave, hot shower, depth finders, and even WiFi were included. He could be self-sufficient for months if he wanted to do so.

He thought of Judd Crowe. They'd met in officer candidate school and became friends because they were both bored with the training. Judd always looked for angles to shortcut things—as he had with the training. Pete finished it as designed, but both of them were eventually commissioned and deployed to the Middle East. Judd didn't cut corners when it came to getting out of trouble. He focused on the problem and worked doggedly to fix it in any way possible.

The air conditioner hummed as it powered up and soon cooled and dried the interior. Pete changed into shorts and a t-shirt and put on his sandals. He opened a Summit pale ale and made himself a bacon, lettuce, and tomato sandwich—this was the time of year to get the best of Minnesota tomatoes.

He went outside and climbed up to the top deck. He settled into a sling chair and finished his beer. The sun had dropped below the tree line to the west, so shadows crawled out from the regional park and surrounded the marina. Sound carried easily across the water. Pete heard the creak of boats around him, the quiet murmur of people, and the chugging of air conditioners. Outside the shelter of the marina, the Mississippi rushed along in silent power. In contrast to the lush green of the shoreline, a white gull swooped across the marina, probably looking for food as they always did.

The year-round boat community was insular, but Pete was starting to make friends. What he liked about them was they had purposely rejected the typical lifestyle of most other people: suburban homes, expensive downtown condos, and mansions near golf courses. Like the boat people, Pete felt he didn't fit anywhere else.

He looked at his watch. Karen and Tim would arrive soon. Pete thought of Karen's mother. She'd left Pete, saying that he "brought her down." That came from a line in a popular rock tune of the times— probably as deep as she was capable of thinking. Still, she was one of many women in his life who'd left him or he'd been forced to leave. He pushed the thoughts from his mind. Not a great way to prepare for meeting Karen.

This time, he'd remain calm.

Pete looked up to see Karen's Prius turn into the marina parking lot. She parked and walked across the lot with Tim at her side. Karen led by a step and moved with a purposefulness that Pete admired. Like him, she was assertive and didn't let people push her around. Maybe that created the problems between them: they were both strong-willed people.

When she lifted her head, she waved at Pete. A breeze blew her black hair to the side, and Pete could, for an instant, recognize the Asian roots in her face. She took a skip and started down the gangplank.

When they came alongside on the dock, Pete called down from the top deck, "Welcome aboard."

"Hey, Dad." Karen wiped off her sandals on the dock and stepped over the gunwale onto the deck of the boat. Tim followed.

Pete hugged Karen and smelled fresh shampoo in her hair. He shook Tim's hand. "Want to come in or sit on the deck?"

Karen waved her hand in front of her face. "Let's go in. I've been in the kitchen all day at the restaurant. I want cold air." She followed Pete inside the cabin. He offered each of them a beer, which they accepted. They moved from the galley to the salon and sat. Pete took the wooden deck chair. Brown tinted windows kept the glare of the sun out and left them in a soft darkness.

"How was your day?" Karen asked him.

"I'm going to South America. Ecuador." He waited to see her reaction.

Her forehead wrinkled. "Leaving again? Seems like you just got back from Myanmar."

"An old friend of mine died there. I want to look into it. Besides, you know me. I'm an investigator—or a snoop, as you call me." He tried to make it funny, but the words sounded lifeless in relation to the problem that sat silently between them.

"Hey, who'll play Grand Theft Auto with me? I got GTA 6, you know," Tim said.

Although Pete always lost to Tim's younger fingers and agile brain, Pete enjoyed playing video games with him. It gave him one way to connect to Tim. "Keep the joysticks warm for me, okay?"

"Make sure you get your hair cut before you go," Karen warned.

"Huh?"

"It's too long; makes you look old." She looked out the window twice, crossed her legs, shifted in her chair, and said, "Uh, Dad. I guess we should talk about the restaurant, huh?"

A knot formed in Pete's stomach, but he forced himself to breathe slowly. "How are things going?"

Karen hesitated, then turned to Tim.

"We're still leaking cash," he said. "We've got a deadline at the end of this month. We're behind on the mortgage payments, and if we don't come up with the balance owing, we lose everything."

"I thought you cut your overhead." Pete's voice took on an edge that he didn't intend.

"Of course," Karen said. "But the costs just keep climbing."

Pete stood and took a drink from his beer to slow down his racing thoughts. Then he asked, "So how much money are we talking about?"

"Uh, fifteen thousand."

"That's a lot. Have you checked with your parents, Tim?"

He twirled one of his dreadlocks between his fingers. "Already talked to them. They've helped as much as they can."

Pete looked out the window at the docks and watched as people walked by, pushing plastic carts filled with groceries. He turned back to them. "I don't know."

"We'd pay you back," Karen said.

"I already gave you ten thousand. I don't want to—"

"I hate doing this, Dad. You know that, but we're desperate."

"I want to help, but I can't keep bailing you out. I never got any help from my father."

"Oh, drop the pity party," Karen shouted. "So your dad was a creep. You don't want to be the same, do you?"

That hit him hard, right in the chest at about heart level. He hated the thought of being like his father, of not helping, but just throwing money at the kids wouldn't help either. Pete worried the restaurant was a losing effort anyway, no matter how much money was pumped into it.

He spoke each word carefully. "No, I don't want to be like him. But I also won't rescue you every time you ask."

"But this is an emergency," Karen said.

"I know," Pete said to stall them.

"Oh." Karen raised both arms and slapped them down along her sides. "You told me what happened in Southeast Asia and how you learned that Asian people help each other, more than Americans ever do. Well, we're of Asian heritage—or are you still repressing that, too?"

"I don't want to talk about it now." A passing cruiser moved behind the stern, and Pete could hear the engines gurgle as it passed.

"You never want to talk about it," Karen said. "That's the problem. You never want to talk about anything. Let's work together to help Tim and me." When Pete didn't respond, she shouted again, "Because your problems are hurting us."

"I have to think about it." Pete squeezed between them and slid open the glass door that led to the deck. He walked to the stern and climbed up to the second deck. A hot breeze came off the river.

He was torn between the two of them: Judd and Karen. He owed both of them something. From his experience as an investigator in many places in the world, he knew there were dark holes and dangerous people out there. Probably as many in Ecuador as anywhere else. He could stay home and no one would criticize him for it. But Judd and Pete had a history. And to himself only, Pete recognized the anger he felt. Even in death, Judd had, apparently, cheated fate again.

Five minutes later, he came down and entered the salon. Karen and Tim sat in the dusky interior in silence. Pete said, "I need some time to think. Can't promise anything." He knew it was the temporary way out —leave the country to avoid having to make a decision right now. Karen would have to live with it.

She took a deep breath and stood up, almost as tall as him. "I was hoping we wouldn't fight about this. We've been getting along so much better."

"I agree." He looked her in the eyes. "But our relationship shouldn't be dictated by money."

"Of course not, but this is our life." When he didn't respond, she continued, "So, go to Ecuador. Have a safe trip. How long will you be gone?" Her voice sounded flat.

Pete ran his hand over his hair. "Just a few days, probably."

There were a few minutes of awkward silence until Tim moved toward the sliding door. He opened it and stepped through. Karen followed him, and Pete hurried behind her. She gave the door a strong shove, and it struck Pete in the forehead. It hurt like hell, and a gusher of blood erupted from his head.

"Oh, Dad. I'm so sorry," Karen wailed.

Tim rushed back into the galley and found a towel on the granite counter. He handed it to Pete, who pressed it to his forehead. Soon the towel was soaked with blood. "Let's get you to an emergency room," Tim said.

Pete nodded, as he could sense how serious the injury was. He picked up another towel from the kitchen and followed them out to the dock and their car. This was a hell of a way to end a conversation with his child.

Chapter Three

Pete waited at the Minneapolis/St. Paul International Airport for his flight to Miami and then to Quito. Above his left eye, a large bandage itched where it covered the six stitches he'd received at the emergency room. A blue bruise streaked across his forehead.

Maybe it was a good thing for him to be leaving right now. There was wreckage here in Minnesota. It would be good to take a break from Karen's request for more money.

His plan was simple: meet with the director of the Export-Import Bank in Quito, Oswald Lempke. Maybe he'd have contacts with local police who might be willing to help Pete. Judd's wife, Deborah, had already left the country. Although he knew the police or the bank had probably searched Judd's house, Pete wanted to do his own investigation.

He left Minneapolis, arrived in Miami, and left again for Quito for a flight of less than five hours. He'd learned the country was in a similar time zone, which would eliminate any jet lag and make his work easier for the short time he'd be in Ecuador.

As usual, the bank had provided Pete with extensive research about the country, which he scanned during the flights. Named Ecuador because it straddled the equator, it was about the size of Colorado but held an incredible amount of diversity. It had world-class wildlife and geography that included the Andes Mountains, some of the highest active volcanoes in the world, steamy Amazon jungles, and a long Pacific coastline of beaches and fishing villages that looked out to the fabled Galapagos Islands six hundred miles offshore. It attracted a diverse group of outdoor tourists and adventurers and, increasingly, American retirees looking for a pleasant climate and cheap living.

The country had been stable for years. Huge reserves of oil and natural gas in the Amazon drove the economy to allow the government of President Rafael Correa to pour money into infrastructure like schools, roads, and social security programs. He'd done that by defaulting on the nation's debt, renegotiating oil contracts to Ecuador's advantage, tightening the tax system on the rich, and turning to China for new loans. The government fostered new industries, anticipating the time when the oil and gas would eventually run out.

Pete's jet dropped into dense clouds that obscured the ground. The plane approached the Mariscal Sucre International Airport twenty-two miles outside of Quito. Once under the clouds, Pete could see snow-capped mountains and volcanoes—some smoking with twisting, pearl-colored plumes—ringing the valley of the city. The volcano's slopes, covered in green velvet, dropped down into hidden valleys. As the plane banked into its final descent, the sun blinked off the snow in a flash.

The city was draped over a high plateau, and it looked from above like someone had spilled a chocolate malt. Cocoa-colored fingers dripped into the valleys between the volcanoes. As he got closer, Pete could make out shapes in the tan mass: boxy houses painted in pale colors of ochre, yellow, burnt sienna, and even blue. They stacked against each other up the hillsides in higgledy-piggledy confusion.

After landing and clearing customs, Pete worked his way through the immaculate airport. The first thing that struck him was the altitude. Although he had taken acetazolamide pills to help, at 9,350 feet above sea level, Quito was the highest capital in the world, and Pete felt it. He stopped walking to catch his breath. He felt tired.

Advertising on the walls reminded him of the ancient Incan empire that had existed here. The research from the bank recounted how the Incas had spread, through war, from Peru into Ecuador in the 1400s to reach as far north as Quito. The Incas forced the indigenous people to adopt their language, Quechua, and to worship the sun. Some of their sun temples still existed in the valleys around the city.

By 1534 the Spanish conquistador Francisco Pizarro had conquered Peru, and his generals moved north to Quito. After hard fighting, the Spanish overran Quito and within fifteen years controlled most of what is modern Ecuador. They called it the Royal District of Quito. About two thousand Spaniards had subjugated about half a million indigenous people and, in the process, killed tens of thousands of the locals.

As he rode through the narrow streets of Quito in a taxi, Pete saw the continuing struggle of various religious beliefs from the past: magnificent cathedrals and monasteries squeezed next to shops offering the services of local shamans or healers who still spoke the Incan language and worshipped both the sun, *Inti*, and Mother Earth, *Pachamama*.

The healers were known as *yachacs*. They practiced an ancient combination of superstition, myths, and a belief that the volcanoes were powerful entities, associated with earthquakes, eruptions, and thunder.

The cab exited the Avenida Libertador Simón Bolívar and turned into the city. The air smelled fresh and dry, as if it were eternally spring. For the month of September, it surprised him. Pete marveled at the capital. It was the best preserved colonial city in South America.

The cab driver spoke good English and introduced himself as José, the "friendliest driver in Ecuador." He had learned the language from the American nuns who taught at his school. Pete chatted with him, asking about the sights passing by the windows.

José changed the subject as they passed an American chain hotel, the Marriott. "We like Americans here," he said. "We use American dollar as our currency, *como no?*"

"Right."

"Many years ago your oil companies rape environment, and we were mad at you. Now they are more careful, but we have new enemy."

"Who's that?" Pete leaned forward over the seat.

José turned down the pan pipe music on the radio. Serious talk was coming. "Chinese. They are taking over country. Our president and government are still corrupt."

Pete had seen corruption all over the world in his work for the bank. "What do you mean?"

"President Correa turned his back on many traditional markets. Instead, he loaded our country, like a burro, with billions of dollars in debt owed to the Chinese. It is based on future oil sales, and now Chinese are involved in many oil and mineral companies."

"I suppose you worry about oil for the future."

"*Claro*, because the supply of oil in the ground is limited, of course." José glanced in the rearview mirror and cleared his throat. "I believe Chinese *puercos* will do anything to make money."

Pete shrugged his shoulders in agreement.

José squinted into the mirror. "Are you Chinese?"

Pete's eyes jerked up to meet José's. "No, why do you ask?"

"I can tell you have Asian blood. I hope you not Chinese."

The driver annoyed him. Pete quit talking and looked out the window. "Can you just get me to where I'm going?" he snapped.

In twenty minutes, the taxi stopped in front of an old colonial building two blocks from the main plaza on the Avenida Cristóbal Colón. At one time, the building must have boasted a brilliant white marble façade, but now it looked gray, its corners crumbling. He entered through carved doors. Some signs of affluence still remained: the brass door handles gleamed in the sun, the red tile floor looked expensive, a large stone fountain in the courtyard burbled with water, and pink lilies floated in the pool. The courtyard was open to the sky, and Pete could see the sun peeking over the western edge of the roof to light up the row of curved arches that led around the second floor of offices. In the shadows behind the arches, doors remained closed.

His steps echoed against the stone walls of the hallway. Pete came to a stairway. The steps were low, and as he climbed to the second floor, he felt the effects of the altitude again. When he reached the top, he was panting.

At this level the signs of financial accomplishment were even greater: wooden floors had been polished, potted palms stood guard before every mahogany door, and beside each one a gold sign boasted of the tycoons' lairs. Pete reached a double door with a sign that read *Export/ Import Bank of the United States of America. Please ring for admittance.*

He pushed the button under the sign. When he heard a faint buzz, he opened the right-hand door, stepped inside, and knew immediately he was on American turf. A painting of a cabin on a lake surrounded by woods and a large framed photo of Manhattan hung on the walls.

An Ecuadorian woman came from the back room, heels clicking across the floor, and smiled at Pete. She extended her hand. "Welcome to the bank. Are you Pete Chandler?" Her hair was thick, shiny black, and pulled into a tight bun behind her head.

"Yes. Is Mr. Lempke in?"

"He's expecting you. Follow me. Would you like some of our excellent coffee?"

"I feel kind of light-headed."

The woman chuckled to show white teeth against her caramel-colored skin. "Of course. It takes a while to acclimatize. I suggest some *mate de coca* tea. It's made from coca leaves that are used to make cocaine—after much processing. This tea is drunk by everyone." She led him down a narrow hallway to a large office in the corner. Probably because of the high altitude, the office felt chilly and dry. In a corner fireplace flames wiggled above burning logs, but Pete couldn't feel any heat.

Chapter Four

A voice behind Pete startled him. "Chandler? Welcome to Quito."

Pete spun around to see a small man standing before him. The man wore blue running shoes, which explained how he'd been able to come across the wooden floor silently.

"Oswald Lempke," he said. He shook Pete's hand and pointed to a stuffed chair in front of a desk.

Pete lowered himself into its depths. He smelled leather, and it surrounded him like a luxurious cocoon. Lempke sat on the opposite side of the desk and crossed his legs.

"How was your trip?" Lempke asked. He wore wire-rimmed glasses with photo-gray lenses. They must have been old because the lenses hadn't completely cleared, so Pete had difficulty seeing Lempke's eyes.

"It was fine. I came because of Judd Crowe's death. He was a close friend of mine."

"Unfortunate business," Lemkpe said. "One of our best men here at the bank. A real genius with computers and tech issues."

"Did Judd work in this office?"

"No. We have a satellite office farther from the plaza. Cheaper rent, you know." Lempke spoke with a slight lisp and enunciated every word. "How's my old friend, Martin Graves?"

"He's fine." Pete wanted to get on to the questions that bothered him about Judd's death, but he found the conversation with Lempke was comforting in an odd way. "I understand you worked in Minneapolis?"

"Once, for a short time. I'm originally from the East Coast. Worked at the bank in Washington and was transferred to the Twin Cities. I loved it there."

"I've also worked all over the world in various security positions."

Lempke straightened his body in the chair. "In some ways, I miss those days. The bank's work here is much more difficult."

"Let's talk about Judd."

Lempke sat back in the chair. The receptionist came into the room carrying two cups on saucers. She set one of coffee before Lempke and a cup of *mate de coca* tea in front of Pete. He drank it quickly. It tasted bitter, similar to herbal tea, and smelled like damp grass.

"What can you tell me about his death?" Pete asked.

"I don't know much about it. Local police handled everything. Judd had gone to a town called Baños, which is famous for eco-tourism. He was alone on the ride—a metal basket that ran on cables across a deep gorge. Ecuadorians built it as a tourist attraction because it spans a deep river gorge. Somehow, Judd fell when he was over the river. It rains a lot down there and it's foggy, so things could've been slippery."

"Any witnesses?"

Lempke's head twisted back and forth once. "There was an operator who has given a statement to investigators. And the local police were more concerned about getting emergency help to Judd at the bottom. They didn't interview anyone else."

Pete frowned.

"Each town has a small police department and not much more. Many of them are corrupt and incompetent anyway. In terms of law enforcement, Ecuador is far behind what we expect in America."

"What kind of work was Judd doing for the bank?"

"As you know, we lend for risky investment opportunities that private banks wouldn't touch. Judd was in charge of all our computer data services, from loan reviews to compliance issues."

The lenses on his glasses had cleared, and Pete could see sharp blue eyes. "Why was he in Baños?"

"He'd gone on vacation with Deborah. It's a popular spot for outdoor activities. Didn't you serve with Judd in the military?"

Pete's head tilted back. "We served in the Criminal Investigation Command. Went through OTC together and got to be good friends. He loved to break the rules, and I liked that about him. But when it came to our duties, he was all business."

"I understand he saved your life."

Pete hesitated. "Uh, yes."

"I did some checking on you, and the story I heard was you two were interrogating a local warlord that you thought had been cleared of weapons. But he jumped you and put a knife to your neck until Judd pulled out his service weapon and shot the man."

The fire hissed in the corner while a log cracked in half. Pete didn't respond. If that's what Lempke believed, that was all right. There was no need for Pete to reveal any more. Instead, he pulled out the card Judd had sent him. "Does this make any sense to you? Any idea why someone would be threatening him?"

Lempke glanced at it. "No. Of course, I don't involve myself in our employees' personal lives. Judd had an unfortunate habit of offending people, if you know what I mean."

"I do."

Lempke looked away. He glanced at a crossword puzzle that rested on the arm of his chair. He must have been working on it before Pete arrived. "What are you going to do?" Lempke asked.

"I want to look at his house. Where was his body taken?"

"His house has been searched already—nothing of interest to his death was found. Deborah had his body taken to a funeral parlor here in Quito. You just missed the funeral service." Lempke shrugged. "An unfortunate accident. A good man who was steady and did his job."

"I'd also like to see the scene where he died."

"Sure. I'll get a driver from the bank to take you down to Baños." Lempke glanced at his watch and stood. "It's been a pleasure to meet you, Pete. My secretary can give you the other details." He walked away from Pete.

"Look, Lempke, you may not have the time, but the bank has sent me down here to investigate Judd's death. I'm going to do that until I resolve the case."

"Call me Oz. Like the Wizard of Oz." He smiled briefly. "Don't get upset. I know he was a friend of yours, but what's there to 'resolve'?"

"Can I get any help from local law enforcement?"

"Not very dependable."

"Don't you have contacts here that I could tap into?"

"Sorry. I run a bank. We don't get into trouble and have no need for—" his eyes dropped to the desk, "—investigators. To tell you the truth, I think you're wasting your time down here."

Pete felt pressure building in his chest.

Lempke's secretary clicked on her high heels into the room.

"Agent Silvio Castillo is waiting to see you, sir. Remember, he's here to talk about Mr. Crowe?"

Pete stopped. "Who's Agent Castillo?" He whirled around to face Lempke. "What's this about?"

"I don't know," Lempke said.

"I'll stay."

"Uh, sure." He waved at his secretary. "Show him in, Consuela."

She brought back a tall man dressed in an expensive, double-breasted suit. He was dark skinned with straight black hair, silvered along the temples. He removed a white Panama hat and placed it on the arm of the chair Pete had just vacated. Castillo's posture was military, and he gripped each man's hand. "Thank you for meeting me, Director." He spoke excellent English. "One of your employees, Mr. Judd Crowe, has come to our attention. I am investigating about some concerns we have."

Lempke responded, "Unfortunately, Mr. Crowe died a few days ago. An accident when he fell into a deep river valley."

Castillo frowned and dropped his head for a moment. Then he continued, "Yes, I'm aware of that, and it troubles me greatly."

"It also troubles us," Lempke said with a lisp. "He was a good and loyal employee of the bank. But there's nothing we can do about it now."

Castillo cleared his throat and shifted to stand on his other leg. "I work for the Secretariat for Multidimensional Security in this region. It was established in 2005 to increase our law enforcement ability across borders. Traditionally, in Latin America we have relied on local police. In today's international climate of crime, that's not adequate." He pulled out a leather notebook from inside his suit coat. On the cover was a hand-painted copy of the Mona Lisa. Castillo opened it and flattened a page.

Pete stood up. What did this have to do with Judd? he wondered. It didn't sound good. "I'm curious. What does your job include?"

Turning to Pete, Castillo said, "We handle broad defense and security issues, terrorism, drug trafficking, infrastructure protection, and cyber security."

"You must be busy," Pete said.

A brief smile creased Castillo's lips. "Tourism security also." He closed the notebook. "And who are you?"

Pete introduced himself and explained why he was there.

"You came all the way down here for an accident?"

Pete's back stiffened. "Yes I did. You might not understand the friendship I had with Mr. Crowe."

"This sounds suspicious to me." Castillo took a step forward. "Are you looking for the money also?"

"What the hell are you talking about? No. I've got my own reasons to be here, and they're none of your business."

Lempke sliced his hand down through the space between Pete and Castillo. "All right. That's enough. The last thing I need is a fight in my office between two strangers."

Castillo looked out from under his dark eyebrows. "Obviously, you don't understand why I'm here." He glanced at Pete but continued, "Mr. Crowe is at the center of our investigation."

"What do you mean?" Lempke asked. "I hardly think he was a terrorist."

"No, I don't think he was," Castillo said. "But we were contacted a year ago by your Treasury Department, specifically their Global Illicit Financial Team, in relation to a company he ran."

"A company he ran?" Lempke's face flushed red. "What the hell are you talking about?" His words tumbled out. "Mr. Crowe was the chief IT supervisor for the Export/Import Bank of the United States here in Quito."

Castillo said, "Yes, but perhaps he ran it secretly. It is called the Dow Cyber-Security Corporation." When neither Lempke nor Pete responded, Castillo continued, "It contracted with major companies to protect their computer systems."

"What?" Lempke stammered.

Pete smiled to himself when he heard the name. Same old Judd with his crazy sense of humor. "Who were his customers?"

Castillo tapped his finger on the notebook. "I do not know the extent of his business yet. It's one reason I'm here to talk with you. Development is booming across Ecuador and Peru. Perhaps he wanted to 'get in on the ground floor,' as you Americans say, in the security business."

"Well, even if he had this company, what's wrong about that?" Lempke crossed his arms over his chest.

"It's more complicated." Castillo removed a computer printout from the inside pocket of his suit coat. He walked over to Lempke's desk. "I will share this with you." Castillo unfolded the paper and smoothed it with his palm. He set the notebook with Mona Lisa's face on top of a corner to hold it down. "Look at these transactions."

Pete stood on one side of Castillo while Lempke moved to the other side. Pete read a series of entries:

Pay to account: U885673-2: 170,500 NS
Pay to account: U347884-3: 340,000 NS
Pay to account: U347884-3: 275,300 $
Pay to account: U556900-7: 850,000 NS
Pay to account U342000-6: 382,010 $
Pay to account U990069-14: 435,344 NS
Pay to account U2334335-3: 870,555 $

"What's it mean?" Lempke asked.

Castillo stood back. "These are recorded transfers of money. NS means *nuevo sols*, the Peruvian currency. With the present exchange rates, we estimate this represents millions of American dollars."

Lempke's face flushed pink. "So what the hell does this have to do with Mr. Crowe?"

"These are bank transfers representing investors' money going into his accounts for the Dow Cyber-Security Corporation. There are undoubtedly many more, but these are the initial results from our investigation."

"Still doesn't mean a damn thing." Lempke shuffled backward into the office. "I'm mad as hell that he didn't inform me, but starting a company isn't a crime. I don't see how this could possibly have anything to do with my bank."

"How were you able to get this information?" Pete asked.

"The Secretariat has broad powers of investigation." Castillo smiled. "But then, this is South America. Through my family and friends, I have additional contacts at the highest levels in my country. Unlike in your country, we are not tied by ridiculous laws of privacy. I can get whatever information I need."

Lempke turned. "So why are you here?"

"I had hoped to talk with Mr. Crowe, but since he died, I thought you may have further information about his activities."

"Well, I don't, and frankly, it's none of your business as far as the bank is concerned."

"You make him sound like a criminal," Pete said.

"Maybe this will help you understand our concerns. There is a prominent Chinese businessman here in Quito. His name is Xiong Lo."

At the mention of the name, Lempke snorted, "I know him. Shady. What do you want with him?"

Castillo lowered his voice. "In our preliminary scan of Dow Cyber-Security Corporation records, Mr. Lo came up as one of the largest investors. I don't know what is going on, but his presence makes me suspicious."

Lempke said, "Here at the bank, we wouldn't touch him with a ten-foot pole." When Castillo frowned, Lempke explained, "American idiom. We don't trust him."

"Why would Mr. Crowe deal with someone like Lo?" Castillo spoke slowly and let the words dangle in the air.

"To make money," Pete ventured. "He always wanted to get rich."

"Yes, I can understand that. But where did all the money go?" Castillo spooned out the words for Pete to follow.

"Huh?"

"Besides the deposits into Mr. Crowe's accounts I showed you, other records indicate he withdrew almost as much cash in the past two months." Castillo looked from one man to the other. "There has been a huge increase in investments from the Chinese into our economy. Much of the inflow is for illegal activities. What you call 'money laundering.'"

"Wait a minute." Pete's voice rose. "I fought with this guy in the Middle East. I'd trust him with my life." Anger threatened to overwhelm him. From bad experiences in the past, Pete tried to keep it in check. But Castillo had already charged and convicted Pete's friend. If Judd were alive, he'd already be locked up in a damp South American jail cell and probably hanging by his thumbs.

Oswald Lempke paced to the large window behind his desk, filled with small panes of glass pieced together in a lead frame. He stared outside at clouds crossing the sky.

Castillo folded the printout into a small square and replaced it inside his jacket. "I'd like the cooperation of you and the bank to help us. I assume I could receive it?"

Without saying anything, Lempke nodded his head.

Pete was so shocked that he couldn't talk for a moment. He sensed Castillo would leave soon, so Pete said, "I'm sure we'll find out Judd was completely clean." He didn't trust Castillo, but he obviously had resources and information that Pete could use. "I'll be happy to work with you."

"Good."

Pete ran his hand back over his hair. "By the way, what is it with all of you and the Chinese here? Even my cab driver hates 'em."

"You may as well learn this now," Lempke spoke up. "We're in a war with Chinese competition for investments around the world. In Africa, for instance, their export/import bank has increased lending by eight-fold in less than ten years. They're also trying to buy up everything here." He sneered, "This is the new cold war, and I plan to win it."

"So you're willing to help me investigate the case?" Pete asked Lempke again.

"There really isn't much I can do."

Castillo handed a white card to Pete. "Contact me there."

He picked up the leather notebook and cradled it against his chest. Pete commented on the cover. Castillo held it out to show Pete. "This represents civilization and all that humans have accomplished that's good and beautiful. I have all my case notes in here. If I lose this, it could mean the fall of civilization."

Pete studied him closely.

A smile cracked between Castillo's lips. "Maybe I should say that if I lose this, I'm afraid we'll lose the progress we've made in South America to combat crime. I look forward to solving this mystery." Putting on the Panama hat, Castillo tugged at the brim to settle it on his head.

"Let's be honest, Senor Castillo," Lempke said. "I'm sure your investigation will be above-board, but how are you going to deal with the corruption here?"

Castillo's face hardened, and he didn't respond for a moment. "I have my own reasons for solving this. Corruption—that is life here. But I assure you, I can handle that problem in my own way."

"Like the 'Untouchables,'" Pete said. When it was obvious Castillo didn't understand, Pete continued, "Too bad we can't talk to Judd to clear up this mess, but with the accident—"

Castillo waved his hand in front of his chest and leaned close to Pete's face. Castillo said, "Don't forget the biggest problem we face now: where did the money go, and what was he doing?"

Chapter Five

The next morning at the NH Royal Quito Hotel, Pete hurried into the dining room. Most hotels in Latin America offered a full breakfast to guests. Although he was anxious to continue his investigation, Pete was tempted by the food. Scrambled eggs, smoked trout, stuffed tamales, potatoes, pancakes for the North American guests, and bowls of fresh fruit from the Amazon crowded the long table. He drank coffee with milk.

Pete planned to search Judd's house and follow up with the funeral parlor where Judd's body had been taken. He walked through the lobby toward the floor-to-ceiling windows that looked out to the Avenida 12 de Octubre. While the concierge called a cab, Pete stepped outside. Warm sun flowed around him like water, and he looked down the street toward the main part of the city below. Orange-tiled roofs cobbled against each other for as far as Pete could see. A woman walked by wearing a pink shawl with a baby wrapped in a blanket slung over her shoulder. A wool snap-brim hat perched low over her eyes.

The driver arrived, and Pete told him the address of Judd's house on Fray Rodriguez near the University of San Francisco de Quito. It was an upscale suburb of Quito. Tires crunched over gravel as the taxi merged into the busy street. They turned right and moved onto a four-lane road with a boulevard dividing two lanes on either side. They passed a one-story colonial building with a sign that read *Embassy of Paraguay*. Under arched loggia, four baskets of dying flowers hung in the sun.

The driver reached a roundabout and curved to the right, and Pete saw a statue of Abraham Lincoln sitting in a small park of dried grass in the center of the circle. Four blocks later, he saw a statue of Winston Churchill. He asked the driver about them.

"Those are gifts to the city from the Americans and the British. We never turn down anything free here." He laughed and squirted through a break in the heavy traffic. Buses lumbered alongside the cab, belching diesel exhaust. Reaching a wide freeway called Interoceanica, the driver sped up, and Pete settled back for the ride.

When he arrived at a white stucco house, Pete got out, paid the driver, and walked up a cobblestone sidewalk to the wooden door. He knew the house was empty but still lifted an iron knocker and heard a boom echo from within. Bougainvillea cascaded over the tiled roof, splashing pink and red flowers everywhere. They almost hid a broken wrought iron lamp hanging at an odd angle next to the door.

At the office, Consuela had given Pete an old skeleton key that fit loosely into the keyhole. He turned it around twice before the lock clicked open.

He stepped into a cool entry space with a closet on the right side. A mirror hung from the opposite wall, and Pete saw his reflection. The wound on his forehead looked horrible, still blue and black.

Through the entryway, he moved into a low-ceilinged living room. French doors led to an open terrace enclosed by a waist-high wall painted white. A blue awning sheltered the area from the sun. On the terrace, Pete gazed across the valley, the city of Quito, and up the other side to see the Rucu Pichincha volcano. He took a deep breath while he looked around at the stunning scene. In the clear air it seemed like he could see for miles. Prussian blue skies were darker than any he'd seen in Minnesota. Puffy clouds hung motionless around the mountains as if the clouds had snagged on the peaks when they tried to pass by.

A Celestron Nexstar telescope tilted up at the sky in the corner of the terrace. He was surprised Deborah hadn't taken that with her; it was an expensive piece of equipment. Judd had always been an amateur astronomer, even when deployed in the Middle East. He especially liked it there because the air was clear of urban pollution—both exhaust and light.

Back in the living room, a huge vase cradling a bunch of red and white roses took up most of the surface on a table. The stems had collapsed, so the flowers hung upside down and dropped petals on the surface. When a breeze puffed off the terrace, the flowers swayed as if they were still alive. Pete smelled the decaying sweetness in the air.

He worked his way toward the rooms in the back. The master bedroom also had two French doors that opened onto a small wrought-iron balcony, more of an architectural feature than a practical place to stand.

He started methodically searching the room. In the closets, he ran his hand over and underneath the shelves. He poked at the wooden boards on the floor. Were any loose? Pete knew the house had been searched by others, but maybe he could discover something they'd missed.

He flipped the mattress off the bed, crawled underneath, and poked the bottom of the box spring for any spaces that might hold something. He removed each drawer of the chests in the room and searched in the far back recesses.

In a small room that must have been an office, Pete tapped on the edges of a desk. False panels? Knowing that many investigators were lazy, he lay on the floor and inched his way underneath the desk. He pushed at the wooden panels that rested under the drawers. One was loose. Pete lifted it and, like an insect searching for food, his fingers crawled over the inner spaces in his own blind search. Nothing but dust.

He went into the kitchen and continued to poke, prod, and open everything he could see in the room. Pulling out the refrigerator, Pete squeezed around the back and ran his hands into the cavity that held the motor. Cobwebs and dust were the only things he found.

Frustrated, he took a break and walked out onto the terrace. He sat in a tan sling chair. The leather felt warm from the sun. He removed a folded paper from his pocket. It was a copy of the local police report Lempke had given him. It stated that Judd had fallen out of a steel basket ride that carried people across a deep gorge of the Rio Verde toward a waterfall on the far side. Apparently, he was not alone. The lock on the side door was broken, allowing it to swing open unexpectedly. The police had managed to get down to the river bed, recover Judd's body, and at his wife's direction, brought him back to Quito for cremation. The name of the funeral parlor was Descansa Tranquila, and Pete noted the address.

Deborah had been shopping in the town, so she wasn't with Judd. The operator of the ride wasn't paying attention and didn't have much to tell police when he was interviewed. It sounded to Pete like the ride was in a remote area outside of the closest city, Baños.

He thought back to Judd. If there was a clue to be found here, Pete had to get into Judd's mindset. After all, he'd sent the card to Pete indicating something was dangerously wrong. The people involved in his company were an obvious line of investigation also—who was after him?

Pete texted Kendra back in Minneapolis and asked her to check on death benefits that Judd's estate would have gotten. Life insurance proceeds? Pension benefits? Who were the beneficiaries?

His eyes lifted to the mountains surrounding Quito. The city sat in a bowl, as if the volcanoes sheltered it. Even the constant smoking must have become a comforting, steady feature for the people. He looked back into the room and thought of the telescope on the terrace.

A memory of Judd popped into Pete's mind. Judd had stood on an isolated desert dune with a telescope tilted to the heavens. Stars covered the sky like a golden carpet, and Judd swept his hand up toward them. "Hey, Leftenant, know why I love this? Who knows what's hidden up there in those little dots of light? A telescope can reveal their mysteries."

Pete stood and walked onto the terrace to the telescope. It had a long white barrel with black ends. He stooped and put his eye to the lens. Half of the view was black, like it was blocked by something. He tipped the front end down, unscrewed the larger lens, and jiggled the barrel. Something metallic rattled down the tube and clinked onto the wooden floor. A key.

A small key, probably not for a door. It wasn't a car key. Wouldn't be an office key. Maybe for a desk? He picked it up and tried it on the desk in the back room. The key didn't fit. Pete's mind ran over the possibilities. He decided it might be for Judd's desk at the bank office. Or it could be for a safety deposit box in a savings bank.

In ten minutes, Pete left the house. He swung open the front door, and a breeze out of the valley blew through from the terrace. Without the warmth of the sun, it felt chilly. He walked onto the cobblestone sidewalk and tapped in a request on his phone for an Uber ride.

When the ride came, Pete asked, "Do you know where the Descansa Tranquila funeral home is?"

"Descansa Tranquila?" The driver shook his head. Then he reached to a smartphone mounted on the dashboard. He did a quick search and smiled with dirty teeth. "*Sí, sí, por supeusto.*" He drove around the corner and headed up a hill. With the exception of the original main plaza—the only flat space in the city—Quito crawled over the foothills of the surrounding mountains and volcanoes. Roads twisted around the contours like an ancient roller coaster, up and down throughout the uneven city.

They headed up a street so narrow that the taxi could barely squeeze through. People edged along the sides, and the taxi missed them by inches as it bumped over the cobblestones.

Within twenty minutes, the driver stopped in front of a one-story building. Papers blew across the sidewalk, and two dogs lay in the sun next to the door of the funeral home. A neon sign read *Descansa Tranquila*. The double wooden doors looked heavy and were both open.

Pete motioned the driver to wait, and he stepped over the broken concrete sidewalk to go inside. The interior was dark and cool. Paneling lined the walls up to waist height. He smelled lemon wood polish. At the end of the hall, an iron cross with a figure of Jesus on it hung from the ceiling, looking down on a man at a low desk. The man heard Pete and looked up from a laptop. He had shiny black hair, white skin, and drooping eyebrows that looked like collapsed tent walls over his eyes.

"*Bueno, Señor. Cómo estás?*" He stood.

When Pete asked him if he spoke English, the man nodded, and Pete said, "I understand that an American friend of mine was cremated here a few days ago."

The man blinked and continued to smile. "Who did you say you are?"

Pete explained and continued, "The deceased's name was Judd Crowe, and his wife's name is Deborah. I believe the police brought his body here after he died in an accident. The remains have already been sent back to the States."

"That is correct. I received the body." When he turned to look at the computer screen, a flash of light reflected off an ear stud, and Pete saw the tendrils of a blue tattoo disappear down his neck to hide under his collar. "It is unusual to cremate a body in my country. The police brought in the deceased, and the wife identified him, insisted on the immediate cremation, and wanted the remains shipped to the US as soon as possible." The man sighed quietly and continued to smile. "She was very determined. I think she did not like our country."

"Is there a death certificate?"

"Of course." The man didn't move. Finally he said, "I don't know who you are—"

Pete reached into his pocket and brought out Agent Castillo's card. Maybe that would intimidate the man. "Here's who I am," Pete said. "He's my partner in this investigation."

He looked at the card for a long time. "I do not know him, but I know of his agency. What would you like to see?"

"The death certificate."

The funeral director went into a back room and returned in a few minutes. "Here it is."

Pete grabbed the stiff paper from him and read it. It was written in both Spanish and English. It certified Judd's death and had some official-looking stamps on the bottom.

"Do you have a doctor's statement as to the cause of death?"

"In our country, we do not do that for every death. I am licensed to confirm a person as deceased. The police determined the man was dead. That is enough for me, and in my inspection of the body, there was no question as to his death." He passed another piece of paper to Pete. "Here is proof of the shipping invoice. At the widow's request, we sent the remains to Minneapolis in Minnesota to a funeral parlor there."

Pete made a note on his phone and planned to send another text to Kendra to check it out.

"Anything else?"

"What?"

"You know, something you remember that was unusual?" Pete fished for whatever he might find.

"Uh, I remember that his wife was very composed in spite of the fact her husband had just met a violent and unfortunate death." He paused. "But I've seen people react to grief in many different ways. When she left, Mrs. Crowe bought a large bunch of our roses. Said she loved them. When she grabbed them to carry them out, the thorns stuck her finger. Bled a little. Funny, I remember the bright red against her pale skin."

Chapter Six

Later in the afternoon, Pete found Oswald Lempke in his office and said, "I'm checking on Judd's benefits from the bank and who his beneficiaries are."

"I don't think there's much I can do to help, but you can use what you need here," Lempke offered.

"I can't believe Judd would be involved in anything like money laundering."

"Talk to Deborah?"

Pete shook his head. "She left for the States and won't respond to my phone calls."

"Umm." Lempke walked away from the flaming logs in the fireplace. He explained, "The staff always makes a fire in the morning. These people think it's so cold here, but we're at the equator. It's tropical."

"I want to go to the scene of Judd's death. I'd like to talk with the cops who recovered his body. Castillo already sent me an e-mail asking if I would go with him. I told him I would."

Lempke shook his head. "No. Don't trust anyone here. I'll send one of the bank's drivers with you. Castillo's just like all these *caudillos* down here."

"What's that mean?"

"Tough guys, macho men who forgot the world has moved on from the Spanish empire of the 1500s."

Pete wondered why Lempke was so opposed to Castillo. "Okay. I'll tell Castillo no thanks. I'd like to get going right away."

Within an hour, Pete had been back to the hotel, changed to hiking boots, and took a rain jacket with him. The Ecuadorian climate meant that it rained almost every day for short, hard bursts. He put on a baseball cap that said "Somerset Boats" on the front.

The driver picked him up in a small Ford SUV. Together they snaked their way through the morning rush hour as they drove south out of the city. The two-lane road looped below the edge of the city, and Pete looked up to see stacks of square houses that seemed as if they were piled on top of one another.

Pete asked him, "What's your name?"

"Orlando. I am educated at university and work as a currency specialist at the bank."

"Why are you driving me?"

He laughed. "Right now, the currency exchanges are very slow trading. So Mr. Lempke asked if I would drive you. I am happy to show you my country." He pointed out the window at the heavy traffic. "Poor people coming in from the mountains to find jobs. Some are bringing their kids to school. So many people want education that we must offer school in two shifts. One group in morning, another group for afternoon in order to give education to as many as possible." The traffic stopped in both lanes, and Orlando, along with others, honked his horn several times. A roll of toilet paper wedged itself between the windshield and dashboard.

In twenty minutes, they were free of the congestion and followed a new, paved road along sprawling fields of quinoa, maize, sugar cane, and tree tomatoes. A John Deere tractor churned the black soil of one field, but the next field was worked by two oxen pulling a wooden plow.

To the left, Pete saw row after row of immense mountains wreathed in white clouds. A sign along the road said *Parque Nacional Cotopaxi*. "Is that one of the volcanoes?" he asked the driver.

"*Sí*, Cotopaxi. One of the largest. Look, over there." Orlando pointed.

Immense and sprawling, the mountain rose high above the other tall mountains. Its sloped shoulders were wrapped by thick clouds like a shawl. High up, the wind blew, and as Pete studied the volcano, the clouds suddenly parted and he saw the snow cone, bright white around the edges and sloping into the middle where the cone had partially collapsed. The sight was so large and majestic that he was tempted to ask the driver to stop.

"It has been active lately," Orlando told him. "Some tremors and lots of smoke."

"Are you worried?"

He shrugged. "Our scientists monitor it. Besides, it hasn't erupted for seventy years." Orlando threaded the car through deep valleys as they passed more volcanoes. "Volcano alley, we call this route."

"Tell me about this town we're going to. Baños?"

"Beautiful city high in the middle of all these volcanoes. It has always been a weekend spot for people from Quito to go and relax. The Ministry of Tourism has made the city into an eco-tourism spot. We have mountain climbing, whitewater rafting, zip lines, and camping. My family used to come here on weekends. Back then, it took several hours because of bad roads. Now we will be there in fifty minutes."

When they turned around the flank of a mountain, the sky was gray and rain spattered onto the car. Clouds dropped lower, and Pete had a difficult time distinguishing between the clouds and the horizon. It all mixed together into a pewter glow around them. In a short time, the clouds cleared and the sun shone, brightening green fields that stepped up the sides of the volcanoes in terraced symmetry.

The traffic thickened again, and Orlando slowed. He turned down the pan-pipe music coming from the radio.

Pete had heard it at every festival and fair in the US. The music sounded like high-pitched flutes backed by rhythm and guitars. For some reason, they seemed to love Simon and Garfunkel, because Pete had heard their song "El Condor Pasa" over and over. "You guys must love this music," he said.

Orlando turned around with a grin. "It is our national heritage. It comes from Andean folk music as old as the Incas. The bands are very famous and play different sizes of flutes carved from bamboo. This new song is called 'Pachamama.' It means Mother Earth. To the Incas, the Earth and the mountains were holy. Many people in my country still feel this way." He slowed the car. "Here we are."

Pete looked out at several hostels, restaurants, hotels, and sports shops all offering exciting expeditions into the rain forests and rivers of the area. The streets were crowded with tourists, many wearing hiking boots and shorts and carrying large backpacks. A young crowd stood on a corner. Some leaned on walking sticks, while a few drank Ecuadorian beer called Club.

He saw more small, dark people from the mountains here than in Quito. Mostly women, they dressed in the brightest colors, flared skirts, and wool hats that came down to cover both ears. Almost all of them had a blanket stretched over their shoulders to carry babies, woven products, or food.

Orlando stopped and invited Pete to get out.

It smelled damp and fresh when Pete stood on the sidewalk. The sun felt hot on his shoulders. Behind him, the Tungurahua volcano loomed over the small plaza. Several waterfalls shot out of its side to plunge into dark green depths that were lost to sight.

He was anxious to get to the scene of Judd's death. "Where is the ride?"

Orlando pointed between a narrow gap in the mountains. "Down there. Not far."

"Can we get going?"

He nodded and got back into the car. They pulled from the dirt on the side and merged into the stream of cars going south. Within a short time, Orlando crossed to the left side and parked in a small gravel lot. "Here we are." A colonial Spanish-style restaurant perched on the edge of the lot overlooking a deep valley. A sign in front read *La Trucha Perdida*.

Pete stepped out and felt a cool breeze blowing up from the precipice in front of him. He took a few steps to reach the edge, and the sight took away his breath. A wide valley opened before him, and far below, a river tumbled over rocks in foaming blue-gray splashes. It was so deep the river looked tiny. On either side of the canyon, tall mountains lifted straight up, their peaks hidden in dense white clouds.

And everywhere, it was green. Pete had never seen so many shades of green. It looked like soft fur covered everything.

"Follow me," Orlando said. "Watch your step. There are no guard rails here."

As they walked in front of the restaurant, the double door opened and Agent Castillo stepped out. "Ah, you finally arrived," he called to Pete.

"I want to look at the scene of the death."

"I will help you."

38

"Of course, but I'd like to start on my own," Pete said.

"First you must have coffee with me." Castillo clipped off his words.

Pete hesitated. Maybe he shouldn't piss off this guy right away, like he so often did in similar circumstances when he resented being ordered around. "Sure." Pete and Orlando changed course and walked into the restaurant.

The interior was whitewashed adobe and had three picture windows that looked out over the deep valley. Small tables with uncomfortable-looking wooden chairs clustered at the windows. Castillo directed them to one of the tables. They all sat and ordered coffee. Orlando sat at a different table. Castillo removed his Panama hat and set it carefully on the table next to them.

"This scenery is fabulous," Pete said.

"Much of our country is impressive," Castillo said.

"Are you Ecuadorian?"

Castillo said quickly, "No. I'm old Spanish. My family traces our line back to the *conquistadors* who came here in the 1500s."

"That explains your accent. It sounded different to me."

"I am different."

"What about Judd's company? With all your financial connections, can't you trace the cash that left the Dow Company's account?"

"Normally we could, but this cash simply disappeared."

Pete heard the door creak open and someone walking over the wooden floor. When he looked up, he was surprised to see a woman standing next to the table. He took off his hat.

She carried a smartphone and wore a yellow rain poncho. Shiny black hair hung to her shoulders. "*Buenos días, Señor Castillo. No estoy sorprendido encontrarle aquí.*"

"*Igual,*" he responded. He turned back to the window. When the woman refused to be ignored, Castillo turned back and introduced her. "This is Anita Montana."

She smiled at Pete and extended her hand. In English, she said, "Nice to meet you. I'm an investigative reporter with CNN Latinoamerica. Looks like we are all working on the same story." Her skin was the color of cappuccino and smooth. Her nose looked too long, but her face was proportioned well, and her eyes opened wide and large and green, like the color of the mountainsides. She was young, about the same age as Pete's daughter.

"I'm Pete Chandler."

"He was a friend of the deceased," Castillo explained, "and is down here investigating the death for the American export bank."

Montana smiled and asked, "Did you know him well?"

Pete hesitated. Who was this aggressive woman? How much should he reveal to her?

She and Castillo spoke in Spanish for a few minutes until both of them laughed at something. It made Pete feel more comfortable about her. Besides, she was attractive, and he liked the way she laughed—from deep inside, with enthusiasm.

"There is nothing of interest here for you," Castillo told her.

"The fact you're here proves there *is* something of interest for me." She smiled but refused to back down to him.

Castillo waved his hand across the table as if to dismiss her. "*No es importa.*" He turned to Pete. "You should try our cocoa drinks. We're competing worldwide with the best of the chocolate manufacturers."

Pete gulped his coffee. "Aren't we going to look at the scene? I'd like to get moving."

"Of course, we will," Castillo said. "You have to understand how we work in Latin America. There is a procedure for everything, and we cannot ignore any steps. It has been done this way for years. We have coffee, we plan, and then we investigate."

Everyone seemed to agree with Castillo, so Pete waited.

Twenty minutes later, he stepped outside while the others finished. Montana came out and stood beside him. "What are you looking for?" she asked him.

"I'm an investigator for the bank. I want to find out what happened to my friend." Pete still wondered how much he should reveal to this stranger. "What brings CNN out here?"

Anita shifted her shoulders to keep the sun out of her eyes. "It is not often that an American executive dies on a tourist ride." She lowered her voice. "This is what makes me suspicious—if a person like Castillo is involved, that tells me there is something much more serious behind your friend's death."

"Oh?"

"I must explain something first. Although it is improving, we still have a segregated society here. The white people with Spanish heritage still control much of Ecuador and Peru." She paused. "Some would use the word *oppress*. Castillo is very powerful and connected to the highest people in government and industry. So there must be more to this death than it looks like."

Pete frowned.

She smiled as if to impart a secret. "I'm here because if I can break a big story, I could get the promotion I've wanted for a long time."

"What does that mean?"

"I could demand to go to the US. You have a growing Latin American population that CNN wants to reach. It's a much bigger market and has better career opportunities."

"Don't you like Ecuador?"

"Of course. I was educated here at the University of Quito. And I'm one quarter Indian—*mestizo*—as so many people are here. I don't wish you any pain, but—how do you Americans say it?—I smell something like fish about this case." She shifted her feet and revealed shoes worn thin at the toes.

Pete didn't want to tell her about the financial issues involved with Judd's death. "What do you mean?"

"I can't reveal my sources." She smiled quickly. "Do you mind if I ask about the cut on your forehead? I have heard things are violent in America, but—"

Pete reached up to pat the still-sore spot. "Uh, accident. I gave up on fighting years ago." He didn't want to get into the problems with Karen. Instead, Pete explained about his relationship to Judd. "This is personal for me as much as I'm doing it officially for the bank."

She looked at him closely. "I'm impressed. Not many people would do that for a friend." Anita told him that she'd already talked to the operator of the ride, alone, before Castillo arrived.

The sun filled the space around them. At this high altitude, it felt particularly warm. The door to the restaurant opened and the other men filed out. Pete asked Anita about the name on the sign.

"It means 'Lost Trout.' We've imported some of the highest quality trout from the US and grow them here in fish ponds."

"I feel a little lost myself," he said and felt good when she laughed along with him—but he still didn't trust her.

Castillo handed Pete his hat. Pete followed the group across the parking lot to a small concrete building perched on the edge of the cliff. Four steel cables sagged from the structure to cross the valley. On the far side, a second turbulent river crashed out of the mountains through huge boulders and fell straight down to mix with the Rio Verde far below. He could see a red steel basket with four people inside it. It started from the far bank as it came back to the building. All of the passengers had cell phones up to their faces, taking pictures. When the basket swayed over the cavernous valley, Pete could hear people scream.

"This is the ride he fell from," Castillo announced. He wore his Panama hat and a light raincoat. His feet crunched over the gravel as he led the group toward the operator's building.

When they arrived, Pete stepped onto a small concrete platform used by the tourists to wait for the basket. A wooden fence protected the side by the cliff. To the right, inside the structure, an operator ran the engine. Pete and Castillo stood for a minute until the basket came back into the shelter of the structure. Steel clanked as the basket locked into place. Four people stepped out onto the platform. Although it wasn't raining, they were all covered in brightly colored jackets, hoods pulled up and cinched tightly around their faces. They spoke Chinese.

After they moved away, Castillo led Pete down two steps to meet the operator. Anita squeezed into a corner.

Castillo began to question the operator. To Pete's way of investigating, this was all wrong. Too many people crowded around the man probably made him feel nervous. Pete saw the man's hand stroke a steel lever over and over even though the ride had stopped.

Castillo paused to translate for Pete. "He was on duty the day your friend fell, but he wasn't watching. He thinks Mr. Crowe was in the basket with one other man."

The metal basket rested over the platform. The side door was open. Castillo took a step down into the basket and waved Pete in behind him. It rocked gently as their weight settled inside. "Let's go," he shouted.

The operator engaged the engine. He pulled back on the steel lever. The basket lurched off the platform. In a minute, it swayed over the abyss. Pete held his breath at the immensity of the valley and its beauty. It stretched in either direction for as far as he could see. Below, a ribbon of churning water twisted between rocks. Everything else was covered in green vegetation. When they reached the far side, the basket tapped against a huge concrete stabilizer and reversed direction.

Pete looked down and saw a soft field of long grass a few feet underneath the basket. "Too bad Judd didn't fall here; he wouldn't have been hurt."

Castillo nodded. "Look at this basket," he instructed Pete. "See all these grates on the sides? And this guard rail around the edge is higher than my waist. But here's the lock on the door." Pete looked at it closely. It was a thin piece of metal that folded over the frame. If it hadn't been latched, it would've been easy for the door to swing open while over the river. Mist clouded up from the river bottom to cling to the green walls of the canyon. Pete's body tensed at the thought of falling out of the basket.

When they returned to the operator, Castillo pulled Pete to the side away from Anita. "How do we know if this is somehow connected with his security company?"

Pete stopped. "What are you saying?"

"Before you arrived, I talked with the operator alone. Your friend rode with one other man in the basket."

Pete gained a new impression of Castillo. He was better than he appeared. "The director of the bank told me Judd was alone."

"No. The operator says two men. They had gone to the far side, and the basket was on its way back. The operator wasn't paying close attention, but when he looked again, one man was missing. When the basket returned, the second man yelled that the other one had fallen. The operator ran to look over the edge of the cliff. He didn't see anyone, but he came back to the restaurant to report it." He pointed to the Lost Trout. "The second man had disappeared. People in the restaurant called the local police from Baños."

"And they went down into the river valley to retrieve the body?"

"Not exactly. When the local police arrived, some other officers had already made it down to the river. It's not easy to get there. They recovered the body and transferred it immediately to Quito." Castillo pulled his leather notebook out of his coat pocket to read his notes. "At Quito, the widow identified the body, the death certificate was attested to, and the body was cremated."

"If the local police didn't retrieve the body, where did the other cops come from?"

Castillo shrugged. "Not sure yet. I will find out."

"What about the person who was in the ride with Judd?" Pete interrupted. "Did anyone find out who it was?"

"The operator did not pay much attention to him. A tall man, white, with the hood of a rain jacket pulled around his head. In the confusion, he disappeared somehow."

"Can you get more facts from the local police?"

"Possibly. But these local people have a long history of corruption and independence that even I may not be able to break open." Castillo sighed.

"Can we talk with those officers who found the body?"

Castillo shook his head. "As I tried to explain to you, I don't know where they came from. And we cannot talk to them now, because no one can find them."

"What?"

His eyes narrowed. "They were not the local police and had already left for Quito with the body when the real local police finally arrived. No one knows who they were. Now can you understand why I am so interested in this investigation when you couple this with Mr. Crowe's missing money?"

These were not the answers Pete had anticipated finding. How much should he trust Castillo? He was part of the government, but he seemed to be fairly honest. Since Pete had few resources in this country, he might as well work with Castillo—use him for help and access to the secret places Pete might have to go.

Chapter Seven

The next morning, Orlando picked up Pete on his way to Lempke's office. This time Orlando drove a Chevrolet Spark GT, which looked like an inexpensive Prius. In a country with vast oil wealth, most people still drove small cars—in order to fit within the narrow streets. "The bank only allows me to use the official cars for short periods. Today I drove my own car." He wore a crisp white shirt and tight khaki pants.

Since Pete wasn't able to interview the local officers who had recovered Judd's body, he needed a plan.

After several blocks, Orlando spoke. "I listened to you and the agent in Baños. Do you mind if I say something?"

"Go ahead. I need any help I can get here." Although Orlando looked young, Pete sensed intelligence in the man.

"I knew Mr. Crowe—not well, but occasionally we needed the techs' help if our computers crashed. He would provide it."

Pete turned to face him. "Do you think his death may be connected to his work for the Export/Import Bank?"

Orlando shrugged. "I don't think so. He was the genius who ran software. I always thought it was more boring than dangerous."

"Are you familiar with a Chinese guy named Xiong Lo?"

"Of course. He is well known. I have followed his career with some trepidation."

"Why?"

"I believe he is not good for my country." He glanced at Pete with dark eyes.

"I want to interrogate Lo, and of course, I want to find the other man in the basket."

"Mr. Lo may not be willing to talk with you." Orlando looked at the crisscrossing traffic before them.

Pete settled back in his seat as Orlando drove uphill on Avenida 10 de Agosto with two-story colonial buildings crowding in from both sides. Wrought-iron balconies jutted out at the second level, barren of any living thing. From the street the buildings looked dull and lifeless, with few windows or signs of any habitation. But Pete knew from the few days he'd been here that the Spanish style was to turn inward. The interiors of each of these structures probably revealed open courtyards of sun and granite arches and splashing fountains and potted geraniums.

Orlando shuttled from one lane to another to avoid the slower buses and drivers. When he had a clear opening, he pressed the gas to make the engine whine. "The Ecuadorians are all shrimps." He glanced at Pete and explained, "We say that when we mean they're bad drivers."

"What can you tell me about Xiong Lo?"

"He's a well-known businessman here. Our government has been borrowing from the Chinese to finance improvements to our country. That also means many Chinese have come here. Mr. Lo, like most Chinese, wants to invest in businesses."

"What kind?"

"Natural resources, primarily. But it's not limited to that. He is mostly seen at social functions with our dignitaries. The media has covered him many times." Orlando pulled up in front of the office building where the bank had its headquarters. He inched toward the iron gate that led to a small parking area behind the office. Pete got out and flashed his ID to the guard, who nodded and opened the gate.

They climbed the wide staircase to the second floor and walked into Lempke's office. He'd been waiting. The lenses in his glasses were dark, and he waved them deeper into the office. "How was Baños, and how's Orlando treating you?"

"Great. He's very knowledgeable."

Lempke nodded. "And I trust him, unlike Castillo. You can work with him as long as you're here."

Pete didn't want to waste any time. "Can you think of anyone who may have been with Judd on that ride? Who did he hang around with?"

Lempke's eyes dropped. He thought for a moment. "Don't know. He was very private."

"Any enemies?"

"I wouldn't know of any." Lempke's eyes came up. "Of course, maybe that company he was running—"

"Can I look at the records Castillo left here?"

Lempke led Pete toward a credenza in the corner. Intertwined swords were carved into the front of the wooden panel. Lempke removed an accordion file and spread the contents across the table. Pete scraped a chair over the wooden floor. He started to read.

Orlando sat in a chair next to him. "Mind if I look?" he asked.

Pete's first impulse was to say no. But then he thought the young man might be helpful; he seemed to be willing to help. "Here." Pete shifted the file on the table.

Lempke left the office. An hour later, he returned with coffee for both of them. "What have you found?" Lempke asked.

Pete stood up and accepted the cup and saucer. The black coffee released a rich aroma. "I don't know. It's like looking at my bank statement with all the debit card transactions and automatic bill payments— except these involve hundreds of thousands of dollars. And, of course, the number of transactions made by the Chinese guy, Xiong Lo."

"If he's involved, something is wrong."

"I want to interview him. By any chance, can you help?"

Lempke looked up and smiled. "That's one thing I can do for you. I can't stand the guy, but I do have access to him. If he gets a request from the bank, I think he'll be willing to meet with you. But be careful." His lisp slurred some of the sounds.

"Of course." They moved to the leather chairs and sank into them. Pete sipped on the hot coffee.

Lempke leaned forward. "Pete, I've been thinking about this whole mess. I know how you feel about Judd Crowe, but I think you should reconsider. Maybe we should let the professionals take over."

Pete knew where the conversation was going. His reaction was to fight. "I am a professional."

"Of course you are." Lempke set his cup on the table on top of a folded crossword puzzle. "But this is a foreign country. This culture is very conservative, rigid, and closed to outsiders. I think you'll do your usual great job but not accomplish much."

"I came here to find out what happened. I plan to finish it."

Lempke shook his head from side to side. "You've got a fatal flaw."

That got Pete's attention. "What do you mean?"

"Bull-headed. An admirable trait when it's tied to persistence and there's a chance of success. Otherwise, it's a foolish way to work."

Pete felt defensive. "I can decide that. After all, I've had some experience investigating things in the past," he snarled.

Lempke's hand tapped Pete's forearm. "Take it easy. I'm just trying to help." Lempke's eyes crawled around Pete's face. "And call me Oz."

"Let's get back to my investigation. I'll interview Xiong Lo. I appreciate your suggestion to go home, Oz, but I will finish the job here."

"Okay." Lempke grunted as he pulled himself out of the deep chair. "I can make some calls."

A half hour later, Pete and Orlando left the office, hurried down the wide stairway, and walked through the open gate to the street.

Pete said, "That was quicker than I thought it would be. Apparently, Lo wants to meet with us."

"Odd."

"I don't care. This is a possible crack in the case. We have to follow up."

"His office is on Avenida Atahualpa." In the Spark, Orlando shifted into gear, the small engine whined, and he melted into the busy traffic. There was a persistent squeal from the engine—something Orlando said he needed to repair.

The stones in the buildings, some from Incan foundations, were blackened with age. Gargoyles in the shape of condors and pumas hung from the edge of roofs. Orlando wedged through the buildings until they cleared the old section of the city. They headed up to the north. "It's in the embassy neighborhood," he told Pete. Finally, they turned onto Avenida Atahualpa. Orlando slowed, and the diesel fumes from a bus chugging past hung around them.

"There it is. And right across the street is the Chinese Embassy."

"So what?"

"The Chinese are not liked here by most people. Some people accuse them of being like your, how do you say it, *mafia*? In 2012 I was part of a protest by Ecuadorian environmental groups. We occupied the embassy to stop the signing of another mining contract between Chinese companies and our government. The Chinese built the largest dam ever in our country and don't care about our environment. Their largest investments are in mining, oil, and hydropower—they are desperate for energy sources."

Pete noticed lines crease his forehead "And Mr. Lo's office is right across the street."

"How do you Americans say, 'very handy'?"

Orlando pulled around the corner to a quieter street and parked. A protective screen of trees hid the embassy behind clouds of lavender flowers. He pointed up to a high-rise office building across the street. It was about ten stories tall and had blue glass siding that shone in the sun. Instead of a square structure, every other floor had rounded corners that made it look like the glass rippled in the breeze coming down from the mountains.

The street sloped down between tall stands of eucalyptus trees, their pale trunks splotched with brown stains. When Pete commented on their beauty, Orlando said, "They are not indigenous to Ecuador. They were imported to stop erosion as late as the 1960s by your Peace Corps. The problem is, they also use too much water, to the detriment of our other plants." He looked at his cell phone. "We have a few minutes for food. Are you hungry?"

Pete nodded. The sun warmed his shoulders, and his breathing was coming more easily.

Orlando stopped in from of a small restaurant. They turned into it and sat at a low wooden table next to a stone wall made of massive granite boulders. Each one was polished smooth and fitted together in an intricate pattern.

He recommended the potato soup. "Our national specialty."

"How did you become a currency specialist?"

Orlando laughed. "Originally, I wanted to be an archeologist, and I studied it. Of course, everyone in Ecuador has a similar interest, so jobs are hard to find. Your bank offered me an internship while I was at the University of Quito. They helped train me to analyze the changes in currency values that have an effect on our lending."

The soup came and Pete smelled the thick broth, filled with vegetables and, of course, chunks of potatoes. He sipped it. It reminded him of hearty Minnesota farm food. He was surprised Orlando would be proud of something so mundane. "Does everyone eat this?"

"Yes. You must understand the way we think here. Most Ecuadorians are *mestizos*. We are a combination of the white Spaniards and the indigenous Indians. You can see it in me. I have darker skin and a big nose. We are proud of our heritage. Do you know that the most recent change in our constitution gave all the Indian groups autonomy and the right to establish their own schools, worship, and local governments?"

"Our Native Americans also have their own reservations."

"But most Americans are not descended from the native populations. Here, most of us have this in our family history and are happy to preserve it. For many people in Ecuador, the old Incan language, Quechua, is their first language, and Spanish is their second." He waved his arm over the table. "You can see the Incan influence and history all around the country. Much of our food is from old recipes."

Pete nodded.

"What about you?"

"Huh?"

"What is your family heritage?"

Pete avoided his eyes and leaned forward to eat more soup. Orlando sounded like Karen with her interest in the family heritage. "Uh, most came from Europe as immigrants."

"But you seem to have other features in your face. I would guess you have some Asian heritage."

"Well, my mother was from Viet Nam."

"Do you speak Vietnamese?"

"No." He dropped his spoon on the table. "Let's change the subject. I've got more important work to do."

Orlando sat back in the chair. "I am surprised that you do not draw from your heritage. There is much power and wisdom in the ancient traditions."

"I don't want to talk about it." He picked up the plastic-covered menu. "What else should I try?"

A few minutes of silence passed. Orlando looked at his cell phone. "We should go now."

Leaving the restaurant, they hurried to the tall office building to meet Xiong Lo. Inside the building, they reached the seventh floor and were ushered into a quiet, plain office to meet him. The air was cold and dry and smelled slightly metallic from the air conditioning.

Lo met them dressed in a plain suit. Silver hair in a drooping ponytail cupped his flat face. In spite of living in Ecuador at the equator with many sunny days, his skin was ghostly pale. He looked up from a computer screen, and his face cracked into a smile that revealed bad teeth. "Welcome to my office," he said as he came out from behind his desk. He moved slowly, in three-quarter time. "I will offer you fine tea—Chinese tea." He laughed and spoke in English. "I will never become accustomed to Ecuadorian tea." He snapped his fingers.

Someone must have heard him, because a woman darted into the office with a lacquered tray holding teacups and a pot. She set it on a low table near the window, bowed, and inched backwards out of the office.

"It is so pleasing to meet people from the American Export bank." He set a cell phone on the table next to the teapot. They all sat in low chairs.

Pete saw a second table next to him. On the top was a board game with black and white squares etched into the surface. Several polished stones, also black and white, sat inside the squares. Curious, Pete asked Lo about it.

His eyes opened for a moment. "*Weiqi*," he said. "You probably know it as the game of 'Go.' It's at least 5,500 years old and is much more complicated than chess."

"What's the object of the game?"

"To win."

Pete snorted. "Of course. But how?"

"Unlike chess, where you strive to capture the queen, in *weiqi*, we also try to capture the opponent's stones, but with less direct methods. For instance, we depend on psychological strategies, surrounding the opponent before he knows it, and indirect moves to mislead the opponent into a vulnerable position so we can crush him."

Pete thought of the Chinese business culture he'd worked with in the past and decided it would be a good idea for Westerners to become really good at "Go." He tried to start the interview, but Lo stalled as he went through a ritual of compliments and small talk. Pete waited.

Lo's phone chirped, and he answered it and barked a series of commands before hanging up. Lo looked up at them and said, "I want to discuss a topic of mutual interest."

Pete took the opening. "Judd Crowe was a close friend of mine. We know about his cyber company." He stopped to see if the information had any effect on Lo.

His expression didn't change, but his eyes moved between Pete and Orlando. Lo said, "I am curious. How may I be helpful to you?"

"You have been shown to be one of his largest investors. Can you tell us what was going on?"

A thin smile bent Lo's lips for a second, then flattened out. "I have many business interests in South America. Mr. Crowe's looked attractive to our team. Many of my businesses are at the edge of technological advances and I do not want the competition to learn our secrets, so we are discreet in everything. I cannot say much to you."

"You are a venture capitalist, right?" Pete asked.

"We do not use the word 'capitalist' in my country." He grinned. "You are accurate that my backers look for investment opportunities and then we apply our accelerators." He paused to sip from his cup of tea. "Of course, the transition from early proof points to scale is difficult. We also act as incubators for new ventures. Now, you tell me about Mr. Crowe's death. Do you know what happened?"

He leaned forward and set down the cup. His phone rang again. Lo ignored Pete and Orlando to answer it. He spoke briefly in Chinese and clicked off.

Pete said, "He was on a tourist ride south of here when he fell out." He related the actions of the local police.

"Did the police obtain evidence from any witnesses?" Lo asked.

"No. Do you have any idea who might have been riding in the basket with him?"

Lo shook his head. "Why would I have that information?"

"Did you have any contact with Mr. Crowe prior to his death?"

"I had not talked with him for five weeks before he died."

"But you were his major investor," Pete said. "You must have had more contact with him."

A touch of pink colored Lo's face. "I said, no."

"Then why are you so interested in him?"

Lo turned toward the window. Sunlight bleached his face. He arranged his suit coat. It still hung limp across his shoulders. "In our business, adjacent groups can create disruption where technology overlaps, and that can lead to digital innovation. But it requires investment of money. We transferred large sums to the Dow Cyber-Security Corporation that have disappeared. My investors are angry with me and want to know where the money has gone." He looked back at them with dark eyes. "As you can understand, any information about Mr. Crowe would be appreciated by me."

Pete didn't trust Lo, but maybe he could use him in some way. "We can share what we find."

"Of course." A thin smile whisked across Lo's mouth. "Have you found any clues on his computer, for instance?"

"No. I'm sure the bank investigated his computers," Pete said.

"I cannot emphasize enough how anxious my partners are to find answers about their investments."

"I'm sure they are."

He leaned closer to Pete. Lo's face remained motionless, but his ponytail quivered from the tension somewhere else in his body. "You were his friend. Therefore, I will focus on you. Do you like working for the United States government?"

"Uh, most of the time. Why?"

"We have resources that could pay ten times your salary if you help me."

The walls of his office seemed to contract, and the air warmed. For a brief moment, Pete thought about Karen and Tim. Extra money would be helpful to all of them. "Uh, I don't want anything. But we can work together," Pete lied.

"If you can find our money, I could pay you a substantial portion of it in American cash. No reporting to your government. I could match your salary for a year—or more."

He hesitated. "No, no thanks."

Lo leaned back, tilted his head to one side, and in a soft voice asked, "Are you of Asian descent?"

"Southeast Asia."

"Then we have a connection, you and me."

"I don't think so."

"But you are willing to share information, yes? Remember, the cash is always available. Give me your e-mail address, please."

Pete slid his business card across the table. Lo scooped it up and stood abruptly. The meeting was over.

Pete and Orlando walked out of the office building into the warmth of the high Andes sun. "He tried to flatter you," Orlando said.

"But don't you see what I did? I'll pretend to cooperate, get all his intel, give up just enough of what I know, and use it all to find Judd. The technique worked all the time in the Middle East with the warlords."

Orlando stopped talking. His eyes traveled down the length of the eucalyptus trees. "I do not think you understand what Mr. Lo is."

"I think it's pretty clear."

"To say Mr. Lo is a venture capitalist is a joke."

"He's shady, of course."

"He is a gangster—although I am certain his group invests money. Well, 'launders' money is probably more accurate."

Pete shrugged. "I can handle that."

Orlando talked slowly, as if educating Pete. "Chinese are most dangerous. They are totally organized here and can use as much money or force as necessary to get what they want."

Chapter Eight

The text came from Karen at seven in the morning—unusual, since she rarely got up that early. "dad have u made decision??? almost end of month!!"

Pete was drinking Ecuadorian coffee with cream as he perused the breakfast buffet. Yellow mango squares, watermelon, cantaloupe, persimmon fruit with its crunchy black seeds, and the papaya—curved orange slices with red shoulders.

He hadn't forgotten about her and Tim, since he had a palpable reminder on his forehead. Today the stitches were disappearing into the skin, which made it look worse than ever.

He didn't want to be a jerk like his father, who had never helped Pete, but he also didn't want to become an ATM for Karen and Tim whenever they ran into trouble. They were taking advantage of him by pushing him into the decision, and that made him mad. Pete certainly didn't want to jeopardize the progress in his relationship with Karen, but he wouldn't be blackmailed.

He decided to delay. After all, Karen had a couple weeks left. By then he should have figured out Judd's death and could get back to Minnesota.

His investigation needed some answers. A thought flitted through his mind. If someone had wanted to commit the perfect crime, this was it: no witnesses, no body for an autopsy, and no clues on Judd's computers. Pete was certain Judd wasn't a criminal, and he wanted to make certain that was accepted.

He checked his e-mails on the laptop and found one from Xiong Lo, thanking him for the "pleasure of the interview with such compelling people." Pete had to admit that Lo was smooth and could even seem friendly at times. He responded with a thanks to Lo for meeting with them—might as well keep the channel open.

Although Judd's office had been searched by people from the bank and Deborah had removed all his personal belongings, Pete decided to take a look himself. In past investigations, Pete had had an uncanny ability to find things others had missed. He felt cocky—he was really good at investigation.

He called Oswald Lempke and found him in his office early. He sounded out of breath and raised his voice. "What is it, Pete?"

"I want to search Judd's office."

"What the hell for? We've gone over it several times. I told you that."

"I know, but I'm suspicious of some things about Judd's death."

Lempke paused. "Funny you should say that. I'm getting a lot of chatter out of our office in Minnesota. Even the FBI is interested. Probably working with the Global Illicit Financial Team from Treasury. Maybe you should go back there."

"I will soon, but I insist on finishing this, especially now."

"Oh, all right," he sighed. "I'll alert the people at Judd's office to let you in. Give them a couple hours; they move slowly over there." Lempke hung up.

Pete decided to research the news media's coverage of Xiong Lo. Orlando texted him to offer a car for the day. He asked Orlando to come to the hotel. When he arrived, Pete told him to sit next to the narrow desk attached to the wall. Pete opened his laptop and started to key.

Within a few minutes, he'd found old videos from several news sources about Xiong Lo. Pete queued the film and waited. They watched several short news features. For the most part, they looked staged. An opening of a company, a group scene of people waiting to get into a new restaurant, another group of Chinese men in business suits standing before an office. In each feature, Lo was present.

Then Pete found an interview with him. A CNN reporter asked the questions. Pete recognized Lo's office as the setting.

"We know this is not Silicon Valley here." Lo spoke slowly. "But we are convinced this could be more than a two-tech ecosystem. Of course, you understand we do not want to jeopardize our investments. We demand traction numbers near the front end of the project."

"What do you mean?"

"Revenue, number of customers, earnings, for instance." An assistant hovered around Lo, handing him papers and a cell phone at times.

"The government of Peru has floated the idea of privatizing Machu Picchu. Are you interested in buying it?"

Lo's face clouded for a moment; then he smiled. "We are in business to act as a change agent for new investment opportunities. As you know, both governments are changing from the old socialist models. They are offering to privatize various public businesses. We want a sufficient return, but we are most mindful of the people and the environment of both countries. Right now, we are working with the Peruvian bank, Banco de la Nacion, to explore financing partnerships." A second assistant entered the room and whispered into Lo's ear. He looked at the camera again. "We want only to help the people."

The interviewer paused as if she didn't believe Lo. "But if you own the companies, won't the profits go out of Ecuador and Peru?"

"That is not accurate. For instance, we have made significant investments in local construction companies. Obviously, they will build things in your country." The interview ended shortly afterward.

Pete pushed back from the table. "He's a damn good liar. I've interrogated dozens of people, and Lo is one of the best. It might even be pathological since he can lie without showing it. What's that about privatizing Machu Picchu?"

"The Peruvian government has raised the possibility. It would relieve them of the heavy costs of maintaining the site while getting a share of all profits from the company that runs it." Orlando opened his hands. "Of course, there would be massive opposition to the plan from many groups."

They left the hotel with Orlando driving expertly. "Mr. Crowe worked in the satellite office on the far side of the plaza." He looked at Pete's forehead. "May I ask?" When Pete twitched his shoulder, Orlando said, "I know America has a reputation for violence—"

"An accident with a door. It's healing slowly."

Buses of different colors crowded around them, stinking of diesel fumes. Transmissions whined and drivers honked their horns. Orlando drove toward the central plaza.

"I need to walk. Can we stop and get out?" Pete asked.

"Of course, if I can find parking."

In twenty minutes, he found a small parking lot off of Juan Jose Flores Street. When they got out, Pete noticed the roll of toilet paper between the front seats.

Orlando asked, "Hungry?"

"Do you want me to eat more potato soup?"

"No," he laughed.

"I'm okay for now." In the narrow space above the buildings, Pete saw the sky had cleared to a dark blue. They had to walk single file on the sidewalk as taxis rattled over the cobblestone streets, almost scraping their arms. The tight streets opened to one of the many plazas that dotted the city. This one was small but reminded Pete of how far-sighted the Spanish had been to create these open spaces in the crowded cities.

Two-story buildings surrounded the plaza, each one painted white, blue, or yellow. Cars jammed the streets, and Pete noticed that many of them had a roll of toilet paper sitting on the dashboard.

"This is close to where my sister celebrated her *quinceañera*," Orlando said.

"What's that mean?"

"It's a celebration for girls on their fifteenth birthday. It's a combination 'coming of age' and debutante party. Much of life in Ecuador revolves around the cycle of family events. Holidays, birthdays, marriages, and other celebrations. In many ways, we are still quite conservative about most things."

"Sounds nice. I had a fractured family life when I grew up."

"As our country comes into the twenty-first century, we are losing some of that cohesion. Now people would rather go to the mall and shop."

"How about a coffee?"

"There's a shop around the corner. Come on." Orlando led him to a small store that sold groceries and had two wooden tables in the back. On the wall was a sign that read *Volcano Alert*. Below it was a yellow card.

"What's that?" Pete asked as he sat.

"It warns us about volcanic activity. They range from calm white to yellow to orange. When you see red, you run!" He laughed and ordered two coffees for them.

"I know you miss potato soup," Orlando said.

"Hey, I didn't mean to insult you."

They drank quickly and left for the car. Orlando drove through narrow streets that lifted up and over the contours of the land like riding a roller coaster. He pulled to a stop before Judd's office. Pete coughed several times—the altitude was catching up with him again.

At the entrance, Pete looked up at the old wooden door. Above it on either side, two gargoyles in the shape of pumas directed rainwater to the sides. Pete lifted a black iron knocker to let people know they were waiting outside.

In a few minutes, a woman opened the door. She smiled at Orlando, said hello, and looked at Pete's ID. She stepped back into the shadows behind the door. Straight ahead, Pete could see the glow of light from the open courtyard that contrasted with the darkness in the hall.

"You are here to see Mr. Crowe's office?" the woman said.

"Yes, please."

They followed the woman through an arch and down a short hall until she came to a door that had a brass sign next to it that read "Information Technology Services." The door creaked when they pushed through. It opened to one large office with three stainless steel desks. One other man hunched over a laptop on the far end. The woman pointed to the closest desk and said, "That was Mr. Crowe's. He also used that table next to it." She smiled and left.

Orlando called out to the solitary man, "Hey, Mateo. This is an investigator from Minnesota." He introduced Pete and said Mateo was the best geek on staff.

A thin layer of dust had already accumulated on Judd's desk. Pete paused for a moment as he considered his friend sitting at this very spot, still alive, a week ago. What was he planning? Who was he going to meet at the river ride?

"Where do you start?" Orlando asked.

"I don't know. I try to be methodical, but I go by instinct a lot of the time."

He pulled back the wooden chair and sat in it. Pete opened one drawer after another. Most were empty, as he had expected. He also twisted his hand to let his fingers search underneath the top side of the drawers. He felt only dry, cool steel.

The office was quiet except for the sound of running water from somewhere in the building.

Pete searched the remaining drawers and file folders they found, which were few since Judd had probably kept all records on his computer. The lower right-hand drawer had a copy of *People* magazine. Pete lifted it out, thumbed through it, and found nothing. There was also a book, *500 Spanish Verbs*. It, too, was empty.

He pulled open the middle drawer directly in front of him. Loose papers lay in the shallow space. He shuffled through them. Most were computer print-outs with columns of numbers. Some were in software code. Below those, he found folded paper and a thin book. Pete lifted them out, opened them, and flattened them on the desk. One was a travel guide on Peru. Another was a detailed hiking map of Machu Picchu.

"Maybe he was going to visit the ruins," Orlando said. "They get almost four thousand visitors a day."

"Could be."

"Even today, it is still difficult to reach because Peru has higher mountains that we do. It is colder, and they get more rain."

Pete looked more closely at the map and spotted some red dots. He showed them to Orlando.

"That first one marks the *Itinihautpana*, or the 'sun's hitching post.' I do not know what the other one is. It looks like it is on top of a nearby mountain."

Pete folded them up and was about to replace the objects when he decided to keep them. He stopped to think. Judd had sent him the card, he was in trouble, and he would expect Pete to help. Judd also would have prepared for that by leaving clues if Pete needed them. Where would Judd have hidden them?

When they were deployed to Afghanistan and had faced the possibility of courts martial for what they'd done, Judd had devised a secret way to communicate with each other. That's where Pete went next. He lay on his back on the floor and inched his way under the corner of Judd's desk. There was a small space of a little more than a foot between the underside bottom of the lower drawer and the floor. Although the office had been searched, it would take an unusual effort to search this thoroughly.

Pete used his cell phone to illuminate the dark recesses above his face. Cobwebs and dust covered everything—except a spot in the back corner. A small square of paper was taped underneath the drawer. If a person just ran his fingers over it, he'd miss it. But Pete saw it and pried it off the steel.

When he crawled out and was able to stand, he turned the paper over. It read *Banco Ecuador, Plaza Officina.*

Orlando said, "It's a small savings bank on the main plaza. Not far from here."

Pete thought of the key he'd found in the telescope and still kept in his pocket. A bank safety deposit box? "I have to go there as soon as possible," he told Orlando.

They yelled good-bye to Mateo, left the office, and hurried through the courtyard. A hummingbird flashed past Pete's shoulder in a blur of pure blue. Outside, they jumped into the car and headed back to the Plaza Central.

Orlando found the bank, and they walked through the front door. White marble floors led to low counters and a few tellers. A bank officer appeared from behind a door to the left. She wore a blue suit and skirt.

When Orlando explained what they were looking for, she brought them back to her office. She scanned a computer screen for several minutes, then looked up at them. "Yes. Here it is. Mr. Judd Crowe has a safety deposit box at our bank."

Orlando asked if they could see the contents.

"Are you authorized to do so?"

At Orlando's prompting, Pete produced his ID from the bank. He reminded Orlando that the woman could also call Oswald Lempke. Orlando spoke to her for a long time. Finally, she picked up her phone and called the US Export/Import Bank and asked for Lempke. She spoke English and asked many questions. When she turned back to Pete and Orlando, she frowned. "This is highly irregular. But under the circumstances, I will allow you access. I must copy all of your identification."

In ten minutes, they stood shoulder to shoulder in the bank vault. A long metal box sat on the table before them. When Pete opened it, he found a flash drive and two CDs. The labels were white with a blue logo on each that said *Red Electrica del Peru.*

"The main power company in Peru. *Red* is Spanish for network," Orlando explained. "Largest in the country, with their tentacles everywhere."

Pete looked around him as if someone else were watching. He scooped the items out of the box and buried them in his pocket. Something wasn't right about Judd's death. "Let's get the hell out of here."

Outside, Orlando gunned the car away from the curb. The engine screamed in protest. Pete's cell rang.

"Mr. Chandler," Agent Castillo said. "I tried to call earlier."

"I've been, uh, busy. What's going on?"

"There is something very important you should know." Pete could hear his voice drop lower. Castillo spoke fast, and a tingling started in Pete's belly.

"Through the Secretariat for Multidimensional Security, I received a report that the FBI in your country has begun to investigate your friend's death."

"Why?"

"Quite possibly the ongoing financial issues, but it probably has to do with the fact your friend was murdered."

"What the hell are you talking about?"

Castillo sighed as if he were at the end of his patience with Pete. "From all the evidence I've seen, I'm convinced it was not an accident."

Pete didn't want to admit it, but he'd come to the same conclusion. "Why do you—"

"What is more important to me is your involvement. I believe you have not cooperated as you promised."

"Dammit. You can't tell me what to do."

Castillo cleared his throat and said, "You are in my jurisdiction now. If you do not cooperate fully in my investigation, I have the authority to prosecute you as a hostile witness."

"That's ridiculous." His chest felt hollow.

"You must have forgotten: you are not in America anymore."

Chapter Nine

Pete wasn't surprised. Judd's death had looked suspicious from the start. Had Deborah left the country quickly because she was scared of the people who had been after Judd? In some ways, this made it easier for Pete, because now he could look for a motive that might lead back to the killer.

Still, he felt guilty. Maybe he should've come here sooner.

Orlando didn't say anything.

Pete looked at him. How absurd they were: he was lost in a foreign country with few investigative advantages, and Orlando was of little help. He told him of Castillo's threat. "Can Castillo really prosecute me?" he asked.

"I don't know. This is South America. You don't have the same protections you do in your country." Orlando squinted. "I do not trust anyone higher-up. Castillo comes from one of the wealthiest families in the country. They are politically involved at top levels, which is how he got his job at the Secretariat."

"Then he shouldn't be corrupted by money."

"It is not only money with people like him. It is power. The ability to influence an entire country in the direction they want." He waited for a few minutes. "From now on, you must be more careful than ever."

In his mind, Pete pictured Castillo. He moved like a puma: quietly, effortlessly, and powerfully. A modern-day conquistador. "I'll just ignore him."

"No. That is worse. You must pretend to cooperate with him until you have solved this."

"I should tell Oz," Pete said. He stopped before calling Lempke. Castillo would probably have informed him already. There was no need for Pete to add to the confusion at this time.

Orlando drove back to Pete's hotel. He felt lightheaded. How stupid he'd been from the beginning! He should have been more diligent and moved more quickly. There was the card from Judd, after all. He had been worried about something and needed help. Pete stood and looked up at the fluffy clouds. They were cotton white on the top but dark and heavy underneath, like they were pregnant with rain.

"Maybe the flash drive will have some clues," Orlando said. "Or the CDs."

"Huh? Yeah." He felt the chunk of plastic in his pocket. "In the meantime, I'm not telling Castillo about these."

"Probably a good idea."

Orlando arrived at the NH Royal Quito Hotel. The valet offered to park the car. They stepped up into the small lobby. Red couches stretched across the side wall behind two low tables. The smell of fresh-brewed coffee hung in the air.

"*Buenas tardes*," the receptionist called after them as they scooted into the elevator.

In his room, Pete cleared off a section of the desk, propped open his laptop from the bank, and keyed in his passwords. Orlando pulled a chair next to him. Pete slid a CD in the open tray. It contained page after page of indecipherable computer code. The second CD looked identical to the first one.

Then Pete inserted the flash drive. It opened to show only one file labeled "Orion Mystery." Pete double-clicked on it. A long series of numbers and words ran down the screen.

13.583300
72.5313900
1537
Urcuchillay rises November
Coya Raymi
Longest shadow?
Leonce Angrand
452 feet
Elevation degrade=102 feet
2,423.21 meters
Alternate theories

The notes continued, but they didn't make any sense. That was followed by pages of numbers and equations and more computer code. They stopped reading before the end. Pete decided to save the entire document on his computer in case Lempke wanted to keep the flash drive. He removed it to save with the CDs.

Pete pushed back his chair. "Okay, Judd. What the hell does all this mean?"

"Maybe I can help." Orlando squeezed between Pete and the desk to look at the screen again. "I've studied some archeology. It doesn't help, but I did recognize a few things. For instance, Orion is a constellation."

"I know that," he snapped.

"And this word, *Urcuchillay*, is a Quecha word for the constellation of the llama."

"Never heard of it. Something only seen in the southern hemisphere?"

"No. This is found in the Milky Way, but you have to understand the Incan view of the night sky. Most Europeans found constellations by connecting bright stars, like connecting the dots. Incas did that too. They also found what are called 'dark' constellations. These represented gods who existed in the *absence* of stars in the Milky Way. In the dark blotches. So, for the Llama god, the stars Alpha and Beta Centauri serve as eyes for the llama, even though there aren't any more stars to create the body."

"How do you know all this?"

"Ecuadorians are very proud of our Inca heritage. It helps to understand the Inca's religious practices in order to understand the archeology of their civilization."

"What else?"

Orlando pushed back from the computer. "Not much. The Llama rises in the sky in November and was of great importance to the Incas. They offered sacrifices during those times."

"So why the hell would Judd put that in here? I remember he was an amateur astronomer. But you say there's nothing secret about the Llama rising in November; people know that already." He shifted in his chair. "And what about the Incas? Why was he interested in them?"

"They are fascinating. When they ruled during the 1500s, they controlled over ten million people, from Colombia down to the tip of South America. It was the largest empire in the world at the time. They were formidable and feared rulers. The *Inca*, or monarch, was the sun god in human form and was so divine that everything he touched—including the clothing he wore once or the scraps from the food he ate—was ritualistically burned every year. And being a god, he was considered immortal. Who knows? Maybe these powerful rulers are still around right now."

"Here in Quito?"

Orlando grinned. "They ruled here, but the center of their empire was in the high mountain city of Cusco in Peru. The name in Quecha means 'navel of the universe,' since they believed their city was the center of creation. It was so sacred that commoners were expelled every night. The Incas built the *Koricancha* there as the Temple of the Sun. Covered entirely in gold, it was the most impressive monument in the western hemisphere at the time."

Pete interrupted, "So they were the big dogs."

"They had immense and scary power at the time." He pointed at the computer screen. "Look at these words: 'Coya Raymi.' That was a spring festival for the Incas to celebrate the planting of maize, or corn, and potatoes."

"I still don't understand what Judd saw in all this." Pete rubbed the knots in the back of his neck. Tension. He stood and walked to the opposite end of the desk. He opened and poured a bottle of water into the plastic coffee pot sitting on the desk. From a straw basket, he selected the *mate de coca* tea and dropped a dry bag into a coffee cup.

Like a film running backwards, Pete thought of his history with Judd in reverse. What the hell had he been up to? What about the cyber security company and all the money he'd siphoned out of that? That could provide a motive for someone to kill him. What if the killer had forced Judd to reveal the location of the money?

When had Pete last talked to him?

Two years ago. Judd had been back in the Twin Cities for a conference of the Export/Import Bank management. There had been dozens of people from all over the world. Pete and Judd had shared a scotch at the Oceanaire restaurant on the Nicollet Mall. Pete remembered it distinctly because the scotch had cost sixteen dollars for one shot. It had been a hot, cloudless day, and Nicollet Avenue stretched out flat all the way to the Mississippi River at the north end of the mall.

Mostly, they'd relived the history of their close calls in the Middle East wars. As with most military people, a special camaraderie clicked back into place instantly when they met. Old stories, funny things they'd shared, and even the unique military vocabulary came back to them. They didn't speak of the old secret they shared—even though it tied them together more solidly than anything else.

Judd had been excited about his work in South America and told Pete there were big changes coming to some of the countries. "A guy could make a lot of green if he knew how to do it," Judd had boasted. "The economies there aren't as transparent as in the US. But that works in a guy's favor if he can grease the skids in various ways. It's like when the Spanish conquistadors came and took all the gold from the Incas," Judd had said. "It's so easy."

"Uh-huh." He was the same old Judd: irreverent towards authority and trying to sneak in around the edges.

"It's my magic," Judd bragged. "It's just the ol' shell game, man. Fake 'em out, like we did in Afghanistan."

A thud went through Pete's chest; he didn't want to dredge up these memories.

Judd screwed up his mouth to say something important. He laughed hard, and his breath smelled of scotch. "You know what the country's motto is?"

"What?"

"Welcome to the Green Country."

At the time, Pete had ignored it, thinking it was only more of Judd's dreams of getting rich. They'd passed the subject, instead, for stories of their comrades and what they'd been doing after leaving the war zone. Now Pete could have kicked himself for not asking more questions about Judd's business activities in South America.

Pete and Orlando moved to more comfortable chairs by the window. They each sipped tea and looked outside. Two sparrows flitted onto the flagpole that protruded from the hotel over the entrance. Their heads jerked as they watched for predators. In a flash of brown flapping wings, they flew off. A crow swooped past the flagpole and caught the slower of the two.

"His murder changes everything," Pete said.

"What are you going to do?"

Pete stood and crossed to the far side of the room. His first thought was to bring the flash drive to the bank and have their computer experts analyze it. He was hesitant since Judd had obviously hidden the information, but Pete didn't have any other resources. "Do you think your geek friend, Mateo, could look at the data on the flash drive and the CDs and tell us anything?"

"It is worth the try."

That evening, Pete's cell phone pinged several times. He ignored it until it went off again with a new, more annoying set of pings. "What?" he yelled into the phone.

"Back off, Pete." Martin Graves spoke in quiet tones. "What's wrong with you?"

"Sorry. I found out about Judd, and I'm trying to figure out my next move."

"Your job is to find out who did it. Then we'll turn the case over to the FBI."

"Yeah."

"And the other reason I'm calling is to warn you—"

"What?"

"I just got an e-mail alert from IT. They report all security breaches to me immediately."

"Yeah?"

"You've been hacked, Pete. Someone's scooped all the data on your computer."

His breath caught in his chest. All of Judd's data from the flash drive was out there. Out there in front of someone else's eyes—Judd's killer? Not to mention what a setback it was for Pete.

"Better contact IT to get it dammed up right now. And when you're done, don't forget to fill out form GS 1089-23. Washington insists we keep track of all security incidents, and they're a pain in the ass to work with when we don't follow protocol."

Chapter Ten

Pete fought with Oswald Lempke the next morning in his office. Pete pushed his index finger toward Lempke with each command. "I want a report of Judd's friends here, where he hung out, and what he did with his time away from the job. And his enemies."

Lempke pulled himself out of the chair. "Now just a damn minute. My personnel are stretched thin. We've got bigger challenges in our mission here. My mission does not include chasing you around. You're on your own."

Pete stepped back. "I thought you'd help me."

"Up to a point." Lempke turned to Pete and rested a hand on his shoulder. "Frankly, the best help I can give you is a plane ticket back to Minnesota. We're in a foreign country, and you don't have any idea how dark and dangerous things can get here. There's only so much I can do. Let the professionals handle things." His voice lisped.

"You mean the corrupt professionals. Besides, I owe it to Judd to find his killer."

Lempke sighed. He shuffled behind his desk and waved his hand as if to dismiss Pete without another word.

Pete continued, "I also need help right away from your IT to figure out who hacked my computer."

Lempke's head jerked up. "Do you know what the hell you're asking for? Maybe you don't check the news, but the Chinese just hacked the US Office of Personnel Management in Washington, and 21.5 million individual computers were compromised. The Chinese claim it was crooks, not the government. Do you think Washington has time to check into a problem with your computer?" He paused. "And what's this about a flash drive?"

Pete held it up and explained where he'd found it.

"Go ahead. I'll have our experts dissect everything on it." Lempke reached for it. Pete decided to keep it and give it to Mateo himself.

Ten minutes later, Pete descended the wide stone stairway and walked outside. In a thin fog, two iron lamps, glowing yellow, flanked the doorway. Pete could smell dampness in the air. He was surprised to see Anita Montana standing near the door.

She straightened and came to him. Her hands were buried in her pockets. A soft alpaca sweater was draped over her shoulders. She cocked her head to the side but didn't talk.

"Hey, what are you doing here?"

"What else? Following my story."

"Here?"

"Judd Crowe worked for your bank. Why wouldn't I be here? Come on, walk with me."

She linked her arm into his, and they walked up the cobblestone street. The sound of their feet echoed off the close walls. Within a few blocks they'd come to the main plaza of Quito. It was surrounded by the cathedral on one side, the presidential palace on another, and the government offices on the third side.

They walked past a palm tree and sat at one of the green-slatted benches. Mist enveloped them, and the white columns of the presidential palace looked like bones in the light. Neither spoke for a while.

"As you Americans say, I'm wracking my brain trying to figure out what to do next," Anita said. "I thought you might be able to help me."

What was she really after? Pete wondered. "I'm at a dead end. All the usual things I could do in the States, I can't do here."

"If we could trace where Judd planned to go—that could lead to the money and the murderer."

"How the hell do you know about the murder?" He jerked to face her.

Anita grinned. "I'm a reporter. I know lots of things. That's why we should share information."

Pete hesitated. "I don't know you."

"I could help you."

"Maybe."

"You don't sound too optimistic."

"I'm not. I got here too late to save my friend, and now I can't even find his killer."

Anita sighed and slid forward on the bench. She crossed her feet at the ankles. Her pants hugged her legs.

Pete looked at her. In the misty light her features softened. But her eyes were still bright, and there was a tinge of pink at the end of her nose. She took a deep breath, and he watched her breasts push against her blouse. "What are you going to do?" he asked.

A dozen doves strutted past them, gathered, and lifted off the ground to circle into the air. They surrounded the flapping Ecuadorian flag that flew over the presidential palace in the bright colors of corn yellow, blue, and blood.

"Right now, I think the best is to follow Castillo's moves. I've been shadowing him all over. Where he goes, I go. I'm confident he'll lead me to the money—and the story."

That made sense to Pete. He studied her closely. She reminded him of Karen. The same assertive confidence, but he also saw the worn shine on the elbows of Anita's blazer. He sensed her ambition. Anita acted successful beyond what she'd probably accomplished.

"So maybe we can help each other," she said.

"I work alone."

She lifted her face toward him and smiled with ruby lips. "We don't have to trust each other, just share some info."

"We don't want the same thing."

Anita shrugged. "I know my way around down here. Do you?"

She had a point. It wouldn't hurt to share some clues.

"Okay." They exchanged e-mail addresses and phone numbers. "But don't crowd me."

"I have to go," Anita said. She stood.

Pete walked her across the plaza to stand underneath the presidential palace. A small plaque memorialized where an Ecuadorian president had died from stab wounds in the 1800s. Anita flagged a taxi and climbed into the back seat of an old Volkswagen beetle. With a squeal on the damp pavement, it drove off.

Pete took a taxi back to his hotel. Fresh coffee was served in the lobby, and he filled a cup. He had gotten used to the South American way of drinking coffee—lots of cream and even more sugar. He had texted Orlando to ask for his help again.

In his room, Pete pulled back the chair and booted up his laptop. He was surprised when he saw the home office had e-mailed him about his computer, after all. The tech person warned him: *Pete, think of this like you've got a house and everyday people walk by and rattle your locked front door, trying to get in. With a computer, hundreds of hackers are constantly rattling the door and trying to get in. This time they did. Here's how to fix it.*

Pete opened a link to sites that would scrub his computer and add more protection for the future. He downloaded the material and waited for it to finish. He e-mailed the tech on his smartphone and asked him: "Any idea who hacked my computer?"

The tech responded, "No, because it's someone really good."

"It was probably my daughter trying to get access to my bank account." That problem rumbled through his mind. He'd have to deal with it soon.

His computer cleared, and he turned back to it. "Here we go." Pete opened Judd's file.

The possibility that the information was in the possession of someone else bothered him. Would they be able to decipher it more quickly than he could? Beat him in the hunt for the money and the killer?

At the knock on the door, Pete opened it to let Orlando in. When Orlando was seated, Pete scrolled down through the file slowly. He read:

3 weeks left
Peru Ministry of Culture—Javier Prado Este 2465 Lima
comunicaciones@mcultura.gob.pe
perurail 10:30 am
winter solstice
245+39.01 west
https://github.com/federicomarulli/CosmoBolognaLib
9/22 @ 7/21

Pete's coffee had gone cold, and he set the cup on the desk. "Any ideas? He keeps referencing Peru."

"Remember the map you found in his desk? Machu Picchu is in Peru. Could it have something to do with his death? It is the most popular tourist spot in South America," Orlando offered.

"This is more than Judd wanting to be a tourist."

"Open that second web site." Orlando pointed to the entry in the file.

Pete clicked on it and found the Library for Cosmological Calculations. "What the hell?"

He read on the screen:

We present the CosmoBolognaLib, a large set of Open Source C++ numerical libraries for cosmological calculations. CosmoBolognaLib is a living project aimed at defining a common numerical environment for cosmological investigations of the large-scale structure of the Universe.

"What was he doing?" Orlando asked.

"I still don't understand how this could have anything to do with his death."

"And don't forget the entry for winter solstice."

"Why?"

"The Incas were masters at reading the sky and kept exact measurements of the winter and summer solstice. They were the most important days of celebration and sacrifices. They built carefully placed pillars and temples on various mountains to mark both the equinox and solstice." He pushed back his chair. "For instance, Cusco was built on a radial plan that mimicked the sky and pointed to specific astronomical events on the horizon."

"But what for?"

"Archeologists don't know for sure. The easy answer was to mark the seasons for planting and harvesting. But they probably also had deeper and more sinister meanings. Worship of powerful gods that dwelled in the skies, in thunder, and in the volcanoes. Gods that needed to be appeased through animal and human sacrifices at these astrologically critical times."

"Okay, enough of the ancient voodoo. What about Judd Crowe? What the hell was he doing measuring the winter solstice with this numerical library?"

"You said he had an interest in astronomy."

"Right, but why would Judd hide this information unless it was something more than a hobby? After all, it might have caused his death."

Orlando's forehead wrinkled. He didn't respond.

After a while, Pete said, "Whatever, I should go to Machu Picchu."

"I was thinking the same thing." Orlando stood next to him. "It's not going to be easy. The mountains are higher, the rain is heavier, and even though it is a tourist attraction, Machu Picchu is still difficult to reach."

"I have to go. All the clues point to something there."

Orlando nodded and turned toward the computer screen. "You better leave as soon as possible."

"Why?"

"See the 'three weeks left' entry? Judd's death occurred almost two weeks ago now. Can we assume he prepared this data right before that time?"

"And that this entry—'9/22 @ 7/21'—is possibly a date?" Pete added.

"It's still a guess, but today is September fifteenth. What's going to happen on Thursday, September twenty-second, seven days from now?"

Chapter Eleven

September 15, Thursday

Pete turned back to the desk and immediately looked at plane schedules for the trip to Lima and then to Cusco, the gateway to Machu Picchu. There were three seats available for the next day.

Orlando asked him, "What will you do when you get there?"

"I'm not sure. But I've hit a dead-end here, and everything on the flash drive points toward Machu Picchu." He booked a plane ticket. He thought of Oswald Lempke. Pete called the Ex/Im Bank office and caught him as he was leaving for a meeting. Pete explained what he had found on the CD and his plan to go to Lima.

Lempke listened without saying anything. After a few minutes, he added, "We've got a branch office there, not far from the American Embassy in Miraflores."

"Thanks," Pete said.

There was a long silence on the phone. Lempke finally spoke. "What the hell are you going to do once you get there?"

"Not sure. But something about Machu Picchu had Judd's full attention."

"Pete, I know this is personal for you. I admire your loyalty to Judd and his memory, but there isn't a damn thing you can do anymore. Here's what I suggest. Deborah is having a memorial service for Judd back in Minneapolis in a few days. You should go back for that. It's at Lakewood Cemetery, where she has permanently placed Judd's remains in an urn."

"I'm not leaving until I finish here."

"Besides that, there's something unusual going on back there."

"What do you mean?"

"The FBI keeps calling me about Judd."

"You think they've found the missing funds?"

"No. You could be a hell of a lot more helpful investigating there."

"Maybe."

"You're tenacious, I know that. I want to solve his murder as much as you do. But there are players involved who are bigger than we are. Castillo, for instance, has got powerful connections, and he's determined to find the money—no matter who gets in his way. I can't protect you from him." He hung up.

Pete looked out the window of his hotel room. Should he take advice for once in his life? Even if Pete found the killer, what would he do then? Hand the case over to Castillo or someone else?

He remembered the time in high school when he'd started tae kwon do, the Korean martial art, because he was too light for football. He'd become discouraged and quit. His father blew up in anger, calling Pete a quitter. He'd gone back to class, graduated, kept practicing, and was considered an expert now—it was a lesson in not giving up.

He thought of Anita. He didn't like her and thought her self-promotion was amateurish. Pete sensed Anita was scrambling and improvising as she went—something he'd become good at himself. Maybe they could get along.

"We've got some time," Orlando said. "We could drop off the flash drive and the CDs with Mateo."

Pete agreed.

They drove to the IT office again. Mateo met them at his office in the back of the building. He offered two metal chairs.

"Hey, Orlando. What magic can I do for you this time?"

"Pete's got a flash drive and two CDs he'd like you to search." He handed them to him.

"What are you looking for?" Behind Mateo a poster of Friedrich Nietzsche hung from the ceiling to the floor. Across the bottom was a quote: *When you look into the abyss, the abyss also looks into you.*

Pete said, "I'm not sure. There's a lot of strange data on it, but at least most of it's in English. There are also entries in code. Can you tell me what those mean?"

Mateo turned to one of three computer screens spread over his desk. His fingers darted over the keyboard. His face tightened. "This is going to be tough. Right now I have extra assignments on my schedule."

"It's important to get anything off there right away. We think something critical is going to happen in a week," Pete said.

"Ok. But the new story out of Peru is a real time suck."

"What's that?"

"The government of Peru has suggested that Machu Picchu may be for sale to a private developer."

"You think they're serious?"

Mateo shook his head. "At this point, it's only a proposal. They're probably just 'holding a carrot out to the llama.' But if there's any possibility of lending in the equation, the bank could get involved. I'm trying to stay on top of the data."

"But could a sale really happen?" Pete asked.

"The government is so corrupt that if the price was right, they might actually sell it to developers. Maybe Disney, for instance." Mateo laughed.

"McPicchu?" Orlando suggested.

Mateo shrugged. "A buyer could make a fortune. Peru makes a lot of money now."

"But wouldn't it take a fortune to buy it?" Pete said.

"Not as much as you think. Our reports indicate the government would help finance it. The buyer would only need the down payment." He slid back his chair. "This is my life for the next few weeks."

"Whoever can pay the biggest bribes will get it," Orlando said.

"There's a lot of potential stuff all over this for us. That's why the maxed-out effort."

Orlando stood and said, "Pete's investigating Judd's death. Your friend. This could go a long way to figuring that out."

Mateo nodded. "All right. I'll do what I can when I have a minute."

Orlando smiled. "Thanks, Mateo. That's why you're the greatest."

"I know I am."

Later in the afternoon, Pete received a text from someone named Rodney. He responded by calling back.

"I worked with Judd Crowe at the bank," Rodney said. "I have something to tell you about him."

"I don't remember you from all the reports and interviews I've read."

"I reported directly to the Wizard of Oz. After Judd's death, I met with Lempke. He told me to keep my information confidential."

"Why?"

"He said Judd was working on something very sensitive for the bank and he didn't want it leaked to the public. He's obsessed with beating the Chinese."

"I know. How'd you find me?"

"I've seen you around the offices and heard you were down from the States to investigate Judd's death. I miss him and would like to see some justice done. I hoped you might help."

"What do you want to tell me?"

"Not over the phone. I want to meet in private."

"I'm leaving for Peru tomorrow."

"We can meet today. There is a place north of Quito that is quiet. Meet me in one hour. It'll be packed with tourists, so we should be insulated from trouble."

Orlando drove the Chevrolet Spark GT along a twisting two-lane road north out of Quito. Before them rose Cotacachi volcano sprawling across the horizon. They passed through a newer suburb with small western-style shopping centers and car dealerships. Billboards offered American expatriates luxury housing in gated communities, with free dishwashers and air conditioners thrown into the purchase.

The road widened, and Orlando made a left turn at a grove of palm trees. A sign arched over the entrance that read *El Mitad del Mundo*. "Middle of the world," he translated. "In the late 1700s a group of French scientists came here to map the exact position of the equator. See that tower ahead? That was supposed to be the location." He crunched over gravel and came to a stop at the entrance. A guard stood by a turnstile, collecting tickets.

Pete walked to the entrance. He saw the squatty stone tower with a stone globe balancing on the top. After paying, they walked up a straight path toward the tower. "The French actually got it wrong. It wasn't until a few years ago when the government used GPS to determine the true equator that they found this location was off by about 250 feet. Never-theless, they created this monument to the French efforts because they only used the stars."

They would meet Rodney at one of the statues of the French scientists, Pierre Bouguer. Orlando led Pete past several artistic models of Ecuadorian birds with wing spans stretching five feet across. Their eyes seemed to follow Pete as he went past them. They stopped at the Pierre Bouguer statue and waited.

Clots of tourists milled around them. A few feet away, a long painted line on the ground represented the true equator—although it wasn't. People stood with a foot planted on either side of the line while they lifted smartphones to take selfies—lots of selfies.

Orlando and Pete waited for ten minutes. "He sounded anxious to meet us," Pete said.

"I don't know him. I think he worked in the compliance department. Judd would've had some interface with them."

"He said he'd find us."

A lone man wrapped in a gray windbreaker strode up to them. His head swiveled to take in the theme park until he reached the statue. He stopped next to them. "I'm Rodney," he said and stood at an angle, still looking out at the crowds. Pete wondered why all the cloak-and-dagger.

"We should be okay here," Rodney said. He had unusually large ears and blond hair that stuck out at angles like a child had pasted it on his head. Yellow stains circled the inner edge of his collar. "You still trying to solve his death?"

"Yes. What did you want to tell us?" Pete asked.

Rodney's eyes darted from the left to the right. "You should check into this. Judd was working on something with Red Electrica del Peru."

"Oh?" Pete remembered the labels on the CDs.

"One of the largest electric producers. Maybe he got a contract with the company in Peru. I don't know for sure. Judd was so good with computers, maybe he was, like, working on the electric company's systems. He didn't let anyone else know shit about it. I told Oz during my meeting with him, so now he knows. But nobody else."

"Why did Judd tell you?"

Rodney frowned. "He didn't really tell me much. But I think he was proud of it. Wanted to brag to someone. We met occasionally in preparation for the compliance auditors."

"So what does this mean?"

Rodney looked at Pete and held his eyes for a moment before Rodney's gaze flicked away. "I could tell by his excitement that Judd was into something huge. It had the color of money all over it."

"You think he provided security for their IT systems?"

"Don't know. But here's the strange thing: Judd always laughed about it."

"What was funny?"

"Nothing. That's the weird part. He laughed and said it was like the 'Spanish takin' gold from the Incas. So easy.'"

"Do you know what he meant?" Pete said.

Rodney shrugged.

"Do you know which part of the company he worked with?"

"He never said."

Pete straightened and looked out across the park. The sun dipped in the west, and the tower cast a square shadow over the tourists. "Okay. Thanks, Rodney. We've got to go."

With a pale hand, Rodney grabbed Pete's forearm. "Wait. I got more. See, just before Judd disappeared, something changed. He got really quiet at work and didn't laugh about anything. I'd never seen this side of him."

"What do you think happened?"

Rodney's head bobbed down and came up quickly. "I think he was scared shitless."

"Of what?" Pete asked.

"Don't know. He kept mumblin' about how the 'time was finally coming,' like he was waiting for the apocalypse or some shit." Rodney spun around and then moved away from them.

Pete thought of the card he'd received from Judd. He must have had some idea of his killer. He and Orlando waited until Rodney was out of sight and then hurried to the car. Orlando ground the gears as he gained speed on the road

"I don't believe one word," Pete said. "Except for the electric company. How am I going to get access to the Red Electrica del Peru?"

"The bank?"

"Lempke's not been very helpful."

Orlando downshifted to take a corner a high speed. "I have an idea. I know this will be— how do Americans say it?— a 'deal with the devil.' But you should approach Agent Castillo."

"Hell, no," Pete shouted.

"Just listen. You tempt him with some of the information Rodney gave us. He becomes interested and, in return, gets you into the electric company."

"Might work. He knows I was Judd's friend. If Castillo suspects I know more than I really do, I could string him along with that."

"Right."

"How do you know he can really get me into the company?"

Orlando looked at him again and frowned as if to say the answer was so obvious, he didn't need to explain it.

"Wait a minute. He's already threatened to prosecute me. I don't want to end up in some Peruvian jail with dripping water and rats chewing on my toes."

"But what other choices do you have?"

They reached the NH Royal Quito Hotel an hour later. Orlando left the Spark with the valet as they hustled through the lobby. Pete decided to call Castillo, as it was faster and more personal than an e-mail.

In his room, Pete found Castillo's card with the number. He called. No one answered, but he left a voicemail with a couple facts to tease the agent into calling back.

He did, in fifteen minutes. "It is a pleasure to talk with you again, Mr. Chandler. I am also pleased that you have informed me about the Red Electrica del Peru. I am familiar with it. And you are correct that this connection should be investigated thoroughly. But in the meantime, it would be wise for us to meet first. You could give me the information you possess. I will arrange an interview for us at the company's home office."

Pete took a deep breath. "Of course."

"I am leaving for Peru tonight."

"How coincidental. I'm also leaving for Peru. I could go directly to their office."

"Of course. I'll arrange it myself and meet you there."

Just as Pete clicked off the phone, Lempke called. "Get in here right now," he demanded. "You better hear this."

Orlando got the car from the valet, and they raced back to the Export/Import Bank main offices. Orlando thought it best for him to stay in his office. Pete met Lempke in front of the fire that was out and cold.

"I'm waiting for a call from the FBI in Minneapolis."

"What's it about?"

"Judd Crowe."

The phone on Lempke's desk rang. They both jerked even though they were expecting the call. Lempke squeezed between the chairs and hurried to the phone. He answered and waved Pete over. "It's them. I'll put them on speaker phone." Lempke pushed a button, and the voice of the agent in charge in Minneapolis came over the phone.

"Director Lempke, I have information critical to the Export/Import Bank about your former employee, Judd Crowe."

"What's that?"

"Let me brief you about the background of our investigation first. As you know, his widow had the body cremated and returned from Ecuador with his remains."

"We know that."

"Mrs. Crowe placed the urn at Lakewood Cemetery for permanent status. Later, the Bureau received a contact from the Minnesota Department of Commerce, the Insurance Division."

"Yes?" said Lempke, impatient.

"Mrs. Crowe had applied for the proceeds of her husband's life insurance policy."

"Of course. What's the problem?"

"The policy was for two million dollars. Any time there is a large death benefit, the insurance companies routinely investigate the death prior to payout. We don't have the details, but the investigation led to some questions that alerted the Commerce Department. They contacted us to advance the investigation."

"What does that mean?"

"It appears there has been a fraud."

"Didn't pay the premiums?"

"Not exactly."

"I worked with Mr. Crowe and knew his wife. They'd never do anything dishonest."

"Our agents obtained a court order to seize the deceased's remains from the cemetery and run some forensic tests. We just received the results."

"And?"

"The remains in the urn are not from a human being. Our lab suspects it was an animal of some sort."

Pete's breath stuck in his chest. He stepped back. It seemed like the room collapsed in size to a silent bubble, circled immediately around the two men.

The agent continued, "Mr. Crowe faked his death."

Chapter Twelve

Anita's car screamed, as if in pain, when she drove it uphill to the CNN news room. Mechanics had told her there were loose belts on the engine, and she intended to get them fixed. But right now, Anita was late for a meeting with her editor, Enrique Mata.

She parked the car illegally and ran through the double glass doors into the lobby. Her bag flapped against her legs. Anita took the elevator to the second floor and came out to a large room without internal walls. Several desks with computer terminals clustered in a group on one side of the room. A dozen oversized TV screens hung from the walls.

She paused for a moment. Anita loved the smell: part stale, part human scents, and part metallic from the electricity of constant news stories of impending crises.

On the far side, an older man looked up and recognized her. He frowned, and Anita weaved her way through the crowd of desks and people.

"Sorry I'm late."

Enrique waved his hand. Always direct, he said, "Tell me why I should pay for your vacation to Peru."

"You know this story could be huge."

"'Could be' are the words I hear."

"The American's death is really suspicious, particularly with all the money that's missing. There must be something big behind all this. We're way ahead of the competition."

Enrique squinted, triggering a wave of wrinkles to travel across his face. "There's a reason why no one else is covering this." His words hung in the air between them.

"And the American investigator, Chandler, seems tough and really good. Why would they send someone like that down here? I plan to follow him. Besides, he's agreed to share info with me—after I pushed him hard."

Enrique looked up at the TV monitors on the wall. "So, what do you owe him?"

"Nothing. I'll cooperate with him, of course, but if necessary, I'll bleed him dry for any leads."

"You've never been out of the country before."

Anita laughed in his face. "So what? You know I've got more energy that most of your dinosaurs." She swept her eyes toward the floor. "I can handle it."

Enrique's shoulders slumped forward. He spoke slowly, as if he were tired. "Okay. I'm only giving you one week. And I can't justify the full per diem for expenses."

"You're so brilliant, Enrique." Anita smiled and was about to kiss him lightly on the cheek, but the cigarette odor on him was too offensive.

Chapter Thirteen

September 16, early Friday morning

Pete looked out the window of the jet as it crested the peaks of the Andes. For as far as he could see, the jagged mountains stretched to the north. Their gray flanks were topped with snow, and ferocious winds from the Pacific blew across them, carrying white trails down toward the green jungles of the Amazon to the east.

His phone chirped. It was Karen.

"How's it going, Dad?"

"I still haven't figured out everything, but I've learned that Judd faked his own death."

"What? That's crazy."

"Now I'm on my way to Peru. I think Judd is there, and I plan to find him." He waited for the inevitable question.

"Uh, have you had time enough to think about the money?"

He laid his head back on the seat. As with most planes, it didn't feel comfortable. "I really haven't had much time."

"I know, but we're getting desperate. The mortgage payment is due in a few days. Dad, we're up against a wall; we'll lose everything. Could you transfer it soon?"

Something inside his chest shifted sideways. Pete had thought that when Karen became an adult, their relationship would become easier. It hadn't. The challenges had simply changed. "Have you talked to your mother? Can she help?"

"You know the answer to that. I love her, but she's spent whatever she had on astrologers or New Age stuff or whatever."

"Yeah."

Karen waited for a long time. When Pete didn't talk, she said, "I know Grandpa's death really hurt you, and it's difficult to deal with my problems. And I'm sorry about that."

"I wouldn't say 'hurt me,'" he corrected her.

"No, but it upset you. I can tell it still does. Here's a chance to change how he treated you. He never helped you."

Heat spread through his body. "His death doesn't have anything to do—"

"I think it does."

"Dammit. You can't manipulate me with that."

"Sorry. I'm not trying to, but your help for me is part of a larger issue for you. You won't face the shitty parts of your life and change."

"So, dumping more money on you and Tim is going to transform me?"

"No, I didn't mean that. But I do think you should look at how important family is to you—even if you didn't grow up with much of a family."

"Okay, I can't talk anymore. I promise to make a decision in a few days." He mumbled a good-bye and hung up. His body slumped back into the stiff seat, and he looked out the window. He saw puffy clouds sliding under the plane. Up here, everything was carefree. Pete let the thought of his family slip out of his mind.

Instead, he booted up his laptop and decided to run a check on Anita Montana. He Googled her but found very little except social media. It appeared she had few friends, maybe two lost boyfriends, and a brightly-decorated apartment somewhere in Quito. A photo of her wearing a helmet while riding a bike up a narrow trail to a green mountain gave a clue about her hobbies—and strength.

On the CNN site there was more. Anita had graduated from the university in Quito, had worked at CNN for five years, and looked surprisingly beautiful in the official company photo. She'd covered several protests by Ecuadorians against Chinese environmental degradations, and she'd won some kind of a national prize for her reporting.

Pete intended to use her when she could be helpful. He didn't trust her, but she was attractive.

He thought of the weapon that Lempke had authorized resting in Pete's luggage. He was surprised at the bank's small arsenal, but Lempke had told him that conditions occasionally got heated in Latin America. Whatever the reason, Pete was glad to have the Glock G43, the newest subcompact slim line model of Glock's automatic pistols. The bank had also provided the necessary permits to transport the weapon.

In twenty minutes, the jet banked over the Pacific in preparation to land in Lima. The gray-blue water crashed against an endless row of tall cliffs that protected the city from the power of the waves. Lima sprawled as far as Pete could see, convincing him that ten million people really lived on the edge of a desert next to the ocean.

Even at this height, he could make out the colonial plaza, one of the largest in the world. It was bordered by a cathedral, the presidential palace, and the bishop's residence.

The plane streaked toward the international airport. An upside-down yellow bowl covered the city—smog. Although the city worked hard to clean up, the Andes Mountains to the east trapped the pollutants from millions of vehicles.

The plane straightened out, dropped down, and hit hard on the short stretch of tarmac. Brakes and engines screamed in an effort to stop the plane. It taxied back to the terminal, a two-story square of blue glass. Clusters of people tried to squeeze into each entrance.

Pete looked at his watch. Time would be tight. He was scheduled to meet Agent Castillo at the main office of the electric company in two hours. If Lima were like other South American cities, the traffic would be bad. Pete wasn't sure what would happen at the meeting. But Judd's connection to the company was the only clue Pete had—this might be a first step.

While he waited in a snaking line for customs, Pete called Agent Castillo to tell him he'd reached Lima. "It'll be tight for the meeting. Can you hold them until we get there?"

"I will try to do so," Castillo said. "In the meantime, what can you tell me about Crowe's relationship with the company?"

Pete heard warning bells in his head. He said, "It's kind of complicated. It'd be better if we talked in private."

"If you insist. But you were a friend of his. There may be information you have that we would not want the electric company to learn about at this time. I could screen it before we meet with them."

"What do you want to know?"

"What kind of work was Crowe doing?"

"I'm not sure. I think it might have been security work."

Castillo didn't say anything for a few minutes. "That surprises me. What makes you say that?"

Pete didn't want to reveal Rodney's meeting with them. "Well, he ran a cyber-security company, didn't he?" He put an edge to his voice.

"Yes, but the Red Electrica del Peru has an extensive security system already. What more could Crowe have offered?"

"Isn't that why we're having the damn meeting?"

"Relax, Mr. Chandler. We are all trying to find the answer. Are you sure there wasn't more to his relationship with them?"

"I don't know."

"That is very odd. Is there anything else you have forgotten to tell me?"

"No. I'll see you soon." He looked at his watch. Less than an hour left.

Castillo paused, as if thinking. "Yes, yes we will." He hung up.

The ceiling in the customs room was low, and the tile on the floor where Pete stood was chipped. The line shuffled a few steps, people kicked their bags along the floor, and it started to get warm. He finally reached the head of the line. The customs agent waved Pete forward. He offered his passport and visa. The agent studied both, turned them over, flipped through the pages of the passport, studied them some more, scrutinized Pete's face, looked at a computer screen, and stamped the passport several times with a machine that went *ka-chunk* each time the agent hit it. With a jerk of his head, the agent told Pete to move on. While Pete walked past him, the agent picked up a phone and talked quietly into it.

Pete looked at his watch. Forty minutes left. He still had to collect baggage.

The tight area behind the customs desks smelled of too many people and sweat. Fluorescent lights in the ceiling gave a moon-glow to the hall beyond Pete. Funny how shuffling in a line for a long time could make a person so fatigued.

Three security people in brown uniforms with stiff epaulets on their shoulders surrounded Pete. Although they didn't draw them out, each man had a Scorpion machine pistol with a folding metal stock strapped to his leg. The leader wore a flat cap with a brown leather bill. It dipped so low his eyes were hidden. In English he said, "Come with us, Mr. Chandler. Please." He grabbed Pete's arm above the elbow and shoved him toward an opaque glass door behind the customs area.

Pete's first reaction was to resist. So many times in the past, he'd fought with anyone trying to tell him what to do. He held his ground and wouldn't move.

"We will talk in the back," the officer said.

"What the hell's going on?" Pete demanded.

"Routine check."

"No it isn't. I'm not going anywhere."

The other two men formed a curtain around Pete as the first officer pushed him toward the door.

"What's this about?" Other passengers moved past Pete and the men. Like a smooth boulder in the current of a stream, the group didn't disrupt the flow of passengers. "What the hell do you want with me?"

"*No problema,*" the officer assured him and gave Pete another shove.

The men hustled him to the door, one stepped forward to open it, and the group heaved Pete through it. The door closed silently.

Chapter Fourteen

September 16, Friday, noon

The security team force-marched Pete into a hallway. White walls squeezed the space, and the team turned around several corners. More dull metal doors lined more hallways. Occasionally, they passed another security person sitting behind a steel desk. The journey blurred for Pete. They climbed concrete stairs and turned once more into a hallway without windows.

Finally, the team stopped at an open door and shoved Pete into an office. Two metal desks occupied the middle of the room. A folding aluminum chair sat beneath a small window. Pete was directed to the chair. Through the window he could see an enclosed concrete courtyard. A truck approached a loading dock with a raised door. A single man in a uniform waved the truck backward. Lettering on the truck read *El Mejor Carne de Peru. Lopez y Hijos.*

It was impossible to determine where he was trapped in the airport.

He'd been in situations like this many times before, when he was in the military and as an investigator. Pete knew a few tricks that could help him get out. But he'd also miss the meeting at the electric company with Castillo.

The three security men slouched on the desks around Pete. That was a good sign—they didn't seem too serious about Pete's presence. One lit a cigarette and blew smoke at the low ceiling. It spread like a mushroom cloud from an atomic bomb.

Everyone waited. Pete took the opportunity to feel out his captors. "What do you want with me?" When no one responded, he continued. "I work for the US Export/Import Bank. Check my credentials. My visa is okay also. Are there any questions I can answer for you?" The smoke from the cigarette descended on Pete, and it stank like cheap tobacco.

Someone's shoes clomped across the linoleum floor outside the office. A large man turned through the door and came directly to Pete. He wore a brown suit with a white shirt. The cuffs of it were worn to

91

expose loose threads. His shoulders curved around a sunken chest that slid down to a bulging belly.

"What the hell do you think you're doing?" he shouted at Pete.

Surprised, Pete replied, "I work for the United States Ex/Im Bank. I'm here on official business."

"That is—how do you Americans say—a *pile of shit!*"

"The office of our Latin American operations happens to be here in Lima." He stretched the bank's true function for its effect. Pete knew that he must try and maintain some semblance of equality with the interrogator for as long as possible.

"That may be so, but you are here now." The man had a black moustache with gray flecks in it. When he spoke, it remained motionless.

"Uh, *como lava?*"

The man laughed. "*Wash* me? What the fuck you talking about? Your Spanish is shit. You're in trouble." He looked at his wristwatch.

"I don't know what that could be. Tell me."

"I will not waste my time. It is clear to me that you are an industrial spy. Are you really working for the Chinese?"

"What the hell is it with you guys and the Chinese?"

"Shut the fuck up!" His moustache quivered.

Pete stopped. The tone of the man's voice had stiffened. Crazy as the accusation sounded, these guys were not fooling around. He'd have to be careful. He ran his hand across his hair. "Sorry."

"I want to know why you have come to Peru."

Why not try using the truth? Pete thought. "I am an investigator for my bank. I'm here to find out why one of our employees was killed. We have information that he was working with the Red Electrica del Peru."

"That story is a nest of eggs."

Pete didn't respond. It must mean his story was a pile of shit.

"Are you going to tell me the real reason you are here?"

"That is the real reason."

The man took a deep breath. "Is it normal for investigators to have the injury to your face?" He pointed his finger at Pete's forehead. "You Americans are so violent."

"It was an accident. I ran into a door, but it's getting better."

"It is obvious to me that you think we are stupid. Things will become much worse for you now." He glanced at his wristwatch and walked over to a security man wearing a military cap pushed up on his forehead. They whispered together.

Pete said, "I want a phone call to my office or the American embassy."

The big man turned to Pete and laughed. "You must think you are still in America. You are in Peru, *mi compadre*. We do not have ridiculous laws that help criminals. You will not leave or do anything unless I authorize it. If you will not tell me the truth, we have another office for you to visit. My associates here," he waved his hand at the men behind him, "will assist you when you get there—however long that may take."

Pete's chest tightened. So far, they hadn't restrained him. He'd fought his way out of situations like this before. Using his tae kwon do training, he could probably take down at least two, maybe three of them with a few well-executed kicks and jabs. But in this confined space, it'd be tough. Maybe he could attack if only a couple of them took him to the new office.

The man with the cigarette formed his mouth into an "O" shape and blew out a delicate ring of smoke. It quivered as it rose, dissipated, and still stank.

No one spoke for twenty minutes. What were they waiting for? Finally, the large man looked at his wristwatch and sighed. He said to Pete, "It is time to transfer you to our next office. We have some more questions for you."

"I can stay here."

The man's eyes opened wide. "No. You will be more comfortable in the next office." He stepped back. The security man who smoked the cigarette dropped it on the floor, smashed it with his shoe, and approached Pete. The man lifted Pete up and directed him to the door.

The man was careless, because he allowed Pete to go into the hallway first. That left all the other men inside the room. Pete thought quickly and decided to act.

He turned into a classic back L-shaped fighting stance where the feet are turned at an angle to each other. Pete's weight rested primarily on his back leg in preparation for executing a kick with his front leg. He had internalized the teachings of Choi Hong Hi about tae kwon do techniques: speed was more important than size when generating power. When the smoker reached the door, Pete relaxed his muscles.

He raised his leg to waist height, curled his toes back, and executed a front snap kick known as *ap chagi*. It slammed into the stomach of the smoker. He folded in half like a piece of cardboard and collapsed into the room. He rammed two of the security people who came forward to help. They, too, fell in a heap.

Pete recovered in the classic strike/relax pose. No one moved, so he started to run down the hall.

If he could make it to the corner, he'd buy some time and cover to try and escape. Lifting his legs, he shot away from the door. The corner was only a few hundred feet away. He might make it.

"Stop or I'll shoot!" a voice screamed behind him.

Pete kept running.

One of the Scorpion machine pistols barked in a staccato of bullets.

Pete stopped. He dropped his arms and turned around slowly. The interrogator stood at the other end, pointing the Scorpion at Pete's chest. When Pete walked back to the office, the man actually smiled.

"Now you are really in trouble, *mi amigo*."

Pete was about to accept his punishment when he heard yelling and footsteps echoing off the long walls from around the corner he'd run toward. Everyone froze.

In a minute, Agent Silvio Castillo pounded around the corner and stopped in front of the group. He glared at the interrogator. "What is the meaning of this?"

"We suspect this man of espionage."

Castillo showed some identification to the interrogator. The big man fell back a few feet. Castillo barked, "I will take jurisdiction of this case. It is obvious you clowns cannot perform your duties. This man," he pointed at Pete, "is in my custody from now on. Understood?"

The interrogator nodded.

Castillo turned to Pete. "Did they hurt you?"

"No. The service has been great in this luxury hotel."

The interrogator interrupted, "What about my man? Chandler has injured him."

"Fool. He probably deserved it for his stupidity. He should not have tried to move Mr. Chandler to the next office."

How did Castillo know that? Pete wondered, but he didn't care so long as he could get out of the airport.

Castillo led him back through the labyrinth of hallways to come out a small door into the main lobby of the airport. People crowded from wall to wall. Castillo threaded his way through the mob with Pete following him by watching the Panama hat. Overcast skies gave the lobby a matching pearl gray tint. They headed for the parking lot beyond a two-story window that formed the eastern wall.

Outside, Pete smelled dampness and salt air. The wind blew warm. He could tell it was going to be a hot day. A black Mercedes glided to a halt at the curb beside the front entrance. Castillo stepped up to it and offered Pete the open door. They both settled into the back seat as the driver pulled away from the curb.

"Thanks for the rescue," Pete said.

Castillo smiled and studied him. "You are always having trouble, yes?"

"Not really." Pete was grateful for Castillo's help, but now he was even more in his debt. He didn't want to be in that position.

"Those jokers at the airport are fools," Castillo said.

"What about our meeting at the company?"

"Since I had to rescue you, we will be late. I hope they will wait for us."

"Why would the thugs at the airport think I was involved in industrial espionage?"

Castillo took a breath. "Our governments desperately need the investments from the foreign companies, but with those investments come other, less desirable aspects."

"Like what?"

"Some investors come to steal our resources. That is what the Secretariat I work for tries to prevent and explains my concern about the case." He shifted in the seat. "And that is where you come in."

"Oh?"

"What was Judd Crowe working on with the electric company?"

Castillo kept asking the same questions. "I'm trying to figure it out," Pete replied. He didn't want to tell him about Rodney's information. Later, it might prove to be a bargaining point with Castillo.

"But you were a close friend. Surely you know more about his activities than anyone else."

"I hadn't seen Judd for a few years. He was a genius with tech and computer stuff. So I assume he was working on a security problem for the company."

"It is true they have experienced breaches in their systems."

Pete thought for a moment. Why did everyone assume Judd had had a contract with the electric company? What if he wasn't *working* with them officially? Pete didn't want to raise this with Castillo. "What do the people at Red Electrica say about Judd's work?"

"They are unusually silent on the matter."

"Executives usually are."

The driver funneled through the traffic and into the city. Other vehicles crowded around them. Black clouds belched from the back ends of buses as they lumbered away from stop lights. Even inside the car, Pete could smell the diesel exhaust. Two-story shops lined the streets with colorful billboards. One advertised Inka Cola. Another boasted of the national cocktail: Pisco sours. Throngs of people dressed in reds, yellows, and blues hustled along narrow sidewalks. Beyond the shops, tall apartment buildings formed a backdrop to the human parade below. Some of the buildings had broken windows and stains of dirt along the gray exterior walls.

They passed through an area of small hotels, gas stations, and gambling casinos. They had names like Las Vegas Reunion, Golden Nugget, and Victorian's Secret—all written in English.

The driver turned to the south and drove slowly. In thirty minutes, they came to a long park of grass and flowering bushes. Beyond the park, tall cliffs dropped five hundred feet to the Pacific waves below. Joggers exercised on the winding sidewalk that curved through the park. A huge statue of an intertwined couple stood high in the air among palm trees. On the other side of the road, tall high-rise condominiums stood shoulder to shoulder, each commanding a view of the ocean in front of them.

96

"The 'Malecon,'" Castillo mentioned. "This road runs all along the ocean here." He leaned closer to the window and pointed to the huge statue in the park. "That's by Victor Delfin, one of our most famous artists. It's called *El Beso*, The Kiss." With pride, he continued, "It's reminiscent of the ancient Moche Indian erotic art from six hundred years ago."

Pete looked at the sculpture. On a large platform, a chunky man and woman reclined in a close embrace. In spite of the size of it, the work reminded him of enduring love with the obvious addition of sex.

At the end of the park, shops descended into a depression in the ground as if they had slid down the sides of a giant bowl. They occupied different levels as the road spiraled down into a maze of more stores.

Castillo offered, "That's Larcomar, one of our largest shopping malls. Right here next to the sea. Beautiful, isn't it?" Two vendors walked by, pushing three-wheeled carts piled high with rolls of tan burritos.

"Is this Miraflores?"

"Yes. But look closely; it is about to change."

The driver turned into the dense, crowded streets behind the high-rise condos. Palm trees waved above small houses squeezed next to each other. Some were Tudor style, Spanish colonial, English cottage. Orange tiled roofs covered most of them. Under curved arches, brick sidewalks led to partially hidden gardens with flowers that gushed like fountains behind the homes.

"These little neighborhoods are all going to be torn down," Castillo said. He shook his head. "The land is far too valuable. In their places will go high-rise condos and office towers. Many people will make a lot of money." Pete thought of Lempke's comment that the Ex/Im Bank was fighting with the competition to fund some of this development.

The car sped from the corner and passed a restaurant. An umbrella shaded a woman sitting alone. She had cocoa-colored skin and shiny black hair and wore a hat so white it competed with the snow Pete had seen in the Andes.

"We are almost at the main office of Red Electrica del Peru," Castillo said. He shifted the Panama hat in his lap. "We must be prepared for this interview."

"I agree."

"Is there anything you have forgotten to tell me about Judd Crowe?"

Pete wondered if Castillo knew more than he admitted, or was he really still fishing? Pete still didn't want to reveal anything from the flash drive. He thought of the time he'd first met Castillo in Lempke's office. Castillo had had lots of financial records about Judd's company. Could he have more records about the relationship between Judd and the electric company? He asked Castillo.

"I tried to research that but have been unsuccessful. That puzzles me."

"Why?"

"In our countries, almost any information is available to me as an investigative agent."

The car cruised through the winding streets. The neighborhood had a European feel to it. Inside the car it was quiet and smelled of leather. Castillo asked more questions of Pete, many of them the same ones.

Pete decided to push back. "Now I have some questions. Did you forget to tell me anything about Judd and his security company?"

Castillo moved his Panama hat from one knee to the other. He turned to face Pete. "I can tell you this. The executives at the electric company are very upset. Be prepared for them to be angry with you."

"Me?"

"Yes. They know of your connection with Judd Crowe."

"So what?"

"They are very connected with powerful politicians here. They believe you may have been involved with Crowe, and they are putting pressure on our government for me to prosecute you. I warned you about that."

Pete studied his face. Nothing moved. "That's ridiculous."

"You say that, but I am not convinced. Nor are the executives. You see, they believe your friend got access to their internal computer systems and customers' accounts."

"Why? Did he steal their money?"

"That is what is so troubling. It appears he had access to millions of accounts, but he didn't touch any of them."

"Then what was he doing?"

Chapter Fifteen

September 16, Friday afternoon

The Mercedes whispered to a stop before a tall, gray stone building. From the outside, it looked like a Spanish cathedral. Two bell towers topped the front corners, and a vaulted arch sheltered the front door. There were a few hints at modernity—set into a recessed cavity in the stone, Pete saw an ATM machine.

He'd be walking a tightrope inside: avoiding any responsibility for Judd and his actions while trying to get as much information out of these people as possible. Was his friend really guilty of hacking into this company?

He followed Castillo out of the car and walked across the narrow sidewalk. Two wooden doors towered over them. On the right side, a gold plate said *Red Electrica del Peru SA*. The air felt heavy and hot as the sun cut through the yellow cataract of pollution in the sky. Castillo pushed on the door. Even though it was three inches thick, it opened easily.

Inside, the lobby stretched for a half block. Palm trees stood along the walls. At several intervals, arches provided openings in the stone to access offices along the sides of the lobby. Men hurried across the marble floor dressed in black suits that matched their shiny hair. They walked with their heads bowed, as if they worked in a cathedral.

Castillo removed his Panama hat. He carried the leather notebook with Mona Lisa on the cover. They walked to a set of elevators and waited for one. "I will do what I can to protect you," he told Pete. "But they are very angry about the breach of their system. It could be a potential national security problem."

Pete didn't say anything. A few days ago, Castillo had threatened him with prosecution. Now he acted as if he'd save Pete.

The elevator arrived, and they rode to the third floor and stepped out to a deserted hallway. Red carpeting muffled their steps across the marble floor. Wrought iron torch holders stuck out from the walls, holding dull light bulbs now instead of flaming torches. Pete could smell the faint odor of a cleaning product.

At the end of the hall, a male secretary met them and smiled. "Welcome to Red Electrica del Peru," he said. "They are waiting for you inside." He motioned toward a closed door. Castillo turned the knob in the middle of the door and stepped through. Pete followed him.

Two elderly men stood inside and offered their hands to shake. They had skin the color of cappuccino, long noses, and black hair streaked with silver. They led Pete to a tray of pastries, tea, and black coffee. Since it was afternoon and Pete hadn't eaten much except the stuff that was called "food" on the plane, he grabbed two pastries. The man who did all the talking introduced himself as Filipe Luciano. "You are right on time," he said, in excellent English, to Agent Castillo.

Pete wondered what that meant. Castillo had said they'd be late.

Luciano explained about his name. "My mother was Peruvian and my father from Italy. He moved here in the fifties and became involved in the state energy company. In the nineties when Peru privatized the electrical system, I became vice president of our company. Therefore, I will conduct the questioning."

Pete poured himself a cup of thick Peruvian coffee. It smelled fresh brewed. The waiter next to the table offered to add a spoonful of cocoa to sweeten it.

Luciano's voice dropped. "We have much to discuss." Without another word, he led them to an open area where heavy sofas rested on a thick rug. "Sit," he ordered. Five other men in black suits came out from the corners of the room and sat in various places on the couches. Coffee cups lined up in a straight row on a table. Agent Castillo followed them.

Pete sat at the end of a sofa. The leather was slippery. Castillo perched on a sofa on the other side of the table and opened his leather notebook.

When they were all settled, Luciano spoke. He enunciated each word and spaced them in an even pattern. "As vice president of Red Electrica del Peru, I am in charge of many aspects of our company, including security issues. These colleagues are part of my management team." While balancing a cup and saucer in his hands, he took small sips. "In Peru our company dominates in hydroelectric generation. Our facilities occupy the central part of the country, from Cajamarca in the north to

Cusco and the Andes in the east, down to Arequipa. We have spent hundreds of thousands of dollars to ensure that security for all our facilities is impenetrable." His words sounded like a clock ticking. A person next to him handed over a thick folder of papers to Luciano.

Waving the sheaf of paper in the air, Luciano's face tinged red. His cup clattered when he set it on the table before him. His voice rose in volume, and he turned to face Pete. "Agent Castillo has been very helpful. He told us that a former employee of the Export/Import Bank, Mr. Judd Crowe, is a suspect in several possible crimes. And that you, Mr. Chandler, were a close associate of his."

"I wouldn't say a close—"

"Do not interrupt me. We know Mr. Crowe breached our system. Our experts were able to trace his attack from a laptop located at the Export/Import Bank. Agent Castillo has verified that the laptop was used exclusively by Mr. Crowe. What we will determine now is how he did it, and for what purpose." Luciano waited for Pete to respond.

Pete looked around the table at all the suits. "I don't know what to say."

"Start with how Mr. Crowe accessed our system."

He chuckled. "I don't have a damn clue."

"Mr. Chandler, I don't think you appreciate the predicament you're in right now." Luciano's voice took on a hoarse edge. "You are not in the United States, and although we are a progressive country in all aspects, we treat criminal suspects seriously here."

Pete jerked back in his seat. "Criminal suspects? That's ridiculous. I haven't done a damn thing wrong. I'm working for my bank to solve the mystery of Mr. Crowe's death." He glanced at Agent Castillo.

No one spoke, but all eyes focused on Pete. A thought came to him. Maybe he should've taken Lempke's advice and gone home. Here he was in the depths of a private stronghold with a group of powerful strangers. He felt trapped again. "I want to call the United States Embassy," Pete insisted.

Glaring at him, Luciano's voice rose to a shout. "No."

"Why do you think Judd Crowe got into your system?"

"Esteban," Luciano called to one of the other men. "In an effort to save time, educate Mr. Chandler."

A slight man with a thin goatee came over in jerky strides. When he held up his hand in the air to get the group's attention, his index and middle finger were stained yellow from cigarettes.

"As you know, I have been tasked with providing cyber-security for the company. Like all institutions which must keep data private and protect their facilities, we have worked for years to develop sophisticated walls to keep criminals out."

He stared at Pete. It was obvious they had all condemned him.

Esteban continued, "The basic defense is called encryption codes."

"What does that mean?" Pete asked.

"You know them as passwords or log-on words. Your encryption software converts those words to prime numbers." A few people frowned, so Esteban explained. "Remember, a prime number is one that can only be divided by itself or the number one. For instance, three and seven are prime numbers. Next, the software multiplies two prime numbers to the reach a semiprime number."

"Why?" Luciano said.

"Because at that level, it is almost impossible for hackers to go backward to determine the original prime numbers in order to determine the passwords. It's like 'unfrying' an egg—easy to start an omelet, but impossible to put it back into the shell."

"But we have such powerful computers now," Castillo said. "Couldn't they work around the clock to break the encryption code?"

"They could, but it would still take thousands of computers millions of years to determine the two original prime numbers."

"Then what is our problem?" an elderly man on the side asked. His necktie was pulled up tightly against the wattles hanging from his throat.

Esteban looked at him. "I haven't finished yet." He turned back to the main group. "When a customer pays a bill, for instance, the software scrambles a credit card number or a bank account number with the encryption code. That is sent to the company's system or to the internet."

"Making it virtually impossible to crack the encryption coding and gain access to our records." Luciano finished for the professor.

"How big are these semiprime numbers?" one man asked.

The professor said, "The largest I have ever seen ran to five hundred printed pages."

The group muttered.

"How in the hell could Judd Crowe have broken in?" Castillo said. He wrote something in his leather notebook.

"We are not certain," the professor said, "but I have not finished my lecture. As you know, in modern communities we are linked by computer networks for everything. Our electric power grids, the city water supply, air transportation, and of course, all the commercial activities, including our entire banking network, for instance. If someone can gain entrance to one grid, it may become possible for them to jump from one grid to another." Esteban paused. His voice cracked. "You can understand the potential national security crisis if a terrorist were to breach our defenses, particularly the electrical system."

"But you just told us our encryption codes were unbreakable," the man in the corner reminded everyone.

The professor frowned. "Every grid has three components to its security: technology, processes, and people. I have told you about our technology, the encryption codes. These are very secure. Processes refer to the way we give people access to the grid. Only a few people have authority to access the technology. Their backgrounds were checked thoroughly, and we continue to monitor those employees. I can assure you from our internal investigation about this crime, no one from this company has compromised the system."

"That leaves people," Luciano said.

"Yes. Always the weakest point of any system," the professor continued. "So, how do people compromise the grid? We can control almost everything about access to the system except for removable media. This means objects like CDs and thumb drives."

"Why are they a problem?" Pete said. "Aren't they used only to store data? As I understand, the encryption codes wouldn't be contained on a thumb drive."

"You are correct, but you do not understand the potential problem. I will give you an example from research in ultra-paranoid computing studies. Suppose an employee finds a thumb drive left by someone else on his desk. If the device has the company logo printed on it, there is a seventy to eighty percent chance the employee will insert the thumb drive into his official laptop to check it out. He will enter the system with his password and log-in." The professor raised his stained finger in the air. "And, *voila,* if a virus has been planted by a criminal on the thumb drive, it gains access to the grid as a result of the employee's actions."

"Can the virus crash the system?" Castillo asked.

"It could. More common is that a malware program will replicate by inserting copies of itself in the hard drive or data files. Malware can infect an entire grid this way for the purpose of pirating CPU time, corrupting data, or stealing private information."

Luciano said, "We have over ten million customer accounts. Almost all pay electronically by giving us entry into their bank accounts."

The group leaned back into the couches and considered the possibilities. Pete was somewhat relieved. There wasn't any evidence he'd used something like a thumb drive—even if he knew how to plant a virus on it, which he didn't.

"Here's another example from research where the scientists ran a test. A CD with the business logo on it and the word *salaries* handwritten on the label was dropped outside each of the companies' branch offices. Most of the CDs were ignored. But the researchers found that there was a one hundred percent chance that at least one employee would insert the CD into their company computer and log in to see what was contained on the CD."

Luciano nodded and tried to interrupt.

The professor spoke louder. "You can easily see that if a hacker planted a virus on the CD, he would be able to get past the security perimeter easily. The hacker didn't even have to break the encryption codes—the employee 'invited him in.'"

Castillo cleared his throat. "This has been interesting, but I am searching for thousands of American dollars that disappeared from Crowe's company. What does that have to do with your company?"

"Did Mr. Crowe steal anything from the company?" Pete said.

Luciano shook his head.

"Did he access customer accounts?" Pete felt more confident. "Did he shut down the power to the entire city of Lima?"

"Well, no."

"Then what's the problem?"

Luciano whispered, "He got in."

"There is a grave potential for a national crisis," Esteban said. "We do not know what he planted in our system. He could shut down the power in the country."

"Did he have a contract with you to provide cyber-security for your computer system?"

The professor said, "Never. My team would not need help from someone like him."

"But he got access somehow," Luciano said. He turned to Pete. "And you are not going to leave until we find out *how* he did it and, more importantly, *why* he did it."

Pete wondered how much he should tell these men. The gibberish on the thumb drive didn't seem to be part of any electric company connection. Pete didn't understand the code on the CD. And how could he convince these men he didn't have anything to do with the problem?

Luciano came toward Pete. "We have a close association with the government prosecutor here in Peru. We have already instructed him to consider charging you with aiding and abetting industrial spying under our penal code, Supreme Decree Number 053-2005 EM."

Pete looked from one man to another. "Isn't your prosecutor independent of commercial interests?"

Luciano grinned. "You are in Peru now, Mr. Chandler."

It sounded so ludicrous, but no one was smiling. He studied Castillo, who was supposed to protect him. Castillo's head dipped forward, concealing his face.

"I, uh—" Pete started to say.

"The simple truth will be the best," Luciano insisted. "You have exactly five days from today to come up with the answers we need. If you do not cooperate, we will authorize the Supreme Attorney General to indict you."

Castillo nodded. "Our goals are the same in this case," he said. "The truth."

Pete realized Castillo's assurances of protection were bullshit. He'd lied to Pete. He decided to stall for more time. "I have some information on my laptop that might be helpful. But it's in my hotel."

Then he remembered the CDs. Both had the electric company's logo printed on the labels. The CDs wouldn't have meant anything to

Lempke's investigators, so they'd probably ignored them. Could Judd have dropped dozens of CDs outside the offices of the Red Electrica del Peru? At that point, Pete knew Judd was guilty and how he had breached the company's security.

Chapter Sixteen

September 16, early Friday evening

By evening, Pete had been "released" by the electric company's men. In order to get away, he had promised to retrieve the information on his laptop and get it to Agent Castillo as soon as possible.

How long could Pete stall? Could he solve Judd's murder—or faked death, as it now appeared—in less than a week and get out of the country? He decided to ask Oswald Lempke for help.

Pete registered at the Atton San Isidro Hotel. The lobby soared two stories tall and had white floors and walls. Metal chairs containing red and yellow cushions lounged around the lobby in clumps for conversation. As the clerk handed Pete the card for his room, he reminded him happy hour was just about to end. He pointed to the small bar at the end of the lobby. "Try our national drink, Pisco sours."

Pete smiled. "Is there a question?" He walked to the square bar with high metal seats surrounding it on three sides. He deserved a drink after the day he'd gone through.

Pete sensed the executives at the electric company were serious about their threats. Powerful interests that were critical to the country—like electricity—might be able to influence the attorney general.

He ordered a Pisco sour. The bartender put lemon juice, sugar, and Pisco liquor into a blender. It whirred for a few minutes, and he poured the cloudy drink into a short glass. Pete sipped it and thought it tasted like a Margarita. He devoured the appetizers offered for happy hour. His favorite was a circular stack of mashed potatoes called *causa*. Layered between the potatoes were grilled lobster chunks. The bartender told them it was also a common food for dinner in many Peruvian homes.

What could Pete give to Castillo to keep everyone satisfied? The data on the thumb drive should do it. It didn't have anything to do with the security breach at the electric company and didn't seem to make much sense anyway.

Pete ate and sipped his drink. Outside the tall windows, palm trees shaded the interior. A row of thick bushes studded with orange-red berries lined the sidewalk. Pete asked the bartender if he knew what they were.

"Goji berries. They're grown all over and are used in herbal medicine, which is a huge industry in Peru. They're supposed to help you become calm and enter separate worlds."

"Is this something New Age?"

"No. The use of medicinal herbs is very old here. Much of it can be traced back to the Incas. It's still used across Latin America by shamans and healers."

"Do people still believe that stuff?"

The bartender shrugged. "I've lived here all my life and have seen some things that would be quite strange to someone like you. Do these drugs really open a portal to the spirit world that trained people can enter?"

"Sounds like the discussions in my dorm when I was a freshman in college—while some guys got high. Talking about the Incas, does anyone know what the purpose of Machu Picchu was?"

"Not really. There are lots of theories, but no archeologist or historian has proven anything. Was it a religious sun temple? Some think it might have been the summer retreat of the royalty. Maybe it was a fortress—the last holdout of the Incas when the Spanish came up the Sacred Valley to steal their gold and kill them. The odd thing is, nothing about Machu Picchu has ever been recorded in Incan records. That's why it's called 'the lost city.'"

"Until Hiram Bingham discovered it in 1911."

"Right. But in the 1500s the Spanish started to work their way inland from Lima and up into the mountain holdouts of the Incas. They were after more gold."

"So the Incas retreated?"

"Yes. They passed the rainforest on the Plain of Ghosts and built Machu Picchu behind three-mile-high passes, granite canyons, tropical jungles, and dangerous rivers with rapids."

"Did the Spanish get to Machu Picchu?"

"No. Maybe Machu Picchu was the last hidden hideout of the Incas."

"And their ghosts live there to this day?" Pete laughed.

"Actually, there are a series of hiking trails that cover the mountains around the entire Sacred Valley. Tourists think of these sites as just separate cities. But the Incas saw things much differently. The cities and the trails were considered organs and vessels, the circulatory system of a living thing. The Sacred Valley made up one big living body. Call it a ghost if you like."

Pete resumed eating until he was full. One last Pisco sour and he'd go up to bed. He thought about Castillo's "rescue" earlier at the airport. He remembered something odd: the guy who'd interrogated him seemed uninterested in actually getting information from Pete. Was he playing a role in threatening him? The guy kept looking at his watch, like he was waiting for someone—Castillo?

It was a set-up. But Pete hadn't revealed anything of value to the agent.

He decided to call Oswald Lempke. When he answered, Pete told him about being grabbed by security at the airport, Castillo's "rescue," and the interrogation at the electric company.

Lempke shouted, "Why didn't you call me for help? What the hell were you thinking?"

"They wouldn't let me call anyone. And I can take care of myself."

"Pete, you don't know what you've gotten into. These are powerful interests in a corrupt country. They will deal with you like dealing with a pesky fly." He was silent for a moment. "So what did you tell them?"

"Nothing. For one thing, I don't have any idea why Judd hacked into their computer system. I'd like to find out myself. And I didn't reveal anything about the stuff on the thumb drive. I'm here to ask for your advice."

"My advice? My advice is to get the hell out of here. Especially now that the Peruvians are after you. They won't let up till they get what they want," he lisped.

"To hell with them. I'll stay one step ahead. My plan is to get to Cusco and then up to Machu Picchu. Something there interested Judd. I don't know exactly what I'll do, but I'm convinced the answers are up there. Maybe the data on the flash drive is some kind of a code."

"You're wasting your time, Pete. I've tried to be respectful of your skills, but now you're going off the rails. You believe all that astrological crap? Good for uneducated primitives six hundred years ago. And worse, you're in a shitload of trouble. I'm not going to be responsible for you putting the bank at risk." Lempke hung up.

Pete eased off the bar stool and went through the lobby. It was dark outside. He needed a walk to sort things out. He left the air-conditioned lobby and stepped into a warm evening. It smelled moist.

Eucalyptus trees lined the streets. Tall high-rise hotels and condos stood in silent rows. A woman in a raspberry beret followed a Pekinese dog on a leash along the sidewalk. They both walked with the same jerky movements. Fog on the sidewalk parted around her legs as she went by Pete. On the street all he could make out were crisscrossed shafts of yellow light from the cars poking through the thickening fog.

He turned around to watch the woman. He caught a wisp of red and then she disappeared.

Chapter Seventeen

September 17, late Saturday afternoon

Pete slept late and couldn't manage to get himself out of bed in spite of the pressures on him. He showered, dressed, and noticed the cut on his forehead looked better. Less purple and more pink. Pete went down to the restaurant of the hotel for a very late lunch. Its ceiling was two stories tall, fronted by a floor-to-ceiling glass wall that opened onto an outdoor patio. Red and yellow umbrellas sheltered the wrought iron tables from the sun, creating circles of shadow under each table.

He slouched in a chair and ordered Peruvian coffee with a spoonful of cocoa to sweeten it. He added cream also. He'd learned to drink it sweet when he was in Southeast Asia.

He twisted sideways because the iron chair hurt his back. He was furious with himself. From the start, he'd suspected something odd about Judd's "death."

He called Martin Graves. Luckily, he was still in his office.

"How are things going, Pete?"

"Like shit. I've hit a brick wall."

"Well, the FBI here has been busy. They took Deborah Crowe into custody for questioning. So far, she's lawyered up and won't talk. Everyone believes Judd is hiding in the US. The attempt to scam the insurance company almost worked. With the money, they could both disappear into Costa Rica or someplace hidden."

Pete sighed. "It's all over, and I've wasted a hell of a lot of time here for nothing."

"That's what the FBI thinks."

"Yeah?"

"Judd's hiding here until he can grab the insurance proceeds."

"Marty, something doesn't make sense about that. Judd also scammed millions from his company in Ecuador. Where's that money? I disagree. I think Judd's still down here."

Graves didn't respond.

"What about all the cryptic data on the flash drive that points to Machu Picchu? You think I should ignore that?"

"He was an amateur astronomer. A tourist. That's all. It has nothing to do with the insurance scam or any other money."

"You're wrong." His face felt hot.

"You're just upset because you thought he was your friend. You're not thinking clearly."

Pete pushed back his chair. Graves made a painful point. Like flood waters cresting a dam, he began to think about Judd's actions. Pete felt angry. Judd always got away with everything. When he deserved to be punished, he wasn't. Trickles of flood water turned into gushers.

The killing in Afghanistan was the worst example. Because of Judd's inattention to duty, he'd ended up killing the Afghan soldier instead of simply arresting him for trial. It was really an execution. When the CID questioned Judd first, he'd lied and made up the story of how the soldier had attacked Pete. Judd said he'd killed the man in order to save Pete. By the time the investigation got around to interviewing Pete, Judd's version had solidified as truth. The investigators were busy, and besides, they didn't care much about the death of a "camel jockey" in the midst of so much death. Pete still felt guilty for his lack of courage to tell the truth.

And Judd was guilty, too.

Pete took a deep breath to cleanse the thoughts from his mind. He switched to picturing the scene of the ride over the river. How had Judd faked it?

He remembered getting into the basket as it lurched over the side of the canyon and sensed all the shades of green as the basket traveled over the river. At the far side, it bumped against the concrete block that held the cables in place, and the basket reversed direction. Pete had looked down. The ground was only a few feet underneath and was covered by long grass. That's where Judd had jumped out to escape up the embankment to the road above.

Pete wondered about the police who'd "found" the body by the river. Castillo had given the most likely explanation in an earlier conversation with Pete.

"I know how my country works. Remember, those two police 'disappeared' themselves. I'm sure they were bribed to follow the plan—if they were even real police officers. I distinctly remember the operator for the ride telling us he looked over the edge of the cliff but didn't spot a body near the river."

"So there never was a body?" Pete had asked.

"I always thought it was odd that not one person we interviewed could say they actually saw a body down there. Since Judd disappeared from the basket, everyone assumed that he fell down into the canyon."

Pete frowned. "But how——?"

"The police at the bottom of the valley informed the local police from Baños about what they found—and then whisked the body off to Quito. The Baños police never went down to the river."

"Wait a minute. I was at the funeral home and talked to the manager about the cremation. You can't tell me he was in on the plot also?"

"I wouldn't be surprised," Castillo said.

"Impossible."

"Think about it, Pete. If you were setting this up, you'd only need a few people to accomplish it: the second man in the basket, the two police, and the director of the cremation service and an assistant."

"But he confirmed the cremation. Described Deborah Crowe. He knew all the details, and after all, the remains were shipped back to the US. I saw the death certificate."

Castillo nodded. "So did I. It certainly fooled me—for a while. Everyone involved has disappeared, probably paid off. I can't figure out why there was a second man in the basket with Judd."

"I'm not convinced there ever was a second man. But as we all investigated it more thoroughly, it became obvious the death was a murder —we assumed a second man pushed Judd out of the basket," Pete said. "They needed a second man in order to commit a murder—which led us all in the wrong direction."

Pete realized how close he'd come to working with Castillo in spite of their different goals and distrust for each other. Maybe the agent could still help.

Pete finished his meal and went back to his room. Inside, he threw open the drapes to see the glow of the fading sun covering the city like a saffron mist. He gazed over the roofs and the many treetops. From this height, he could look down on dozens of gardens. Many intersections in the city had fountains. It looked more European that Latin American.

Pete sat by the window and turned the facts from the investigation over again. Judd seemed to be amassing money for a reason. Maybe the insurance fraud was simply a way to add more to the money he'd stolen from the company instead of providing a way to disappear in the world. And it had something to do with Machu Picchu.

The sun suffused the room in a glow. Thoughts bounced through Pete's mind, but they were like huge rubber balls—soft and mushy. He couldn't get his hands around them in a coherent pattern.

Pete reached into the mini bar and pulled out a bottle of Cusquena beer. He sat in front of his laptop. He'd study the flash drive data again. Maybe the information would look different somehow.

Once again, he saw a long list of numbers, computer code, and scrambles of data.

13.583300
72.5313900
1537
Urcuchillay rises November
Coya Raymi
Longest shadow?
Leonce Angrand
452 ft.
Elevation degrade=102 ft.
2,423.21 meters
alternate theories
3 weeks left
Peru Ministry of Culture
Perurail 10:30 am
winter solstice
245+39.01 west
https://github.com/federicocomarulli/CosmoBolognaLib
9/22 @ 7/21
Casa concha 2nd

Pete Googled "Casa concha" and found it was a new museum in Cusco, opened recently to display artifacts from Hiram Bingham's discovery of Machu Picchu. The director was named Dr. J. Cabot Wilson. Next Pete opened the link and read again:

We present the CosmoBolognaLib, a large set of Open Source C++ numerical libraries for cosmological calculations. CosmoBolognaLib is a living project aimed at defining a common numerical environment for cosmological investigations of the large-scale structure of the Universe.

He stood and sipped his beer, then sat down again, moved the file off his screen, and opened Google. When in trouble, Google it. Pete read about the solstice and the equinox, winter and summer. Something was wrong. Judd had listed the winter solstice, but Coya Raymi was a spring Incan celebration. That didn't make sense until Pete realized Judd's data must be upside down.

In the southern hemisphere, winter is the same as summer in Minnesota. Judd was probably mixed up and mistaken. Instead of winter *solstice*, he'd really meant the spring *equinox*, which occurs in September in the southern hemisphere.

Pete learned the equinox represents the two times a year when the sun is perfectly aligned straight up in the sky. So there are no shadows during the equinox. Now Pete was really in a box. If Judd had screwed up the data, even these clues were worthless. He stood again and walked in a circle.

Maybe Orlando could help explain some of this. Pete called him and was thrilled when he answered. Pete explained what he'd found and asked Orlando about the Incas, the solstice, and the equinox.

"The Incas believed these times of the year were absolutely holy. They meant the continuation of the empire and the lives of the people. Since they were such special days, anything an Inca person did would be blessed with good luck by the gods of the mountains and volcanoes," Orlando said.

"What about Coya Raymi?"

"The Incan calendar was based on lunar months. The tenth month of their calendar is our September. The Coya Raymi celebration is for the planting of corn and potatoes. It's a great feast time for moon worship and for purification. Sacred idols from other people the Incas had conquered were all brought to the king in Cusco."

"Like what? Human sacrifices?"

"Maybe. More likely they were items like precious stones or gold."

Pete finished the last of his Cusquena beer and dropped the bottle into the wastebasket.

"Hold on, buddy. I'm checking something else." Pete's fingers rippled over the keys on the laptop. In a few minutes, he pushed back and yelled into the phone, "Dammit! I'm right."

"About what?"

"I found what date the spring equinox will occur this year in the southern hemisphere: September twenty-second at seven twenty-one in the morning."

"Okay. That explains his entry of 9/22 at 7/21. We were right about something happening on that day. The sun will rise earlier, probably about seven o'clock, and create a sharp line of light that will illuminate the sacred spots in Machu Picchu until it gets straight up in the sky." Orlando laughed at their success.

Pete pumped his arm in the air to celebrate. He was about to jump up and go into a tae kwon do move, but he stopped. He talked into the phone again. "Wait a minute. Didn't we talk about one of the Inca constellations? The Llama?"

"What about it?"

"You told me that rises in November. That's the wrong time. It doesn't fit, and Judd was not the kind of person to make a mistake like that. He was too technical and too smart." Pete clicked back to the list on the computer screen and saw the entry: *Uruchillay rises November.*

"But he was wrong about the winter solstice," Orlando reminded him.

"Easy to do if you're from North America. But you told me this constellation was a big deal for the Incas. Judd would know that, and he wouldn't screw it up."

Orlando remained silent for a long time. Finally, he said, "The Incas made sacrifices to the Llama constellation at the solstice and equinox. I agree: Judd wouldn't screw up something so important."

116

Pete could feel the claws of hopelessness reach around his back. His breath came hard, and he had to sit down. Something involving Judd would happen on September 22nd, and here he was, sitting in a hotel room in Lima, drinking beer. He wasn't even close to Machu Picchu—or to finding Judd Crowe.

Pete sat at the laptop again and decided to open the link to Cosmo-BolognaLib again. He switched his cell to speaker phone and could hear Orlando chewing on something like crackers.

Pete read through the introduction and still thought it was New Age gibberish. But he kept reading. The site had several links to other pages. He clicked and scrolled again. One page displayed a blue background covered with the white lines of a transparent globe. It turned slowly. Dates and times flowed by like a river of data coming out from within the globe. "Cosmological calculations." What the hell did that mean?

The screen morphed into a set of instructions:

To enter Skyglobe 4.0 you must use password.
Learn more about Skyglobe 4.0 here.

Another link opened, and Pete clicked on it and read:

Since the earth wobbles on its axis and the universe is expanding, the stars precess one another in declination. That leads to an apparent change in their position in the sky. For instance, in the northern hemisphere, Polaris (the North Star) marks north direction. But 2,500 years ago, the star Thuban marked the direction north. Changes in declination cause stars to rise at different times in history. Skyglobe is accurate up to 10,000 years in past/future.

Another click brought Pete to a page that was titled *Orion Mystery*. He stopped. A tingling built low in his stomach, rising into his chest. That could be it. "I think I've got it," he shouted into the speaker phone.

"You do?"

"The Orion Mystery is based on calculations about the Orion constellation and Egypt. Today it doesn't rise high enough above the horizon to be seen in Egypt. But astronomers calculated back to the time of the ancient Egyptians and discovered that Orion did rise in the eastern sky and could be seen. The three stars that made up his belt were aligned perfectly with the position of the three pyramids at Giza."

"But you're not investigating the pyramids."

"No, but don't you see? This program that Judd found can calculate the position of the stars *as they appeared in ancient times.* He could find out what the sky would have looked like to the Incas. I bet if we knew how to run Skyglobe 4.0, we'd find that the Llama rose in September for the ancient Incas and not in November like it does today." He grinned. "All the data really does fit together."

Chapter Eighteen

September 18, Sunday evening

All through the day, Pete tried to get a plane ticket for Cusco, but all flights were full. While waiting, he found a tourist guide to Machu Picchu left in the lobby of the hotel. He paged through it.

From Lima, everyone flew to Cusco, high in the Andes, in order to reach the ruins of Machu Picchu. Travelers had to actually go *down* to get there. Cusco was situated at eleven thousand feet in altitude, while Machu Picchu was at about eight thousand. "When you're there it seems higher because the ruins are on top of a huge cylindrical mountain," the guide book explained.

From Cusco Pete would take a bus or car to the Sacred Valley. Then he would transfer to a narrow-gauge train that journeyed up the Sacred Valley to a little town called Aguas Calientes because of the hot mineral baths located on the edge of the city. Across the Urubamba River, which twists around the foot of the mountain, are the ruins.

Pete could understand why the Incans had built the city sky-high—it was still difficult to reach it, even with modern transportation. There was only one route into the Sacred Valley to get to the ruins. Only one train, run by PeruRail, made the journey into the cloud forest to Aguas Calientes. From Pete's military training, it sounded like a choke-point, and that worried him. Orlando had said that four to five thousand people make this trek during the high tourist season. Luckily, Pete had passed the peak time. It still sounded messy.

He waited at the Atton San Isidro Hotel throughout the day. Every hour, he checked on flights to see if any cancellations had occurred. Pete took a walk outdoors for the third time. He passed restaurants filled with laughing people. BMWs and Mercedes cruised the streets.

He stopped walking. How would he get information about Cusco and the sacred sites in the valley? He remembered the Casa Concha museum and its director. Maybe he would be willing to give Pete the information he needed.

Pete entered the lobby of his hotel and saw the small bar at the far end. He heard the whine of blenders and the tinkle of ice in glasses. Must be the happy hour crew preparing Pisco sours. It was tempting. He waited at the elevator next to a banana palm tree, its shiny green leaves so inviting that he almost stroked them.

His cell phone buzzed. When he looked, he saw it was a call from Karen's mother, Barbara. Pete hesitated to answer. This was the last thing he needed right now. He pressed the green button.

"Pete, do you know what our daughter's going through?" Barbara's voice was shrill.

"I got an idea, yeah."

"Well, can't you do something? What the fuck are you waiting for? She's dying up here."

"I don't think it's that dramatic."

"She and Tim will lose everything."

Pete's neck tightened. "I know the problem. How much can you give them?" He waited for the firestorm.

"Me? You know damn well I've been going through my own changes. Money's been tight, and I need it to pay for my therapy." Her words came faster. "I've got my own diagnosis, but you can amp it up to help our child—for once."

Blood flushed into his face. "God dammit, Barbara. Don't blame me for everything. I'll take my share of responsibility, but you've got some too. I have helped Karen a lot in the past, gave her money before. When does this stop? When is she independent from us?"

"That's our job as parents—to help our child."

"Forever? And why is it that I'm always the one to come up with money?"

"You know I would also, but I'm trying to transform myself. The crystals and my life coach say I should not worry about money. So I don't. I've got enough other issues I'm working through."

Pete held the phone away from his head. He could hear the clatter of her words, but they seemed small. How could those words be so upsetting?

"Karen tells me this is all about that asshole of a father of yours."

"Barbara, I'm going to hang up. You never make much sense, and this conversation is going nowhere. I know Karen has a deadline, but I'm just a little busy down here. I promised her I'd make a decision soon. And I will." He pressed the red button. Within a few minutes, Barbara called back again. Pete didn't answer. The elevator doors opened and he stepped in, trying to leave the ugly conversation on the floor of the lobby.

Back at his room, he searched for plane tickets. He finally found one open seat on LAN, the Peruvian national airline, but it was standby only. Pete booked it. He noticed the time and realized he had to get to the airport as soon as possible. Maybe he'd make it in time. He sent an e-mail to Dr. J. Cabot Wilson at the museum, asking for an interview.

He had already packed his luggage, which rested next to the door. In the lobby, the concierge waved a taxi over from the street. Outside, Pete felt the warm, humid air and smelled fresh vegetation.

The taxi had rust on the lower panel of the door and a dent on the front fender. Pete jumped into the back seat. The driver glanced back at him with small eyes. His hair looked wet, as if were greasy. He nodded at Pete's instructions, and the cab leaped into the traffic. He swerved through dense clusters of vehicles, always finding a slice of open road. When the driver came to stop lights, he reached between the front seats and pulled up on the parking brake. After the light changed, he clicked it back down and sped forward.

"Don't you have any brakes?" Pete shouted from the back seat.

"*Sí, sí. Tengo los frenos.*" He pointed down at the parking brake.

Pete sat back and hoped he would survive the trip. His cell phone buzzed, and he saw a text from Agent Castillo. He insisted on meeting with Pete, who agreed to meet in Cusco.

The car screeched on the pavement in front of the Jorge Chavez International Airport. Cars were prohibited from parking at the entrance, so Pete scrambled out of the car, pulled out his luggage, and paid the few dollars' fare. He hurried across the parking lot. At the sliding glass door to the airport, Pete stopped. The last time he'd been in this airport, he'd been arrested.

Pete took a breath and plunged into the crowded hall. He dodged large groups of passengers until he reached the LAN airline counter. Pete spoke quickly.

The clerk studied the computer screen before him. He shook his head but continued to read. Pete's shoulders dropped. If he didn't get to Cusco tonight, would he be able to leave for Machu Picchu the following morning? That would delay him another day from reaching Machu Picchu by September 22. He looked at his watch. The last flight would leave in less than two hours. Even now, by the time he made it through security, he might miss the plane.

Pete turned to the clerk again and explained how important it was to reach Cusco today.

"I understand," the clerk said and went back to reviewing his computer screen.

Pete waited for ten minutes.

Finally, the man looked up at Pete. His eyes were large and looked tired. He nodded and pushed a boarding pass across the counter.

"*Gracias, gracias, Señor.*" Pete tried his best Spanish, grabbed the boarding pass, and spun around to hustle to the gate. He raced to the security line, found it shorter than he'd expected, and plopped his luggage on the tile floor to wait. He inched forward and kept checking his watch.

Compared to the security in the United States, the screening was minimal. As Pete stepped through the metal detector, he faced two men in tan uniforms with dark brown berets slanted across their foreheads. They converged on him. Pete's breath stopped in his throat.

The first man had a salt-and-pepper moustache. A patch on his shoulder said *Guardia Civil del Peru*. He looked Pete up and down and glanced at a clipboard in his hand. "Humph," he snorted and waved Pete past him.

He boarded the small jet that would take about an hour to reach Cusco. Within ten minutes, it lifted off and banked over the Pacific and then rose to the east. Golden light from the setting sun filled the cabin, and Pete relaxed in the warmth. In a half hour, Pete looked out the window. Gray mountains stretched as far as he could see, their peaks covered by cold, white snow. The Andes spiked higher than he'd expected. He could see plumes of ash-colored smoke trailing off at an angle from some of the mountains. Active volcanoes.

The jet gained altitude as it came to the mountains. It threaded its way through them and suddenly dropped toward a large plateau set amongst the peaks. Pete spotted small fields at crooked angles to each other, tan, green, and mustard yellow. He heard the engines protest as the pilot reversed them and raced toward the short runway. Two rough bumps and the plane slowed down. It looked dry. Pete could see one-story houses go by the window. They were sand-colored, with terracotta and orange roofs. They looked like they were made of clay, red brick and dust.

They entered the Alejandro Velasco Astete International Airport. The name was longer than the building itself. Like so many of the airports in Peru, it had been built at a time when tourism was about half of what it was now. Pete pushed his way through the crowds. It smelled stale and warm.

That changed when he came out to a small parking lot, where a line of taxis waited. The air was crisp, clean, and smelled dry. The last of the sun lit up the roofs of the buildings to the east in orange squares. Small yellow lights twinkled from the houses that were cramped against each other, trying to hang onto their position on the sides of the mountains that surrounded the ancient city.

Pete slowed his pace and wandered down the line of cabs. He pulled out his phone to check on Uber. Finding nothing, he looked for a taxi with the least dents, thinking it might offer the safest driver—if there was such a person in the country.

He found one and piled into the back seat. The driver left the curb and turned onto a road that rose and fell as it twisted through the city. Two-story tan buildings crushed against both sides of the road. In the twilight, Pete saw brown mountains that ringed the city. Some had snow on the peaks. There didn't seem to be one level place anywhere, and the roads followed the contours with sharp turns. The sky turned magenta, and more lights came on as he got closer to the main plaza, the Plaza de Armas, in the center of Cusco.

He Googled Cusco on his phone and learned that one of the reasons the Incas had built here was that even though it was very dry, there were seven rivers coming out of the mountains. So the city always had a good water supply. They'd also built aqueducts to supply their fountains.

The houses were stacked on each other up and down the hillsides. Most of the red tiled roofs had turned black at the edges. Dark green

Victorian lamp posts stood at all the corners and were lit with amber lights.

Pete continued to read: in the 1500s when the Spanish had first arrived here, Cusco was the largest city in South America at about 50,000 people.

Outside the taxi, he saw shops that sold blankets, jewelry, ice cream, coffee, and furniture squeezed next to each other like kernels of corn on a cob. On the second floor above each shop, beautiful wooden balconies hung over the sidewalks. The driver turned again and again, although there didn't seem to be any square corners in the city.

One block from the Plaza de Armas, they stopped before the Royal Inka Hotel. Out of the cab, Pete pushed through a crowd of people strolling along the narrow sidewalk. Inside it was quiet, and soft Peruvian flute music played from somewhere in the back. A pipe band with a rhythmic swish soothed Pete after the frenetic trip to get here.

Incan art covered the walls with large, grotesque characters painted in various poses. One showed the gold face of a king, his head surrounded by the full circle of a golden crown. The intricate details added to the overall effect of the piece—his head looked like the rising sun.

A fountain bubbled next to the desk in the lobby. After checking in, Pete stopped at a small, dark bar to have a Pisco sour, or two.

The waiter was friendly and spoke excellent English. "Most of our guests are from the United States," he said. "May I welcome you to our magnificent city. This is an Incan city. Everywhere you go, you will find historical artifacts, and even in the newer architecture, you will see the Incan influence. Many of the people who live here are descended from those ancient Indians."

"Have you heard about a new museum called Casa Concha?"

The waiter's face brightened. "Of course. It is very famous. When the American Hiram Bingham re-discovered Machu Picchu, he stole many artifacts—contrary to his agreement with the Peruvian government."

"Re-discovered?"

"Yes. The local people always knew Machu Picchu existed. In fact, a few families were still cultivating small fields up there when Bingham climbed into the clouds. But they didn't understand the archeological significance of the site. Today we have retrieved most of the artifacts he stole, and they are in the museum. You should go there to understand the full glory and mystery of the site."

Chapter Nineteen

September 18, Sunday evening

Sitting in his office in Quito, Xiong Lo sipped his fifth cup of tea. Normally, he wouldn't drink this much at night as the caffeine kept him awake. But tonight, there was much to accomplish before he left for Cusco—and much at risk.

The office was cool in spite of the crowd of assistants who hovered around him. One filled his teacup, another took copious notes on a laptop, another woman prepared his luggage, and one made arrangements for a hotel once Lo arrived with his team in Cusco.

With so much on the line, everything must be done correctly and nothing missed. Xiong Lo prided himself on mastering every detail of an operation. Like in a game of Go, one must plan strategy for dozens of moves in the future.

Lo walked to the window and gazed out over the twinkling yellow lights of the city below. He traced the positions of other buildings up the slopes of the mountains surrounding the city. At night, it looked like they were suspended in mid-air. A half-moon shone in on Lo and colored his face pale.

Using an encrypted phone, Xiong Lo made contact with his team.

I am leaving Quito tonight. I will use our jet to reach Cusco very late. All must be prepared before my arrival. I will bring four members of the team. I expect the rest of you to be ready for us.

We have lost track of Chandler and, as a consequence, we have lost the trail of Judd Crowe. Besides that, Agent Castillo is undoubtedly heading to Cusco also. We must beat all of them to Machu Picchu. Our investors will not wait any longer before they take the full consequences on us for the missing funds.

His assistants in Cusco replied,

We will have everything prepared for your arrival. Should we also procure the arms? The machinery?

Xiong Lo exploded and wrote back,

How many times have I instructed you? Of course, we must be able to assert our control—with any weapon we possess. Yes, be fully armed. The machinery is also required. How many times have I told you about this?

The assistant was still confused.

What is our first target?

Lo replied,

We will track Chandler. Sooner or later, he will lead us to Judd Crowe. Use any means necessary to obtain information from Chandler. We do not have time to be polite anymore, and he has not cooperated anyway.

Chapter Twenty

September 19, Monday morning

Up early in the morning, Pete finished the hotel breakfast and the last of his *coca de mate*. The altitude at Cusco was affecting him more than he'd expected. So far, drinking lots of liquids and the tea had held off any sickness. He wanted to get started for Machu Picchu as soon as possible. But first, he needed to learn more about where he was going. The museum at Casa Concha would help.

Pete also needed transportation into the Sacred Valley and to make reservations for a hotel at Aguas Calientes. Since it was a small town, tourists filled up the rooms quickly, he had been warned by the waiter.

"Can I get there in a day?" Pete had asked him.

"No. It's a long way up there. The Incas built Machu Picchu at the end of the valley in order to hide it from their enemies. Besides, there is one train line going in and one coming out. PeruRail runs only a few trains each day. You must book a fare on the train also."

Pete listened to the waiter's advice and, in spite of his need to get moving, he felt calmer. His phone buzzed with a text message. It was an order from Agent Castillo: *Wait for me at Cusco. I will be there on Tuesday morning.* Pete debated whether to wait for him or not. He could certainly use Castillo's help right now.

In the meantime, Pete mapped the location of La Casa Concha and found it was only a ten-minute walk from the hotel across the Plaza de Armas. He read more about the museum.

Hiram Bingham had been a part-time faculty member at Yale University when he found Machu Picchu in 1911. All the artifacts he took out of the country went to the Peabody Museum at Yale, where they had sat for over a hundred years. A few years ago, President Garcia of Peru had asked President Obama if he could help recover the artifacts that rightfully belonged to Peru. President Obama was able to persuade Yale to return most of the items. The new museum was named La Casa Concha because it was created in an old colonial mansion.

Pete figured if Judd had included the museum on his flash drive, there must be something important there. A clue to Judd's plan?

He left some *solis* for a tip for the breakfast service and hurried through the spacious lobby. Outside, cool air surrounded him. It smelled dry, and the sun streaked in over the tops of the mountains on the east side of the city. At this altitude, the light was brighter as it bounced off the tan stone of the ancient buildings. Pete blinked and started toward the center of Cusco.

When he reached the Plaza de Armas, Pete clung to the south side on Calle Plateros. The buildings were two stories tall, and the first floor of each was set back from the street so the second floor created a balcony that hung over the sidewalk. They sheltered him from the sun.

At the corner, he passed a jewelry shop with small French windows. Next to it was an ice cream shop, an adventure travel agency, and a clothing shop that offered real alpaca wool blankets and sweaters. Walking under a loggia, he entered a shop called El Pico del Andes. The glare of the sun and its power up here reminded him to get a hat. He found a floppy white cotton one that fit. He paid and left for the museum.

He crossed into the plaza. An enormous fountain in the center arced water into the air. The water broke up into hundreds of sparkling diamonds as it fell down. A woman wrapped in colorful blankets and wearing a snap brim hat made of green wool pushed a stroller toward him. A baby was tucked inside. The woman held out a wooden rack hung with earrings and necklaces.

"*Para ustedes. Muy bonita,*" she said.

"*No, gracias,*" Pete said and waved her away.

To the right, he spotted a Starbucks coffee shop on the second floor of a building. Heavy, smooth stone blocks provided a foundation. The building had a carved wooden balcony, with people sitting along its edge sipping lattes and tea. In spite of the Incan and Spanish history, modern civilization had finally reached Cusco.

He walked past a bed of peonies blazing in the sun like a festival designed to show off the colors of Peru: lavender, fluorescent pink, coral, and cardinal red. Pete looked up at the Spanish cathedral that dominated the entire plaza. *The Cathedral Basilica of the Assumption of the Virgin* read the sign at the foot of a dozen stone steps at the base of the church. Since it was a mouthful to say, that proved it was built by the Spanish.

Pete also read that the cathedral was started in 1560 and was built on the ruins of the Inca king's palace. It took almost one hundred years to complete it. He stopped walking and bent his head back to take it all in. Two square towers rose from the front corners of the red stone building. On each side a smaller church sheltered the main edifice and emphasized the mass of the cathedral. Even the stones in the foundation reminded people of the power of the Spanish empire. Gray granite squares of immense size, stolen from Inca palaces, supported the church.

Seeing the immense structure explained why the Spanish had built it. Since the Inca king was the center of Inca religious beliefs, the Spanish wanted to replace that belief system with the Catholic religion.

A man approached him and offered shallow wooden bowls decorated with intricate Incan artwork. Humans and animals had grotesque faces drawn in square shapes and surrounded by geometric designs. "Only three hundred *solis*," he said.

"*No, gracias, amiga,*" Pete said.

"You're almost fluent," the man laughed. "But it's *amigo* with an 'o.' I'm a man."

"Hey, I'm trying." Pete laughed with him, and it felt good to relax for a moment. Although the temperature wasn't hot, the sun burned along his bare arms. "Sorry, I need to get going." He turned away from the man and looked at the map on his phone. Pete crossed in front of the cathedral and started downhill along a narrow street that led away from the plaza. Several small wooden balconies jutted out of the second floors over the cobblestoned street. Pete had to stop to catch his breath.

He'd read in the tourist guidebook that Cusco had been built by the Incas in the shape of a puma. Cats were thought to be able to give better access to present-day life. Birds represented in Incan art gave access to the gods in the sky. And serpents gave access to the dead for help and regeneration. Pete stopped at the corner and looked down a long street. A street sign said, "This was the royal road from the king's palace to the sun temple." It was labeled *Avenue of the Sun.*

Pete breathed deeply and realized the ancient Incas must've been in great shape from climbing up and down all day at this altitude.

The guidebook had said,

The Sun Temple was the center of the Inca religious practices. When the Spanish first saw it, they were amazed at the architecture and all the gold that covered everything in the complex. The Spanish took the gold. A lot of it ended up in the cathedral on the plaza; the rest went in the pockets of Pizarro and his lieutenants. It only whetted their appetite for more.

The walls on the left side of the street contained large granite stones laid as a foundation. They were smooth and fitted together so carefully there wasn't any space in the cracks between the stones. Pete stopped and ran his finger over the cold rock. It was the original Incan wall, and since they didn't have the use of mortar, the stones were carved perfectly in order to stay upright. No one knew how the immense blocks had been transported. The Incas were advanced in many ways, but they didn't have the wheel.

Pete looked at the time. He had a half hour before the appointment with the director of the museum. Pete decided to call Lempke.

"What are you going to do there?" Lempke asked.

Pete told him about the museum. "As soon as I can, I'll get transport up into the Sacred Valley. I'm worried that I won't get on the train to Aguas Calientes; I don't have a ticket yet. They look like they're booked, and they only run a few trains a day."

"Maybe this is a sign for you. You've worked your ass off on this case. Judd has betrayed us all, but he's disappeared. You might think about going back to the US."

"No, dammit. I've come this far."

"Why are you so persistent, Pete? You came originally in response to the card from Judd. But things have moved far beyond that. What can you possibly do now?"

Pete thought for a moment. "I don't know. I came to help him 'cause we were so close at one time, and it sounded like he was in trouble. Then he scammed all of us. Now I'm just too damn mad to let go of it. I want to find Judd and confront him."

"Take my advice: don't waste any more of your time." Lempke hung up.

Pete turned around and walked back up the royal road past the cathedral again. He looked at the map on his phone. The museum was two blocks behind the plaza. He breathed heavily and trudged uphill.

While he walked, Pete thumbed through the documents on his phone and found the list from Judd's flash drive. There was a name that made no sense to Pete, so he decided to check on it. He Googled Léonce Angrand.

Pete waited for the information. When the page opened, he read. "Angrand was the French vice counsel to Lima in 1838. He is known mostly as a romantic painter of ordinary people and street scenes in Lima. He created an excellent record of what Lima looked like in 1838." Pete's shoulders dropped. What the hell did was that about? And yet, Judd had included it on the list.

Pete scrolled down and found a scholarly article about the artist. He opened it. The essay ran for dozens of pages in small script that he couldn't read on the phone. He decided to study it later and keyed off his phone.

Two blocks beyond the Plaza de Armas, Santa Catalina Ancha Street curved slightly. He reached a two-story building with a flat roof. The windows were barred. Whitewashed walls rose over carefully carved stones in the foundation. Two large wooden doors with old iron studs in them were shut. A smaller door in the side of the double doors stood open. A sign next to it read *Museo Machu Picchu. La Casa Concha.* He stepped through and entered the old mansion.

Once through a second door, he paid the museum admission and was allowed to walk out into a large courtyard open to the sky. Granite arches held up both stories and ran the entire length of the courtyard. Stone paving led across to a dry fountain in the middle. There weren't any plants or flowers to soften the harsh glare of the bright sun against stone. Pete squinted as his eyes adjusted to the light.

He hurried across the courtyard. The stones looked the color of dried mustard, and his shoes clapped over them as if they were disturbing the heat that rose to grab at his legs. Under the shelter of the arches, the change in temperature was startling, and Pete understood why the Spanish had used this design for their homes.

He stopped to consult the paper map the attendant had given him at the entrance. To the left was an arched opening with two wooden doors whose tops matched the curve of the stone arch. He climbed a stairway covered in red carpet. It smelled like new wood.

Judd's flash drive had referred to Casa Concha 2nd, which Pete thought meant the second floor. Besides, Dr. Wilson's office was also on this floor. Pete found signs pointing to the administrative offices and followed them. He looked through the first door that opened onto the museum and the artifacts inside. He stopped, overwhelmed at what he saw.

In dozens of glass cases, wall mountings, tables, and book racks, there were hundreds of artifacts. Pete didn't have any idea where to start —and he didn't have time to browse.

He reached the offices and found Dr. J. Cabot Wilson sitting behind an ornately-carved wooden desk. Pete introduced himself and thanked the director for meeting with him.

"No problem." Wilson flew out of his chair as if he were lonely for American company. He gripped Pete's hand and pumped it vigorously. "Welcome to La Casa Concha."

"How long have you worked here?"

"Since the beginning. When Yale University agreed to return these items, part of the deal we cut was that an American curator would be in charge for the first five years. That's me." He wore a pressed button-down shirt with the Yale logo on the pocket. Underneath, Pete could make out an athletic build.

"It's a beautiful building."

"Those damn Spaniards knew how to live, huh? This was a man-sion, typical of the richest *conquistadors* of the time. They stole so damn much gold from the Incas, they couldn't spend it fast enough. Kind of like our dot-com companies in Silicon Valley today. Anyway, we got title to this and decided it was a perfect site for the museum." He looked out the door and encouraged Pete to follow him.

They stopped before a long chart that explained the history of Hiram Bingham's discovery of Machu Picchu and his excavations. Wilson clapped him on the back and said, "Let's start with a history lesson."

Pete read,

Bingham was originally looking for the hidden city of Vilcabamba, where the last of the Incan emperors, Manco Inca, was supposed to have fled with his court and his riches in front of the marauding Spanish. Instead, Bingham heard about another mysterious "lost city" in the clouds at the top of a mountain that could have been the actual city the emperor fled to for hiding. The sacred Urubamba River curved around a spur at the foot of the same mountain, and to the south of it stood another mountain—one of the most sacred for the Incas: Salcantay. The combination convinced Bingham the rumors of a different lost city in the clouds were true—perched above him, overlooking the vast rain forest below.

Bingham hired a few porters to help pack supplies on mules, and they started up. The climb was slow, hot, wet, and difficult. They had to slash the vegetation aside to make any headway while grabbing onto tree limbs or roots to pull themselves upward. Besides the heat, they fought incessant clouds of mosquitos. Unlike those in New England where Bingham lived, these were invisible, and he didn't even feel the bites until he stopped to rest. When he turned over his arms, they were covered with small red welts.

Pete shifted his weight to the other leg. It was fascinating material.

After days of struggle, Bingham reached the summit and crawled under a stone arch. It led to a slippery trail that opened onto a sight that has beguiled millions of tourists ever since—who still enter the ruins through the same archway.

But it didn't look like the modern version. Trees and bushes grew over most of the ruins, poking their limbs through the windows in the walls. Some farmers tilled the few flat spaces on the far side of the city. Gray smoke twisted up from the slash-and-burn farming they practiced.

Bingham was thrilled. He immediately realized what he'd discovered: a city unknown in the Incan historical records and unseen by any previous explorers. He named it Machu Picchu after one of the mountains that rose above the city from the rain forest like a giant green finger, as if it were pointing the way to the sacred spot.

Bingham came back several times and excavated hundreds of boxes of artifacts from the ruins. His agreement with the Peruvian government was restricted, but Bingham ignored that and smuggled out over twice as many pieces as he reported to the government for shipment back to the Peabody Museum at Yale. At least he wasn't looking for gold, as the Spanish had done. Bingham was an amateur archeologist but understood the historical value of the precious treasures he'd unearthed.

Wilson led Pete into the first room. The walls were painted dark brown, with track lighting on the ceiling. Several photos of Bingham and his party were framed and hung around the room. He looked like the original Indiana Jones. In fact, the creator of the film had said he'd modeled the character after Bingham.

They walked over an ochre tiled floor and found a glass case filled with the original documents and maps that were used in the excavations. Squares were drawn in a grid system over a map of the ruins. A note beside it offered viewers a website for more details.

"Bingham followed the rules of recovery for the time," Wilson said. "He's the one who named many of the spots in the city." He pointed to the map. "Here's the Sun Temple and the Temple with Three Windows. And here's the 'Hitching Post' of the sun. The Incan word for it is *Intihuatana.*"

"What's that?"

"It's a tower of carved stone at one of the highest points in the city. It was used during the solstice and equinox. The Incans measured their seasons with this. At the equinox, the sun stands directly above the Intihuatana and doesn't cast any shadow. At the solstice, it's the opposite and the shadow is the longest. They believed the post could 'catch' the sun, so they called it the 'hitching post.'"

"And they made their decisions based on the position of the sun?"

"Right. It represented the holiest time of the season. Only the most important actions were taken at those precise times."

"Like September twenty-second?"

"Yes." Wilson straightened his back. "How do you know about that?"

"That's the time I must be at Machu Picchu."

Wilson studied him. "Who is going to help you get there?"

"Uh, I don't know exactly."

They moved into the next room. Rows of shelves held items of pottery glazed in colors like cobalt, leather, sand, and white. Intricate designs and pictures curled around the pieces. The next shelf showed vases used for carrying water or *chincha*—beer. Hair pins, tools, shallow bowls, carved bones, bead-covered pieces of cloth, and worn sandals all crowded along the shelves.

Next they walked in front of several glass boxes set on pedestals. Inside each one were intricately carved royal headdresses—all made of solid gold. Unlike European crowns with a simple globe to cover the head, these had triangles of gold that stuck up from the back of the crown to suggest rays of sun emanating from the royal head. Earrings hung in squiggles like writhing snakes from the lower edges of the crowns. Images of pumas decorated the band that covered the king's forehead.

"This is just a hint of the immense treasure the Incas must have possessed," Wilson whispered. "Can you imagine?"

They finally moved on, and after a half hour of viewing, Pete had come to like Wilson. He was a little stuffy but seemed genuinely anxious to help Pete. Besides that, Wilson was probably bored with his work— he might jump at the chance to get out of the museum.

"So, what are you really looking for?" Wilson stopped and faced Pete.

"I'm not sure."

"What?"

How much could Pete trust this stranger? "How familiar are you with the Sacred Valley and Machu Picchu?"

Wilson laughed. "Familiar? I wrote the book. I know this history forward and backward, and I've lived here for three years now. Do you need help?" he asked again.

Pete did need help. He explained, briefly and with a lot of things left out, that he needed to be up at the site on September 22. "What I really need is a guide. Someone to help me get there and explain to me what I see once I'm there. My employer is willing to pay you."

Wilson's face lit up. "And I can handle the job of guide. I love this subject, anyway. Call me Cab. When did you want to leave?"

"As soon as I can."

"I hate to be so petty, but can you take care of all the expenses?"

"Of course. You've got transportation?"

"Yes."

In the last room, they stepped up to a full-scale model of the city built across a long table. It revealed the entire site in three-dimensional detail. Cab stooped down and studied the model. Pete followed his actions. He was startled by the differences in altitude even within the city. Some points were hundreds of feet higher than others. Stone stairways climbed over everything between stone walls and abandoned rooms. Around the perimeter, the mountain fell straight down for thousands of feet. Perched along these precipices were over 600 terraces of fields held up by stone walls. Pete asked Cab about them.

"Quite an engineering feat," he said proudly. "They are like upside-down cups. At the bottom, the Incas placed loose rock for drainage. Over that, they laid gravel, then leaves and vines, then added soil to the top. The entire city was watered by an intricate aqueduct system, and there were approximately sixteen fountains throughout the site. Since there wasn't much flat space for farming, they built theses terraces around the edges to grow food. And they also acted like claws to grip the edge of mountain and prevent the city from sliding off."

He pointed out some of the famous spots in the ruins: the Temple of the Condor, the Royal Tomb, the Main Plaza, the Royal Palace, and the nobles' houses.

Pete read from the plaque next to the model. There were over 150 buildings of stones fitted together with a precision that 500 years later made it impossible to fit a knife blade between them. It was all the more impressive because the Incas didn't have iron or steel tools, and they didn't have the wheel.

He shook his head, amazed at the abilities of these ancient people. "Did Bingham excavate the entire place?"

Wilson straightened up. "No. He uncovered a lot of it, but there were large sections that have never been unearthed. It's a mystery waiting to be discovered, I guess."

They circled the model. Pete imagined the Inca people and their emperor, who probably sat on a litter attended by slaves that offered sacrifices of animals, gold, and prisoners to the sun gods. Drum beats echoed off the stone walls, and bells rang across the empty valleys. Spooky stuff.

After another half hour, Pete urged Cab to leave. "If you're going with me, we don't have much time."

"Of course." Wilson hurried back to his office. "I'll pick you up on Tuesday morning, early. We have a long way to go."

Outside, Pete paused on the street to adjust his hat. The sun had passed to the west, and shadows grew from the buildings around them. Behind him, parked with two wheels up on the sidewalk to make room in the street, Pete saw a large Audi—unusually large in comparison to most of the other cars. He started the walk back to the hotel. Nothing in the museum had jumped out at him as an obvious clue, even though Judd had indicated something of importance was located there.

He remembered he had to book a hotel in Aguas Calientes—for two now. He crossed the Plaza de Armas, turned left, and walked three more blocks to the hotel. The old sidewalks were clean of litter, and a slight breeze blew down from the mountains that surrounded the city. Cars squeezed beside each other in the street, jamming together in a swarm of grunting engines and high-pitched horns.

Pete stopped to take a deep breath. From the corner of his eye, he saw the Audi again. It drove past quickly and turned the corner behind the hotel. The darkened windows prevented Pete from seeing anyone inside. He paused to take in the beauty of the blue sky and the billowing clouds above. No wonder the Incas thought this location was the "navel of the universe." It certainly was beautiful. He turned and walked into the lobby.

Three Asian men converged on him from the dark edges of the lobby. One said, "Mr. Chandler? Come with us, please." He wore a floppy hat and sunglasses.

"Wait a minute," he barked. "Who the hell are you?"

One of the men grabbed Pete's arm and twisted it up behind him. It hurt. Two of the men jammed his body between them, forcing him to move forward.

"I'm not going anywhere with you," Pete said.

"Mr. Chandler, you never want to work with us. Mr. Lo is waiting."

Pete decided to cooperate for now and allowed them to maneuver toward the elevator.

"We have meeting for you," the first man said. His English was not good, and his breath smelled of garlic. He was larger than most Asian men and looked down on Pete with a few inches to spare.

Waiting for the elevator, Pete thought about breaking free. The lobby was empty, but two hotel clerks worked behind the front desk. Could Pete get their attention? Then he thought of Lo. He decided to stay and see what Lo wanted. Maybe he knew something Pete could use.

They rode the elevator without another word. Even though Pete tried to get information out of the men, they remained silent. He had never seen any of them before.

The doors opened on Pete's floor, and the first hint of sweat streaked down the sides of his chest. How had these guys known where to go? Had they broken into his room? Sure enough, they stopped before his door. The large man pulled out a swipe card and leaned forward.

Pete decided he wasn't going to meet Lo while being jammed up by these thugs. He took a chance. He twisted to the left, raised his right leg, and delivered a side-snap kick into the back of the other man. He fell into a heap on the floor with a groan. The two other men swarmed forward and pinned Pete against the wall. The man in front of Pete rammed his knee into Pete's groin.

Pete felt a shock course through his body as if he'd been electrocuted. He crumpled onto the floor and rolled to his side to curl up in pain. Bright yellow and blue lights flashed before his eyes.

When the pain dropped to a manageable level, Pete found himself thrown on the bed inside the room. The large man was tying his arms to the bed posts. Someone else tied his legs. His head cleared, and Pete realized he lay spread-eagle across the bed, tied down, totally vulnerable. He swung his head from left to right but couldn't spot Xiong Lo.

No one spoke. In five minutes, the door creaked open and someone walked into the room, footsteps scraping softly on the wooden floor. Pete strained to sit up. He couldn't and fell back against the bed.

A face came into his view, and Pete looked up to see Xiong Lo bending over him. Lo's ponytail drooped over his shoulder.

"Mr. Chandler, you seem to always get into trouble."

Chapter Twenty-One

September 19, late Monday afternoon

The red haze cleared from Pete's vision. "What the hell are you doing here?" he mumbled.

"I will ask the questions, under the circumstances." Lo nodded while one of the men pulled up a chair beside the bed. Another handed Lo a paper cup of steaming green tea.

"You hurt me and you'll pay for it," Pete said.

Lo smiled with one upturn of his lips, then became serious again. "We do not act like American thugs, but you won't cooperate with me as we agreed to do back in Quito."

"What does that mean?"

"You promised to share information about Mr. Crowe with me, and you have not done so. I am not happy about our partnership. My investment group does not like it when agreements are broken. Not only has Mr. Crowe broken his, you have also."

"Go to hell. Partners don't kidnap each other and tie them up."

Lo blew twice on his tea and sipped it. "Our methods have proven to be effective. This is only an introduction. If you cooperate with me, we will be true partners again. What I want to know is still the same: what did Judd Crowe do with our money?"

"I don't know."

"But you are a long-time associate of his."

"No. I don't know what he was doing in South America. I came to help him."

"How were you going to help him?"

"I don't know." Pete knew it sounded ridiculous.

"We have learned that you have some digital data from Mr. Crowe. Why didn't you share that with me?"

"Digital data?" Pete struggled to understand, until he remembered the data on Judd's flash drive and the hack on Pete's computer. "I . . . I couldn't make sense of the data. So what was there to share except gibberish?"

"I find that hard to believe. What does the data tell you?"

Pete tried to shrug, but his shoulders were immobilized. "Nothing."

"What else do you know that you have not told me?"

"Nothing."

Lo leaned back as the large man approached the foot of the bed. He removed both of Pete's shoes and socks. He left for a moment and returned with a worn leather case, opened it, and removed some small needles. While he held them up and selected two, Lo said, "Acupuncture is an ancient cure for chronic pain. But if the techniques are used incorrectly, the procedure may actually cause pain. Extreme pain. Luckily for you, it will not cause your death."

Clearing his throat, the big man leaned down, and Pete felt a sharp prick on the side of his foot. Red hot pain knifed up his leg. It twitched involuntarily, causing more misery.

"What did Judd—"

"I don't know," Pete yelled. "He's still alive."

"What?" Lo stood up and leaned over Pete's face.

"He faked his death. We're up here following him. But I don't know his plans or where he is." His face dripped with sweat. "We think he's going to Machu Picchu."

"How do you know this?"

Pete's tongue swelled, and his teeth hurt. "FBI." He wiggled his hands and felt the left one loosen from its bonds.

"Crowe is at Machu Picchu now?"

"Yes, yes—no. I don't know for sure."

Lo's forehead wrinkled. "Does it have anything to do with the privatization or the sale of Machu Picchu?"

"I don't know."

"Prove to me that Mr. Crowe is going there." Lo glanced at the other man, who removed the needles from Pete's foot.

Pete's mind swirled. What could he say? He didn't want any more pain. He explained how the FBI in the United States had discovered the fake remains in the cremation urn and how that had led to Pete's conclusion Judd was still in South America. "You know who Agent Castillo is?" When Lo nodded, Pete continued, "He's also coming up here to-morrow. That proves he also thinks Judd is somewhere around here." His head flopped back onto the pillow, wet against his neck.

The Asians gathered somewhere away from Pete, and he could hear their mumbled voices rising and falling in the peculiar cadence of Asian languages. Lo came back into Pete's view.

Lo's voice dropped. "Unfortunately, you have still not given me all the information you know about Mr. Crowe." He shrugged his shoulders and backed away from the bed.

From the corner of his eye, Pete saw the large man with the leather case approach the end of the bed again. The man laughed and raised the needles. Pete screamed, "Wait! I gave you everything I have." He felt a cold hand grasp his right foot.

Then Pete remembered the Glock 43 he'd hidden under the pillow beside his head. If he could loosen his arm enough to reach it . . .

The large man stretched out Pete's ankle and turned it to the side.

Red haze threatened to cloud Pete's vision again. He thrust his left hand high under the pillow, touched the square edges of the pistol, and tried to grab it. His fingers slipped.

The man grunted and leaned over Pete's ankle. "This won't hurt." The man laughed.

Forcing his hand to close, Pete got two fingers around the Glock, which was enough to pull it out from under the pillow. He knew he couldn't get a shot, but the sight of it might be enough to startle the Chinese and get them to back off.

Luckily, the G43 was one of the lightest of the Glock line of pistols. Pete managed to get his hand around the grip enough to point it toward the men at the end of the bed. "Back off," Pete screamed.

They did.

He struggled to slip his hand further through the loop around his wrist. It worked, and he got a better aim at the men. He ordered them to leave. Lo smiled but came nearer toward the bed.

Pete thumbed off the safety and pulled the trigger. In the room the blast deafened him, but it worked to clear out the Chinese. They stumbled over each other on their way out. The door shut and Pete, drenched in sweat, leaned back on the bed.

The door of the room burst open, and two uniformed men from hotel security stormed through the opening. They were followed by Anita Montana. People shouted, and Pete heard the scuffle of feet across the floor.

Then Anita was next to him, undoing the ropes that bound his arms and legs to the bed. She lifted him up, and he inched back against the pillows to sit upright. He swung his eyes around the room. The Asians were still gone.

A man from hotel security sat on the edge of the bed and patted Pete's shoulder. "You do not want to fool around with those men. They're gangsters. We have worked for years to keep our hotel safe. Are you all right?"

"'Fool around' with them?" Pete tried to laugh, but the lower half of his body still hurt. "They attacked me."

"We are able to provide a doctor for you if you want one."

"No, I think I'll live. Just a few pinpricks in the ankle. Damn, do those hurt!"

The security people stood, feeling assured Pete was okay, and they left.

Anita remained and said, "What did they want?"

Pete blinked at her. "And how did you know to come in here at just the right moment?"

"I told you I would be shadowing you. I followed you to the hotel and the museum, and I saw those two thugs grab you in the lobby. I should have acted quicker, but when I thought you might be in trouble, I alerted the security." She smiled at her success.

"Thanks. Xiong Lo is mad as hell about Judd and the missing money." Pete carefully swung his legs off the bed, moved to the edge, and stood up. His legs felt rubbery, but he remained standing. He looked at Anita. He was unable to prevent the gush of warmth spreading in his chest. "Thanks, thanks for your help."

"So what are you doing up here?"

Pete pretended to be confused. He shook his head to buy some time. It seemed like everyone knew Judd was going to Machu Picchu. He told her that.

"When?"

Just like his daughter, Anita pushed Pete. He didn't like it. "Not sure."

"Or you won't say." She walked toward the door. "I'm sure I'll see you along the way." At the door, she turned back and said, "Do you have a way to get up the Sacred Valley?"

"Yeah. Yeah, I do."

She came back to him. "You need tickets for the train and for admission to the site."

"Working on those."

Raising her hand, she pointed to the wound on his forehead. "Too bad. The scuffle outside has re-opened this. I'll help put a new bandage on it if you'd like."

He picked a bandage out of his suitcase and handed it to her. She dabbed at his forehead with a warm wet towel covered in soap bubbles. She dried it, spread a new dressing over his skin, and pressed it gently. "Stay out of trouble and this will finally heal."

"It's part of my skill set—always looking for a fight." He could feel the warmth of her close to his face. He backed away quickly.

"In the meantime, let's get our transportation figured out." She moved to the desk and keyed on her phone. "We could take a public bus into the Sacred Valley, but it will be a long, slow ride. There are many small towns along the way, and the bus will stop to pick up people at every intersection."

"Wait a minute. *We're* not going together."

"Okay. It's up to you. You also have to book tickets on PeruRail for the ride into Aguas Calientes. That will be tougher since they only run a few trains each way every day." She keyed in the website and waited for it to load. "Do you remember what Lo asked you?"

Pete snorted. "I can't remember much of anything." There was one thing Anita might be able to help explain. "He kept asking where Judd put the money and if it was connected to the sale of Machu Picchu."

"This guy is an insider. If he's interested in the possible sale, does that mean it will happen? I can't believe Peru would actually sell it, but why would Lo be so insistent about getting that information?"

"And remember, it really wouldn't take a lot of money as a down payment to own the whole thing. Maybe Judd has enough money from all he stole, and Lo is worried he'll get beat out by Judd."

"Although the government will make a show of competitive bidding, the truth is the deal will be made behind closed doors for the highest bribe," Anita said.

The bandage on Pete's forehead itched. He scratched around the edges, careful not to disturb it. "Judd has been clever, as usual. His 'death' threw off everyone on his trail for a long time."

"But now we're all closing in. What will he do?" Her phone beeped. She swiped the screen with her finger and grunted. "I can't get two tickets. The trains are narrow-gauge and don't carry a lot of passengers. If we'd been here two months earlier at the height of the tourist season, we'd have to wait for weeks. I hope we can buy them at the last minute in the station."

"Thanks, but I'll figure it out."

Anita shrugged. "By any chance, are you hungry? There's a great restaurant around the corner."

He did feel hungry. "Sure, I guess we could go there."

They rode the elevator down to the lobby, walked out into the late afternoon sun, and turned to the right. A block away stood a small corner restaurant called Andes Organic. Anita led Pete down the sidewalk past several parked cars. Each one had a roll of toilet paper on the dashboard or in the back window.

At the restaurant, they found a wooden table and ordered two Cusquena beers. "Why don't I order some local food? You can try authentic Peruvian cuisine," Anita offered.

Pete agreed. In a half hour, they'd finished a delicious dinner. Pete had something called *cuy*. It tasted like chicken and was smothered in gravy, potatoes, and green beans. They drank Peruvian coffee afterward. He was starting to warm up to Anita, but he was careful not to reveal too much to her.

They walked back to the hotel. She paused in the lobby to say goodbye. "I'll watch for you tomorrow. By the way, how did you like dinner?"

"Good."

"I ordered *cuy* for you. It's baked guinea pig, a delicacy in Peru. Most of the mountain people raise the pigs as food for their families. The name comes from the sound they make when they squeal."

"What?" His stomach turned at the thought of eating a small rodent-like animal.

She laughed. "You should trust me more."

"After that? Never." He turned and hurried into the hotel.

At his room, Pete's phone pinged. It was a text from Mateo back in Quito. He had found something strange on Judd's CD.

chk your computer!!!! immediately
CANT BELIEVE IT !!!

Pete booted up his laptop and opened a longer email from Mateo.

NEVER seen anything like this code!!! have no idea what is about chking it out— worries me!!! here is example

```
// Data declarations
Extern int dword_10001A90(8); //weak
Extern char *off_10001AB2; //weak
Extern char byte_10001A89(3); //weak
Typedef struck (
HMODULE Handle_Ntd11D11
Dword field_4
Int (_stdcall *proc_1strcmpiW) (LPCTSTR 1pstring1, LPCTSTR 1pstring2)
SIZE T (_stdcall *proc_Virtualquery) (LPCVOID 1pAddress, PMEMORY_BASIC_INFORMATION 1pBuffer, SIZE_T dwlength)
BOOL (_stdcall *proc_virtualprotect) (LPVOID 1pAddress SIZE T dwsize, DWORD 1pf101dProtect)
FARROC (_stdcall *Proc_GetProcAddress) (HMODULE hModule, LPCSTR 1pProcname)
NYSTATUS (_stdcall *proc_ZwClose) (HANDLE handle); //weak
) obsfucatedImports;
//obfuscated strings
// see Scramble_Bytes and Scramble_words
//obfb – asci (byte)
Extern BYTE obfb_Kernel32dll_aslr(48); //weak
```

Chapter Twenty-Two

September 20, Tuesday morning

Cab Wilson picked up Pete in a Toyota Yaris. Cab shifted into second gear, and the engine strained, but it climbed the narrow road out of Cusco and into the mountains. "We're over 12,000 feet in altitude here," he said. "It will get easier as we go on, but first we have to go even higher before we descend to Aguas Calientes at about nine thousand feet."

Pete had contacted Agent Castillo and agreed to meet at the small town. He'd have to be careful with Castillo, but his access to many things would be valuable.

Pete and Cab started at seven fifteen in order to beat other tourists leaving for Machu Picchu. Surrounded by the orange and blue colors of sunrise, Cab weaved through the north end of the city. It smelled dry and fresh, like a new day often does. Small women snapped open blankets to spread on the ground. They stacked piles of produce on them.

The streets twisted to the left and right but always climbed upward. Most houses had orange tile roofs, and a few had iron bulls mounted on them. When Pete asked about those, Cab said, "From the Spanish conquerors. It was supposed to bring good luck."

Pete turned to look almost straight down on the city from the height they'd already climbed. It nestled in a saddle between several mountain ranges. "It's bigger than I thought."

"Archeologists think it's the oldest city of its size in South America."

Within five minutes, they'd left the city but kept climbing. Thick stands of pine trees clustered in green and gray clumps over dry earth. The road straightened, and Wilson was able to go faster. Mounds of worn granite, as large as houses, poked out of the grass.

"There's something coming up that will interest you," he said.

In another ten minutes, he turned onto a gravel road, looped around an outcrop of stone, and came to a jagged wall of immense granite blocks. They were stacked to the height of three stories and carved to fit together in intimate embrace. "It's called *Sacsahuaman*."

147

"Sexy woman?" Pete repeated Cab's phonetic pronunciation.

"If the Spanish hadn't stolen most of the stones to build their churches in Cusco, this sight would be more famous than Machu Picchu."

Cab slowed to a stop in a gravel parking lot. A woman wrapped in a red sweater, wearing a turquoise skirt and a straw hat, stepped over to Pete's door. At the end of a rope, she led a dirty llama that was almost her size. She wanted him to take her picture—for money.

"Why are we stopping?" Pete asked.

"This site always makes me impressed at the enormous—"

"I know, but we don't have time to waste." He twisted from one side of his seat to the other.

"We'll only be here for a few minutes."

Pete shouted at him. "No, there isn't time. I want to find Judd. He's screwed everyone—me included. I can't wait to look him in the eyes."

"Okay, I get it." Wilson pulled the gearshift down into reverse and backed slowly in a semi-circle. "It was originally used as a fort, with two towers on the ends. The long wall you see is built in a jagged fashion to resemble a bolt of lightning." He turned onto the paved road. "So much of Incan planning and design mirrored the sky and the stars—"

Pete interrupted him. "I have to check in with my tech guy." He texted Mateo but didn't get a response. "Cab, you don't seem to understand that I've got to get up there fast. You promised you could do that."

"Hey, back off. Is there something you're missing about this road? Doesn't it look slow and winding?"

The small car felt stuffy. Pete rolled down his window and smelled the pine trees hugging the side of the road. "All right. I get your point."

Cab focused on making the hairpin turns as they crested a pass in the mountains. Pete looked at him and felt sorry for his outburst. Muscles stood out in his arms while he gripped the wheel. In anticipation of the heat in the valley, he'd recommended they both wear shorts. Pete watched as Wilson expertly worked the clutch and gas pedals alternately.

He thought about Anita Montana. What information could Pete get from her? She was ambitious and seemed to work hard. And she was attractive also. Pete pushed that thought out of his mind. There had been a handful of women in his life who had taken his heart for good.

But they were gone now. One had died, and another he'd reluctantly left in Southeast Asia.

He remembered Anita's explanation of how important family still was for many people in South America. Family, for him, had been pretty much a disappointment. As he got older, that loss bothered him more. There was Karen, of course, but the relationship was still in repair, held hostage by the decision about money. It frustrated him that Karen seemed to equate his love with his generosity.

Pete looked out the window at the Andes Mountains. The jagged edges looked like a row of serrated knives with the blades turned out and stacked together with their points touching at the snowy peaks. He remembered that the Incas believed the mountains were living things, perhaps gods themselves. They breathed and moved and talked with the sound of wind and thunder and volcanoes.

Pete realized there was nothing he could do to speed up their progress. He leaned his head back against the seat. "When are we going to get there?"

Wilson laughed. "No patience. Wait till you see the beginning of the valley. I love this part of the world."

The road widened into a modern freeway although it had only two lanes. Cab picked up speed. Clouds, caught on the peaks, floated around them, creating mist on the windshield. Two red-and-white tourist buses lumbered up the grade in the opposite direction. Exhaust followed behind each one, and they growled like huge beasts in pain from the work of climbing the mountain.

Pete spotted small adobe houses perched on the slopes. Terraced farms overflowed with plantings that turned yellow when the sun broke through the clouds and shined on them.

Before Pete could ask, Cab said, "Quinoa. Sometimes they grow potatoes also. They originated here, you know."

"Yeah. Along with corn."

In ten minutes, Wilson cut across the lanes and drove into a gravel turn-out. He stopped next to a line of wooden shacks. Each one had a worn wooden table inside—a market for the people who lived up here. They got out of the car, and Pete could smell moisture in the air. He turned around to face the Sacred Valley and gasped at the beauty.

On either side, for as far as he could see in the morning mist, mountains sheltered the valley. Unlike the Rockies in the United States that were preceded by foothills, these mountains rose straight up from the floor of the valley for thousands of feet. Snowy peaks capped several of the closest ones. Beyond them, even higher mountains thrust upward with a heavy, permanent dominance. A few terraced fields clung to the precipitous edges overlooking the valley.

He felt the looseness of excitement in his lower body. Neither of them spoke.

The valley spread where it could find room between the mountains. It was bright green, the color of the first leaves on trees in the spring. Adobe houses dotted the fields and were connected by dirt roads. A river twisted through the fields.

"The Urubamba River," Cab said. "This is the gateway to the Incan valley. They weren't the first to settle here, but they expanded the use of it by farming and establishing cities with forts and temples. We'll see some of them."

Pete was rooted in place. He watched while the sun moved higher and burned off the mist. He could see for miles down the valley, quiet, clear, majestic, and peaceful. Below, small figures of farmers led oxen across the fields. A bus trundled along the gravel road, lifting yellow dust in its wake.

This place was so isolated and protected that, for a few minutes, he forgot about everything else. The hunt for Judd, the mystery, the threat of the others chasing Pete—all dropped away.

Finally, he looked at his watch. Behind him, Pete heard the squeal of a truck's brakes as it inched down the road. He got back into the car, and Cab started the Toyota. "Where do we go now, boss?"

"In fifteen minutes, we'll be down there." He pointed over the edge of the cliff. "The first town is Pisaq. We'll stop for lunch. There's a huge market in the town square you might want to check out."

"I don't think we have time."

"Right, but we'll hurry."

"Can't we drive all the way to Aguas Calientes?"

"No. About halfway down the valley, we'll have to switch to the train. It's the only way to go further."

"Dammit."

A series of switchbacks led them down toward the farms below. Wilson turned off the paved road onto a yellow gravel road. He rolled down both side windows. The air smelled moist and hinted at the hot weather to come later in the day.

They crossed a bridge over the Urubamba River. The noise of the Toyota echoed from underneath the wooden planks, while below them gray-green water tumbled over boulders in the riverbed. The current looked swift as it plunged from the mountains.

Cab slowed as they came to a cluster of adobe buildings. They were painted ochre, pale yellow, and green like the jacaranda trees that lined the road. Some had advertising slogans on the walls. On either side of the road, square farm plots stretched out until they ran into the walls of the mountains.

"The Incas thought this valley matched the shape of the Milky Way. That's why it was sacred to them."

"And I can understand why they felt this was a place they could defend. It would be impossible for an army to come into the valley without being detected."

"See those notches on the mountain over there?" Wilson pointed across the river. "Those were lookout points. They'd flash signals all down the valley by using the sun and pure golden discs." His voice sounded hollow. "Ultimately, it didn't help the Incas. They were doomed from the beginning."

"Except for Machu Picchu hidden way up there."

"Yes. Except for Machu Picchu."

Three tuk-tuks—motorbikes attached to two-wheeled carts— whined past them, kicking up a haze of dust. The cactus along the road must have choked every time a vehicle passed.

They kept driving. Warm air swirled in through the open windows and brought the smell of fresh earth that had been turned over for planting. People walked along the road. Women led mules with boxes roped to their backs. Wearing uniforms of dark green pants and white shirts, school kids skipped past the mules. A man with a straw hat rode the old Allis-Chalmers tractor along the edge of a field near the road.

Sections of the road that ran through busy intersections were paved. Past those, the road returned to gravel. As they progressed into the valley, the soil took on the color of old bricks. The river was never far away, and Pete could occasionally hear it crashing on its way to the depths of the Amazon basin.

Pete asked him, "Did you go to school at Yale?"

"I did. Undergrad, then I got my doctorate in archeology at the University of Indiana. I was originally considered an apostate for leaving New England by my professional friends, but I found the quieter campus refreshing. After all, there wasn't much to do except study."

They caught up to a lumbering commuter bus. Cab dropped back to avoid the exhaust. When it pulled over to stop at a corner where three people stood in the shade of an acacia tree, Cab passed it. They also encountered mules walking beside the road, trucks laden with rocks, cars, tuk-tuks, and motorcycles. Small settlements—crossroads, really—held shops, homes, community centers, and schools. An adobe wall with a closed iron gate hid a hotel behind it. A polished gold sign read "The Royal Inkan Hotel."

"For the tourists." Wilson explained why such a fancy hotel would be located in this farming community. "And more are being constructed each month. It's estimated that more than five thousand people visit Machu Picchu every year."

Pete realized the view from the hotel would be stunning.

In an hour, they came to a widening in the road. Traffic increased. To the right, several roads led into a densely-packed city. "Pisaq," Cab announced. The one-story buildings were sand colored, and many had open windows. As he drove deeper into the center of the town, the buildings grew to two stories tall. He inched his way up a road so narrow the car almost scraped the mirrors on the rough stone of the walls. A woman sat on a small chair, wrapping her daughter's hair with pink ribbons. They waved.

The street opened onto a huge central plaza. Cab picked his way between several tourist buses and found a parking spot on a side street. "Let's go. I'm hungry."

The plaza was filled with colorful tents. Under them vendors offered products from all over the valley: stone artwork, leather jackets, onions, silk scarves, and food, including *empanadas* filled with chicken and spinach. Pete could smell tea brewing near the food stalls and saw a huge caged box. He stopped to watch dozens of furry guinea pigs scurrying through the doors of their home.

"Want to select one for lunch?" Cab stood beside him.

"Uh, no. I've already experienced those. Never again."

"Okay, then let's go across to the corner. You'll like the Blue Llama."

They turned through the narrow aisles between the tents and came out into the open plaza again. Next to a tent selling hats and wool bags, a two-story café stood on the corner. It was painted bright blue, had a wooden balcony with seating, and the open door at floor level invited them inside. Painted across the front was the name: *The Blue Llama*. A row of white gladiolas stood in pots guarding the door.

"This has the best regional cooking," Cab told him.

The main floor was crowded with several rooms branching out in different directions and an open kitchen. He led Pete up a narrow stairway to the second floor. Several large photos covered the walls. One was of the Rolling Stones, one of Marilyn Monroe, another of Frank Sinatra. Each photo had a quote written across it that said, "I love the Blue Llama." The room was empty, and they picked a table on the balcony. The table wobbled because one leg was too short. They ordered Cusquena beer, and Wilson recommended the *chupe de verduras*.

"Who would've known?" Pete laughed. "More soup."

"You can get something else, but this is a specialty here."

"Cab, do you have a family?"

"Divorced. One child in college at Tufts. I miss him, but the position at the Casa Concha was too exciting for me to turn down. I get to work with the original artifacts along with some of the best researchers in Peru. They're very good, you know."

Pete could smell wood burning from somewhere. The sun flooded the balcony and felt hot across his back. He took a long drink of the beer, removed his hat, and leaned back in the stiff chair. "Do tourists support this town?" he asked.

"Not entirely, but as you can see, everyone must come along this road to get to Machu Picchu. The locals know that, so each tourist bus stops in this plaza."

153

Pete looked over the balcony and saw a line of Chinese people step down from the open door of a giant bus. The women wore the latest in fashion, high wedge-heeled shoes, and covered their heads with hats and their hands with gloves. He thought it must be dangerous for them to walk on those shoes over the cobblestone streets.

The soup came, along with local bread. Pete found himself hungrier than he'd thought. He dug into each. In a thin broth, there were sliced fava beans, carrots, potatoes, and quinoa that looked like swollen wheat. It was all delicious. "Good, but a little bland for me."

"Here you are." Cab handed him a serving dish with three cups of dips. "They have over fifty kinds of chilies here. Try one."

Pete ladled a small amount into the soup, stirred it, and continued eating. Better. He wiped his mouth and asked, "What's next?"

"We continue on the road to Ollantaytambo. Another town, but it also contains huge Incan ruins of a temple and fort." He slurped the last of his soup from the bowl. "Beyond that, we catch the train."

"You said the train doesn't run often. Do we have tickets?"

"No. I think we'll be early enough to buy them at the station. There should be room for two of us."

"Dammit, Cab. I can't miss it." He ordered a cup of *mate de coca* to ward off the altitude headache that threatened. When served, it was darker yellow than the tea served in Ecuador and not as bitter. He added a lump of sugar and drank all of it. He felt better.

From farther up in the valley, deep thunder rolled down its length. Pete looked up to see only the cobalt sky with puffy white clouds. He must have frowned, because Wilson said, "It's called 'slumbering thunder.' The weather changes dramatically in the valley depending on where you are. When we get to Aguas Calientes, we'll be deep in the rain forest. It rains almost every day."

More thunder rumbled past them. It made Pete feel uneasy. He finished his beer and stood. "I want to get going."

"Yes, I know." Cab scraped back his chair, stood, and started down the stairway to the main floor.

They came outside and into the plaza. Six more buses had parked to one side, tourists flooding out the doors and barging under the vendor's tents. "Where'd you say the cash machine was?" one woman yelled at the Peruvian guide who leaned against the side of a bus. Another man mumbled, "I need a God damn beer. Is it too early?"

Cab led him around the corner to find the car. Pete's phone chirped, and he pulled it out of the cargo pocket on the side of his pants. He had a text message. He keyed it open and stopped so quickly that Wilson also stopped.

"Wha—?" Pete croaked.

"What is it?"

His chest pounded. "I can't believe it." Pete couldn't talk. He read the message again:

ali baba after you— dont trust anyone— anyone!!
Sorry I got u down here— go home now!!

It was from Judd Crowe.

Chapter Twenty-Three

J. Cabot Wilson headed deeper into the valley toward the next town, called Ollantaytambo. At least the one-lane road was paved. He drove as fast as the conditions allowed. Green fields bumped against the mountains and climbed the sides, held in place by narrow terraces of stonework. These were connected by faint white trails that crisscrossed the flanks of the mountains.

Pete was still stunned by the message from Judd. He'd disappeared so completely that Pete wondered if Judd had really died. Pete had replied immediately but didn't get a response. He tried a few more times before giving up. Although it was a warning, it created the opposite feeling in Pete. It motivated him to work even harder to find Judd.

"That message you received looks like it made you mad," Cab said. A breeze streamed into the open window, the air heated by the sun and the high altitude. "Are you okay?"

Pete even wondered if the text was truly from Judd, but then, who would impersonate Judd? And why? "An old—" He stumbled on the word *friend*. "Someone I've known for many years. He's the reason I have to get to Machu Picchu by the twenty-second."

"I can tell this is very important to you. I'll do my best to get us there."

Pete nodded. He didn't believe Judd was warning him. Instead, he was trying to get rid of him.

While Pete thought Judd had been hiding, all along he'd probably been watching Pete. He felt uneasy and glanced behind the car to see if anyone was following them. Two motorcycles buzzed up from the rear and passed the Toyota. Both riders wore black helmets that hid their faces.

The part of the message that got Pete's attention was 'ali babas after you.' He was armed and prepared to fight, if necessary.

Cab drove on. Neither of them spoke.

"Are you sure we can get tickets for the train?" Pete said.

"Should be okay." Still, Cab pressed the little car faster. As if to break the silence, he told Pete about the farmed terraces. "By building those high up on the mountainsides, the Incas could take advantage of temperature and moisture differences. Each section of terraces encompassed a different microclimate, allowing the Incas to grow plants that normally wouldn't flourish at this altitude." He waved his hand toward the mountains. "As a result, they can grow crops year-round."

"How do you know all this?"

"This is what I've studied for years. I love the history and the culture of those ancient people. Without all of our modern conveniences or even the Internet, they seemed to thrive. They were healthy and self-sufficient. Who knows? Maybe happier than we are."

As they came closer to the next city, dust rose again, and Pete could see the low profile of buildings set at the base of three intersecting mountains. They dwarfed the human habitation.

Wilson explained, "Two rivers come together here. The mountains made this a natural fortification. You'll see the fort and sun temple soon."

He looked up but couldn't see the peaks lost in the clouds. The sides of the mountains were bare of vegetation. The rock looked chiseled and cold in spite of the heat on the floor of the valley. Pete pulled in his arm from the open window.

Cab slowed as the road snaked into the center of the town. Narrow cobblestone streets branched off in every direction. There were no square corners. Along the side of the street, an open channel carried running water. It was the first time Pete had seen that. "I bet those were built by the Incas for irrigation." He turned to Cab for confirmation.

"You are a quick learner." He laughed. "Except for your Spanish. I've heard you try to speak it, and maybe you should study that a little more."

"I'm an expert on most subjects."

Wilson turned onto a street that ran straight for several blocks. It was intersected by other streets at right angles. The grid pattern was different from the rest of the city, and he said the Incas had constructed this part originally. Cab drove into the main plaza, ringed by shops, restaurants, cash machines, and colonial buildings painted yellow and brown. Several tourist buses rested in the afternoon shade. A line of tourists dressed in shorts and t-shirts that said "Global Action Adventures" stood in front of a liquor store that sold beer and wine. One man at the head of the line called back to the bus, "Helen. I need more *pesos*. I'm all over this beer. It's so cheap."

Cab drove through the plaza and toward the end of town. They passed one mountain on the right and faced two more that seemed connected to each other to create a "V" shape at the end of a steep valley. Fitted between the walls of the mountains, an immense structure of stone and rock rose into the sky. Like the farms nearby, the Ollantaytambo fortress climbed up the valley in set-back terraces. Thousands of stone steps led through the complex and through open doors and under gray granite lintels that looked like they weighed tons.

"This site was started long before the Incas came here. But the confluence of two rivers and three mountains made it a natural defensive position. The lookouts could post themselves on each mountain and get an almost 360-degree view. The Incas expanded the city and added to the fortress. At the top, they built a sun temple, of course."

"It would be easy to spot the enemy. Was this the main town for them?"

"No. But it guarded the royal cities that are farther up the Sacred Valley, hidden in the rain forest."

He pulled the Toyota parallel with the front of the monument. Two tourist buses had already beaten the crowds from the plaza and disgorged dozens of people. Many wore hiking boots, carried backpacks, and balanced themselves on the steps with metal walking sticks. Some of the stones were larger than refrigerators and fitted together so closely it would be impossible to push a knife blade between them. The entire structure had been assembled without mortar and still stood exactly as the Incas had left it when they fled in front of the Spanish conquest.

"This is the site of the largest military victory the Incas had against the Spanish. They were stopped temporarily until reinforcements came. Then Pizarro broke through and chased the Incas back to the other royal cities. That was in 1537."

"Okay, but why are we waiting here?"

"It's important to me, for one thing. When I am near these sites, I feel a spiritual pull from them. The Incas considered everything in their world to be alive in some form: the mountains, rivers, and fields. If they were right, it means these mountains looking down on us are still alive and have memories."

"Okay, okay." Pete waved his hands in front of Cab. "Sorry, I don't know if I can follow all that. Since we didn't plan well, we may not get tickets, right?"

"I think—"

"We may not get on that last train. So we miss September twenty-second at Machu Picchu." Pete's voice rose with his frustration.

"You blame me." Wilson shook his head from side to side.

"Well, you know more than I do about Machu Picchu and how to get there."

He glared at Pete. "I'm doing you the favor. I appreciate the payment, but I could be doing other things. Had you come to me earlier, we would have reached the site easily in time. But now we're under the gun, and—"

"Wait a minute. What was the date you said the Spanish chased the Incas up the Sacred Valley to the royal cities?"

"It was in 1537."

"Yeah," Pete shouted. "Judd's flash drive had a series of numbers on it. I thought they were all measurements, as in decimal degrees. But now I think 1537 referred to the Spanish conquest."

"What are you talking about?"

"Uh, the man I'm after had a flash drive with strange information on it. Now a lot of it is starting to make sense. I don't know anything about the conquest. Can you tell me more?"

Cab frowned at him. "I don't understand, but of course. I'll give you the short version. It's fascinating. Pizarro came originally as an entrepreneur—he wanted to exploit the riches of Peru. He landed on the coast in 1532 with 168 men. It was the luckiest date possible for Pizarro."

"Why?"

"The Incan empire was recovering from civil war. The chief from Ecuador, Atahualpa, had beaten his half-brother for control of the empire, but it had been decimated in the process. He was aware of the Spanish advance, and Atahualpa received them in the northern city of Cajamarca."

"Why would the chief agree to that?"

"Remember that Atahualpa had a battle-hardened army of forty thousand soldiers. Besides, he was now the Inca, the sun-god, and therefore invincible. He actually planned to capture the Spanish and enslave them. But he seriously underestimated the strengths they had."

"Only 168 men? That doesn't sound like strength to me."

Cab turned in the seat and spoke faster. "First, the tribes the Incas had defeated in the civil war aided the Spanish as a way of reprisal to the Incas. The first effects of smallpox—introduced earlier by the Europeans—were killing the locals. The Spanish had technological advantages like horses, armor, guns, and steel swords. The Incas fought with wooden spears and slingshots."

"I'm getting the picture."

"The turning point was when Atahualpa met the Spanish in the plaza of Cajamarca. His army was unarmed, but the Spanish were fully armed and fired their cannons into the crowd. They launched a surprise attack and killed hundreds of the Incas. Pizarro captured Atahualpa and held him hostage, decapitating the empire in one stroke."

"Did he kill the emperor?"

"Wait. An extraordinary thing happened: Atahualpa offered to buy his freedom by filling a room twenty feet by seventeen feet with gold higher than a man's head and then, to fill it twice more with silver."

"Did Pizarro get all that?"

"Yes, although it was a fraction of the kingdom's wealth. After he took the riches, Pizarro had Atahualpa executed in the plaza. He strangled the king."

"And we think our modern-day terrorists are nasty guys." The story drew Pete forward. "Did the Incan kingdom fall then?"

Wilson grinned. "Not yet. Pizarro picked a puppet emperor named Manco Inca. At the ceremony to crown him, the Incas brought out several mummies of prior rulers because they believed the Inca was a god and continued to 'live' even after physical death. The mummies resided in the original ruler's palaces with their families and servants still in residence and all their possessions. Each new Inca could 'talk' to the mummies for advice."

"Now that sounds creepy to me."

"But Manco Inca double-crossed Pizarro, escaped, and attacked the Spanish in Cusco with a huge army, and burned it down. The Incas almost won. But the Spanish managed to beat them back, and in 1536 Manco Inca fled from Cusco into the Urubamba River valley with his army, people, and all the riches of the kingdom. In 1537, the Spanish mounted a campaign to find him and the treasure."

"What happened?"

"They captured Manco and executed him, but didn't find either his capital city or his riches. To this day, both are still lost, except for Machu Picchu. Many archeologists think it was Manco Inca's true capital, hidden in the clouds at the top of the mountain."

"Can we get moving while you talk?" Pete said.

"Oh yes, of course." Cab started the Toyota.

Pete looked up at the massive fort and temple before them. It would have been impossible to get horses up there. The fighting between the Spanish and Incas would have been fierce hand-to-hand combat. Nasty stuff. It was ironic that people were still fighting over this area, especially Machu Picchu. The tourists milling about and taking smart phone pictures while posing in front of the stones didn't realize the powerful forces that fought each other behind the scenes. The possible privatization of the citadel in the clouds had pitted large money interests against each other and also opponents like Agent Castillo, gangsters, and even the United States Export/Import Bank, interested in lending to possible American developers. Pete could sympathize with the doomed Incas.

Cab pulled away from the ruins and drove back through the city.

"What did the Spanish do after they conquered the Incas?" Pete asked. The wound on his forehead itched. At least the itching meant it was healing.

Wilson's lips thinned as he spoke. "Today we'd call it genocide." The car careened around a corner, bumped over the cobblestones, and straightened out on the paved road that led alongside the Urubamba River.

The facts of the dark history seemed to fade as they picked up speed on the road. Sun drenched them and gave the air a copper tint. Farmers looked up from their mules and waved. Pete saw more white trails that crossed the mountainsides at different heights. He asked Cab about them.

"Old Incan walking trails. They lead all over the valley."

"Impressive."

"Yes. Like I've told you, the Incas believed these mountains were gods, a part of the whole earth they called *pachamama*. By climbing to the tops of these mountains, they could experience something god-like and meditate without the distractions from the activities in the valley. Soon you'll see those trails come together for the hiking trail to Machu Picchu."

"I have a friend in Minneapolis who hiked the Inca Trail to the summit."

"I did it once, years ago. The altitude makes it difficult, but even worse are the other obstacles."

"Like what?"

"The scariest for me were the trails that hugged the side of the mountains. On the left side was solid rock. On the other side of the one-foot-wide trail, it dropped straight down into the valley thousands of feet below. If you slipped or if it was wet—"

"No guardrails, huh?"

He laughed. "No, there are no safety standards imposed on the trail like we would have in the US. Besides, it takes four days to finish it for most people. You need to get there faster. Many tourists insist on taking the trail because it is the same one used by the ancient Incas to reach Machu Picchu, and it's still a challenge. And then there are the New Age people. They come that way because the crystals and the voices talk to them on the path. It's a spiritual journey to reach a god-like experience, primarily."

Pete nodded. Normally he didn't think much about those things, but Cab's stories of the Incas had awakened in him a sensitivity to his spiritual side. Without admitting it to Cab, Pete thought of his ancestors on his mother's side. What were they like? He envied the hikers who came for the struggle up the mountains. What a reward to reach Machu Picchu! And although his journey now was filled with much more crass motives—money, swindlers, gangsters, and probably danger—Pete felt himself pulled along by deeper purposes.

Was he here because he wanted to be engaged in the age-old battle to beat the bad guys? A struggle that stretched back in time through the Incas versus the Spanish and even beyond them into the mountains and the mists? Today the battle wasn't as epic but was equally important. Justice must be done to Judd Crowe.

In spite of the cloudless cobalt sky, thunder rumbled down from the mountains ahead of them. "Slumbering thunder," he remembered and noticed that the sun had fallen behind the mountain peaks at the west end of the valley

Along the road, Pete saw gas stations all painted in the same colors of yellow and green. He asked Cab about them.

"Government owned, although much of the oil business is being privatized. People still sell gas on the black market to avoid the government prices."

The road turned slightly, the valley widened, and they entered an area of rolling green hills. He spotted clusters of white buildings with orange tile roofs set in the shelter of the hills.

Cab glanced at him and said, "That is the work of the Peru National Tourism Board. They encourage investment in those beautiful hotels."

They passed dozens of hotel complexes. The air smelled clean and fresh. Pete thought how nice it would be to spend a few days at one of those hotels, relaxing and enjoying the scenery of the valley. To his left, Pete saw the Urubamba flowing by, calm and green at this point.

Within a half hour, they approached a cluster of one-story buildings. A long wooden building sat beside railroad tracks. Finally, they'd made it to the train.

Wilson pulled into a small gravel parking lot surrounded by a chain-link fence. It was filled with other cars, and he had to squeeze the Toyota in an illegal spot. Grabbing their backpacks from the trunk, they started across the lot to a paved road that sloped down toward the train tracks. The road was lined with shops and food trucks. The shops sold mostly tourist items like hats, sunscreen, stuffed llama dolls, and t-shirts that said "I Climbed Machu Picchu." Indian women wrapped in colorful clothing that looked hot to wear called out to Cab and Pete. Most of them also wore modern running shoes.

As they got closer to the tracks, the road narrowed like a funnel and became steeper. Some of the shops sold *mate de coca*, others sold Cusquena beer, and many sold *empanadas* with several choices of hot sauce for dipping. "Hey, Indiana Jones," one of the vendors yelled at Pete in English. "You hungry? Thirsty? I have cold beer." It sounded like a baseball park.

They reached a long concrete platform next to two train tracks. One line must have been for going to Aguas Calientes, the other for the return trip. There were no other roads, airports, or ways to get access to the area at the foot of Machu Picchu. The city itself had only existed as more than a crossroads of dirt trails for about ten years. When the Peruvian government finally realized how rich the tourist industry was and how much money people were willing to spend for access to the ruins, they opened the city for development. Wilson had booked the Mapi Hotel for Pete and himself when they were in Cusco, because the tiny city had a limited number of rooms available.

Cab had jokingly offered the municipal park for tent camping instead of a hotel, if Pete was interested. Cab also reminded him there wasn't any heat and the altitude was almost 9,000 feet. He declined.

The train platform was mobbed with people. Most stood in lines and waited, but many, especially the American tourists, pushed forward. Clots of people formed so densely they threatened to fall off the platform onto the tracks.

Wilson's face colored darker as he snaked through the crowd. "The ticket office is over here," he shouted to Pete from over his shoulder. "Come on. We'll have to push our way in."

In order to allow Cab to maneuver more easily, Pete followed, carrying all the backpacks. He was convinced the train was sold out. They were too late. Everything he'd worked for would be wasted. Pete blamed himself for not taking care of the purchase earlier. Surely, he could've bought these online back in Cusco, or even Lima. He elbowed his way through the crowd but lost sight of Wilson.

At the far end of the platform, an old wooden station had its doors wide open. It contained two long and narrow rooms. One was for passengers to wait, and the other included the ticket windows and a small eating area. The interior was dark wood, almost the color of ebony. A counter offered Italian sodas, coffee, and *café au lait*. A barista stood behind a copper-colored steamer. It hissed when he heated the espresso for a drink.

People jammed the rooms and occupied all the benches. A darkened trail from thousands of footsteps discolored the tile floor. Pete saw that Cab had managed to reach the ticket window. He shouted something to the attendant in Spanish through the wooden slats in the opening. Pete came closer and saw Cab fall back a step and drop his head.

Cab regained his determination and leaned forward again. Back and forth, he argued with the attendant. Finally, he opened the leather bag from his shoulder that he used as a carryall and produced his museum credentials. The attendant took them and retreated into the gloom of the back office.

Pete came to his side. "What's wrong?"

Cab shook his head.

"Are they sold out?"

"I don't think so, but he's lying to me. He must be holding the tickets for someone else. In this country, corruption reigns. Who knows? There might be a wealthy family who was able to reserve the tickets or bribed him earlier."

"We've got to do something." He felt his stomach knot.

"They respect educated people and those with authority. I don't know if my museum ID is authoritative enough, but let's hope so."

The clerk returned. His eyes darted to Wilson, and he nodded and slid two tickets under the wooden slats. He grabbed them, yelled "*Muchas gracias*," and turned to rush back to the platform. Pete followed.

They inched along the platform, looking for PeruRail car number two. The cars were painted blue with yellow trim along the roof. A uniformed porter stood by an open door in the car.

A small woman tugged at Pete's sleeve. He turned to see a vendor smiling up at him and offering to sell a metal walking stick. She held it up to him. "Good price," she said in English. Pete hesitated. He didn't need it, and he was anxious to get boarded before something happened to jeopardize their seats. The woman tugged at his arm again. Pete felt sorry for her. "How much?"

"Only seven American dollars."

He clutched a handful of *solis* from his pocket and handed them to her. She gave him the stick and tipped her hat to him. When she smiled, he could see most of her teeth were missing.

Cab handed their tickets to the porter. He stepped to the side as they climbed two steps into the car and entered. Pete felt his body relax. Padded green leather seats flanked the two sides, separated by collapsible wooden tables so that one set of chairs faced forward and, on the other side of the table, the chairs faced backward. Their seats faced forward.

He settled their packs in an overhead rack. Wilson told him to take the window seat because the ride would be impressive. He agreed, slid in, and settled back into the seat. Pete took a deep breath. Somehow, they'd been lucky and had gotten two of the last tickets for the day. After this train, no more would run until tomorrow morning.

Cab leaned toward him. "See. Trust me from now on." He smiled, but there was steel in his eyes.

The train whistle screamed twice as if in warning. Cars clanked against each other with a loud bang.

"But even you have to admit, we were damn lucky," Pete said.

"Well, maybe." Cab's eyes drifted away to look out the window that wrapped around half of the ceiling. His head jerked back to Pete. "I can't believe—Look, that's probably who the agent was holding the tickets for."

"What?" Pete screwed his body around to see outside. Just behind the train station in an open area of sand, he saw a helicopter hover for a moment. Its blades whirred invisibly, and he could read the lettering on the side: *Group China Financial Industries.* The helicopter landed, and before the blades stopped revolving, Pete saw a pale man with a short ponytail leap from the open door.

Chapter Twenty-Four

Tuesday evening, September 20

Anita Montana sat in the green leather seat of the train, facing the rear. Along with several other passengers, she saw the helicopter raising dust that covered the top of the station house. She stood and pushed her way to the big window to watch Xiong Lo step out of the cloud of dust and hurry toward the station.

It didn't surprise her. In her experience with CNN, she'd interviewed Lo twice in the past. He was as persistent and ruthless as they came, and Anita had learned a lot from watching him operate. The difference was, she remained legal in what she did.

Her insides tingled. With all these people coming together here, the story Anita chased promised to be even bigger than she'd originally imagined. She was convinced the best angle was to stick close to Pete Chandler. He was also persistent and tough—he'd find Crowe no matter what. And that's where Anita would be at the same time.

There were four major TV networks in Ecuador. Anita had seen a reporter from Equavisa when she had been in Cusco. Only one other reporter from Gama TV had followed the story up the Sacred Valley, like Anita. She'd spotted him far behind her in line at the train station. There were only a few seats available on the train, and if she could stall the competition, he'd lose any chance for a ticket.

Anita had called over several of the vendors who always crowded the edge of the station. Within seconds, five hungry sellers mobbed her, each of them pushing a stack of products in her face. She waved them apart and told them there was a man behind her who needed many of their wares. Pulling out some *solis* from her pocket, Anita bought hats, t-shirts, walking sticks, and even purses with crude paintings of Machu Picchu on the sides. She paid for all of them and told the vendors to give them to the man with the red shirt and glasses who stood at the edge of the platform in the line. Their heads turned until they spotted the reporter.

"He will probably pretend he doesn't want the gifts, but you must insist that he take them," she had told the mob. "I know him, and he has much money to buy even more from you for his large family."

They agreed, and the group moved back along the line. Anita watched them surround the reporter, pushing the items at him. He swung his head back and forth, raised his hands as if he were being attacked by the mob, and tried to squeeze forward through them. They had crushed him out of the line, leaving the reporter isolated at the end of the station.

After spotting Xiong Lo while in the train, Anita went back to her seat and pulled out her phone to update her editor. She smiled. When the swirl of dust had settled, she'd also seen the Gama TV reporter still arguing with a large group of vendors.

Chapter Twenty-Five

Tuesday evening, September 20

Pressure built from deep in Pete's chest. With both hands pressed to the window, he watched while he explained to Wilson who Xiong Lo was and what he was after. "He's gone into the station. There aren't any tickets left. He's too late."

Cab shot him a look that said: *Are you really that stupid?* "Of course he can get a ticket if he's got enough money. And even if this guy doesn't get on the train, he's got a goddamn helicopter. It'd be a tight squeeze into Aguas Caliente, but I think he could do it."

"Oh." Pete turned and sat back in the seat. There were lavatories at the end of the car, but the Chinese would look there first. Could Pete keep moving from car to car to avoid them? Maybe—until he reached the end of the cars. He took a deep breath in preparation. He doubted they'd try anything violent again on the train. Besides, the tight spaces on the train actually gave Pete an advantage no matter how many of the Chinese there were.

If all else failed, he had packed the Glock 43 at the bottom of his bag—there had not been any security checks to get on the train. Pete would fight.

"I haven't seen him come out yet. I bet he's in there either bribing his way onto the train or simply ordering someone else to get off," Cab said.

The train jerked and the cars clanked again. The whistle screamed, the sound lost as it shot down the river.

"Okay, let's get ready to face him," Pete said.

Cab didn't take his eyes from the station. He leaned further into the window, and his face glowed green from the tint in the glass. "It might work."

"I wish government investigators in the US were as tenacious as these guys."

Another look from Cab reminded Pete how far he was from his country and its customs.

169

The train jerked once more, and with the steel wheels squealing, it lurched into motion. A porter entered the front end of the car. He wore a baseball cap that said PeruRail in blue letters with yellow trim. He carried a tray of sandwiches in his hand. In English he said, "We're departing, and I would like to offer you refreshments. Fine Peruvian coffee, water, and drinks will follow after this. May I offer you fine refreshments?" He stopped at each table and bent over to listen to the passengers.

Wilson sat back in the seat. "If you didn't want to see this guy, I think you are lucky. I didn't see him come out of the station and get on the train."

"Good, but I'll feel better when we finally get to Aguas Calientes. Right now, I could use a glass of wine." When the porter reached their table, Pete ordered two glasses of the Chilean Sauvignon Blanc. Cab handed several ham sandwiches to Pete and kept two for himself. The ham was tasteless, but he ate both of them quickly, surprised at how hungry he was.

In ten minutes, the train was at full speed—about twenty-five miles an hour. Normally, that would have bothered Pete. But the scenery was so fascinating, he didn't mind the slow pace. The windows in the ceiling, called a vista dome, revealed the mountains that soared above them, their peaks hidden in cloud banks. The train rocked from side to side, and Pete could hear faint clicking from the wheels below.

The tracks paralleled the Urubamba River so closely that it was possible to look down onto the river. At this point, it tumbled over boulders the size of small cars. The rocks were bleached white where the chalky green water crashed against them.

From the west, the dropping sun lit up the valley. Long shafts of light created shadows behind the rocks that had fallen from the sides of the mountains. The ancient hiking paths of the Incas threaded between the rocks as the trails climbed high into the peaks. Sometimes the paths were so old and faint Pete lost sight of them.

Along the river, he saw blue-green agave plants. Cacti with flattened arms grew among the rocks and dirt. He leaned back and sipped his wine. Comfortable and safe, for the moment, Pete relaxed and enjoyed the view. He could understand why the Incas had considered the valley sacred. It was truly a unique place protected by massive mountains. Pete assumed the quality of the light, the dry air, and the fresh smell of everything hadn't changed in hundreds of years. In a way, he felt a closeness to the ancient people who'd crawled over these same rocks and paths.

His mind drifted to the electric company people who had interrogated and threatened him. There must be a connection between the company, Judd, and Machu Picchu. The officers had bragged to Pete they were one of the largest suppliers in the country. Could they have extended their tentacles this far? He asked Cab about them.

Setting down his wine glass, Wilson frowned. "I'm not sure."

Pete pulled out his phone and tried to Google the company. He couldn't get service.

Cab used his phone. "I've got the local service. What was the name of the electric company?" Pete told him, and in a few minutes, Cab looked across the table and said, "They own a major electric generating plant that supplies this whole region at the foot of Machu Picchu. It's on a turn of the river, hidden behind the mountain. Here's an aerial photo." He passed the phone to Pete.

A grainy black-and-white shot showed a huge lump of buildings at a sharp bend in the river. Even at the height from which the photo was taken, the electric plant looked like a cancerous growth on the foot of the immense mountain.

He turned back to the window. The train rocked gently, and he watched the river flowing as it probably had for thousands of years. Lately, he'd been having an unusual dream. He found himself as a child in a large family celebration. Kind of like Christmas, but the party couldn't have been for that, because everyone there was Asian. How could that be? The dream seemed so real to Pete that he could even smell the sandalwood incense burning somewhere in the small house. People smiled at him and talked in words that he couldn't understand. Where did the dream come from?

Cab tapped him on the arm. "Your phone. It lit up. Maybe you've got service."

Pete grabbed it in time to see a text from Mateo back in Quito, asking Pete to contact him. Had he cracked the software on the CD?

"Good news?"

Pete keyed his phone and flicked his finger across the screen, then tried again. Finally, he admitted, "Lost the signal again. We should be able to get one in Aguas Calientes, or an Internet connection. We're running out of time. Doesn't the train have wi-fi?"

"No." Cab patted the space between them with his palms. "Mateo's working on it. Relax. He is a genius."

At the moment there was nothing more anyone could do, but Pete was a man of action. He hated to sit still.

He turned to the window and saw a herd of alpaca. They were smaller than llamas and were grazing in a pasture along the river.

The valley narrowed, and when the train whistle blew again, it echoed off the walls of the mountains. The Urubamba River became more turbulent, and the water leaped above the rocks as if it were straining to escape the river bed.

There were small stone and adobe houses that perched at the edge of the river. They had clay roofs and low stone fences. Many had tiny plots of corn growing in the front yard. The ears of corn, like small green footballs, gave color to the dull rock surroundings. Pete didn't see any cars or motorbikes, nor people at any of the houses.

As they journeyed further into the valley, the wall of the mountain on the opposite side of the train from Pete crept closer to the tracks until the train cars almost scraped it. The passengers on the right side of the car lost their view in the brown blur of the passing rocks.

A few trees crowded next to the river, and Pete noticed their shadows had lengthened to a distance of twice the true height of the trees. He could feel a chill in the air.

Wilson pointed out the window to a pile of gray rocks halfway up the mountainside. "Crumbled Incan ruins. They're all over the valley."

Pete turned to look. "Not as impressive as Machu Picchu."

"No. But many of the other sites are huge and equally astounding. Choquequirao, for instance."

"Never heard of it."

"Its cousin, Machu Picchu, is much more famous. When Hiram Bingham came here, the local people first directed him to the citadel on the edge of the Yanama River. The name means 'cradle of gold' in Quechua. The legends told that Choquequirao was the final refuge of the Incas, thousands who were said to have escaped from the Spanish to reach the hidden city in the clouds. Supposedly, they carried the most spectacular riches of the kingdom, and when the last of the Incas died out, the location of the treasure was lost with them. The jungle grew over the city until it, too, was lost."

"Did Bingham find the treasure?"

"No one has ever found anything. The city resembles Machu Picchu but is not as impressive. One of the most interesting things about it is the hundreds of terraced fields that step down toward the river. On the sides of the stone are mosaics with over two dozen pictures of white llamas. Some of them are taller than humans."

"So the llama must've been a big deal to the Incas."

"Not only the llamas, but the alpaca as well. They provided wool, pack animals, a food source, and even their dung was burned for heat and cooking. There's also an interesting religious hybrid up here that goes back to the time of the conquest."

"They're not all Catholics?"

"Some are, of course, but these mountain people mix the traditional Catholic beliefs with ancient ancestor worship. For instance, in many of those small stone houses you see, you might find the skull of a grandfather, watching over the home."

Pete noticed something that resembled a wisp of smoke curl off the side of the train. The sharp smell of ozone in the air signaled a pending rain storm.

Clouds dropped around the train, causing the sides to look like they were sweating. They rocked along at the same speed through the mist. It glowed silver in the sunlight. Pete noticed more vines hanging from the branches and the trunks of trees. "The scenery is changing," he said.

"Right. We're entering the cloud forest. By the time we get to Aguas Calientes, we'll be in the full rain forest."

"I've been in rain forests in Southeast Asia. What's different about a cloud forest?"

"It's still tropical but has a dense fog at the canopy level of the trees. That's why you see the mist outside."

Pete thought the mist looked like smoke passing by—it softened all the objects outside the window.

"This forest doesn't get as much rain, but the added moisture creates a unique ecosystem of ground and tree ferns and mosses." Cab pointed out the window. "See those spiky plants? Red bromeliads. And orchids grow like crazy up here."

Pete admired orchids but had always thought they were creepy. Their weird shapes and colors made him think of predators. The beauty of orchids was clearly designed to lure the prey into them. What an irony that something so delicate and attractive could be a predator.

"You can also find some of the most exotic birds in South America here: mountain toucans, hummingbirds, tanagers, and quetzals."

"I can't see much anymore. Too bad the light's going."

The rocking of the train, the glass of wine, and the soft shapes that passed by caused Pete to feel tired. He tilted his head back and closed his eyes. Everything in Pete's gut told him it would end at Machu Picchu. Judd's cryptic notes pointed that way.

He opened his eyes and looked out the window. The mist had lost its silver glow as the sun disappeared beyond the mountain range. From the tree limbs, climbing vines and branches intertwined until they looked like the tangle of a spider's web. Water dripped from the hanging edges of the primeval green.

Across from him, Wilson dozed. He'd probably seen this many times.

The valley narrowed into a tight canyon. The train seemed to strain at the altitude, slowing their progress. Pete could see evidence that they were heading into the rain forest. The leaves on the trees became broader and overlapped each other like green shingles on a roof. A few drops of rain hit the windows and ran down in meandering lines.

The tapping on Pete's shoulder startled him. When he turned, he saw Anita Montana standing above him, her hair curled behind her ears.

"Mr. Chandler, I presume?" She smiled.

"You're like a bad penny."

Anita cocked her head to the side.

"American saying, forget it. I don't have to ask what you're doing here."

"I'm trying to help you."

Pete laughed in her face.

"Do you know that Silvio Castillo is already in Aguas Calientes?"

"No, but I'm not surprised. I would like an answer about what Judd Crowe and the Peru electric company are doing."

Anita leaned her hip against the back of Pete's seat. "They are the only power source up here in the valley. If someone were to buy Machu Picchu and develop the area, they'd make the electric company rich. Perhaps the company and Crowe are secret partners for the purchase."

Pete thought about the idea for a moment and couldn't figure out a reason to reject it immediately. He introduced Cabot Wilson and invited Anita to sit with them. She sat next to him, crossed her legs, and tapped her foot to a private rhythm in the space between all of them.

Wilson looked at Anita and smiled often. "We'll be at Machu Picchu in a day."

"Oh? Why?" Anita smiled back at him.

"Pete's not sure exactly. Seems something will happen on September twenty-second."

Pete groaned loudly enough for Wilson to look at him. Pete gave him the worst scowl he could manage. Wilson sat back in his seat.

"What an interesting mystery." Anita drew out the words slowly. "Any clues what that will be?"

"No." Pete stopped the conversation before it went further. He found Anita attractive but young, like a daughter. "Let's hear what information you have," he asked her.

Then the train stopped.

The rocking that had mesmerized him for so long disappeared. The clacking from the wheels stopped. People near him in the car sat up, blinked their eyes from sleep, and looked out the windows. Convinced nothing was amiss, they all sat back. After all, trains do stop on occasion. More rain pelted the windows, and Pete could feel the temperature dropping.

They waited for ten minutes without moving. Outside, the different shades of green took on vivid colors, as if they had been lit with an electric current. The foliage glowed intensely in yellows and reds, caused by the longer rays of the setting sun that hid the blue rays of daylight.

Fifteen minutes later, the train still had not moved.

Pete saw a herd of alpaca in the light from the window. They grazed along the river, heading toward dense cover in the distance. As they moved on, one alpaca was left behind. Pete could hear faint bleating. A strange thought hit him. He remembered the scene in the film *Jurassic Park* when a single goat was tethered as an appetizer for the Tyrannosaurus Rex. Pete smiled as he listened for thunderous footsteps in the rain.

Cab stirred across from him. "Something's wrong. We should be moving by now." He looked out the window as if that could make the train start again. The ceiling lights gave the car a green tint.

"Maybe the track's blocked and they have to clear it," Anita said.

"Probably. A lot of rocks fall down."

"I feel like another glass of wine. How about you?" Pete stretched his arms in the air and looked from one to the other.

"Sure," Cab said.

Pete stood and walked toward the far end of the car to find the porter. That's when the lights went out and everything fell into blackness.

Chapter Twenty-Six

September 20, late Tuesday evening

Pete hadn't been in blackness so complete since he'd served with the Army CID in Afghanistan and his investigation had taken him into a Taliban cave—after they'd been chased out. In the train car, he groped his way back to his seat. His fingers fluttered over the rounded corners of the seats. Once he hit the hair of a lady who had leaned out into the aisle. Pete counted the number of rows he passed until he'd reached Anita on the outside seat. To make sure, he called for her.

"We're here."

Pete tapped the space on the floor with his foot and slid into the seat across from Anita and Cab. Several people switched on the lights on their cell phones. The beams crossed over the ceiling of the car. A few murmurs bubbled up from around the car. Someone at the end of the car said, "Y'all should see the darkness just before a Texas twister hits. Worse than this here stuff."

Another person must have stood up and tried to walk down the aisle. Even with his phone light, he stumbled and cursed. "Sit down," a woman shouted. "You almost poked me in the eye, you idiot!"

The darkness remained, and an electric surge ran through the car—but not power for the train. It was a panicky feeling as people started to become afraid.

"Somebody do something, for God's sake," a voice shouted.

"Stay calm. It'll be okay."

"Go to hell! I'm not going to sit here all night."

Someone followed the beam of light from his phone and made it to the door of the car. He pounded on the wood, screaming for it to open. Pete had been in situations of mob chaos. In the Middle East, during the war, he'd experienced panic in crowds. It was dangerous.

From the train car ahead of them, Pete saw a faint shaft of light, bobbing back and forth as it moved closer. He heard someone shout, "Stand back." The door to the car opened, and the porter stepped around the passenger. The porter wore a clip-on light attached to his baseball cap. The light poked through the darkness, following the direction of his head. Faces and windows lit up one at a time as the porter surveyed the car.

"Please remain calm," he told the passengers. "We have experienced an electrical failure of some kind."

"Why don't ya'll have a damn back-up generator?" the Texas man yelled.

"We have never experienced anything like this before. I can assure you we are working on the restoration of power as quickly as we can. In the meantime, I have some candles for your use." He started to distribute small white candles to each table.

"Is the entire train dead?" Pete asked.

"Yes. We have called our supervisors, and the fault is not with PeruRail. It is probably caused by an interruption of the power from the generating plant. There is a big one up the river at Aguas Calientes." The porter cocked his head to the side. "They have never failed in my memory."

Two hours later, the lights popped on, the train rumbled to life, and people cheered and clapped around the car. With a jerk, it started to move forward.

They reached the deserted train station at Aguas Calientes. Pete helped Anita lift her bag, and they followed Wilson onto a concrete platform sheltered by a corrugated plastic roof. They walked toward a one-story station and pushed on the creaking wooden door into the waiting room. It was quiet, and their footsteps echoed off the walls.

Outside, the passengers trudged through a small city of colorful tents covering a market. Now the vendors were gone, their stalls empty of produce and artwork. All that remained were vacant boxes.

Dull yellow light from iron street lamps led the three over a wooden bridge. Pete could hear a stream gurgling below and felt the structure tremble with the weight of the crowd crossing it. At the end, Cab stopped, retrieved his phone, and keyed in the address of the El Mapi Hotel. He couldn't get a signal.

Anita looked up at the tangled streets and dark shapes and pointed into the dusk to the right. "I think I remember the map from when I looked earlier. Two blocks straight, then we go through a narrow alley, and at the end, we should be at the hotel," she said.

She was correct. In ten minutes they reached the hotel. Anita was booked into another hotel one block down the hill from the Mapi Hotel. With Cab, Pete checked in, rode a shaky elevator to the fourth floor, and, in spite of his anxiety, collapsed into a deep sleep.

Chapter Twenty-Seven

September 21, Wednesday morning

Pete awoke later in the morning than he'd intended, but he was exhausted by the previous day's difficulties. After cleaning up, he took the elevator to the open-air walkway on the main floor of the Hotel El Mapi. Ferns taller than Pete bordered the edge of the walkway. As usual in Latin America, the breakfast buffet was huge. Fresh fruit dominated the menu, while the colors of the fruit were challenged by cut flowers from the region stacked in several vases. Wilson was already seated at a table by the back.

They selected breakfast items and sat to enjoy the meal. Pete could hear the whirr of an espresso machine grinding Peruvian coffee beans. On the far side of the dining room, floor-to-ceiling windows looked out onto the narrow street that sloped sharply down to the right. Even in the dark of the previous night, Pete had noticed that all the streets sloped in some direction. There were few level places anywhere in the city.

Aguas Calientes had been a tiny town at the intersection of two rivers, the Urubamba and the Rio Vilacanota. The city had grown one hundred percent in the last ten years as the tourist interest in Machu Picchu exploded.

By ten thirty they had finished breakfast. Pete glanced out the window and sucked in his breath. He nodded, and Cab turned to look also.

Three of the Chinese thugs who'd attacked Pete in Cusco stood several feet down the sloping road, peering inside through the window. They apparently didn't spot Pete.

"Who are they?" Cab asked.

"Friends of mine. They were probably in the helicopter at the station."

Wilson, his face pale, looked back at Pete. "What the hell are they doing? Following you?"

"Sort of. There are several people looking for Judd Crowe."

"What are you going to do?"

Pete shrugged. "I'll take care of them, if I have to. Now I'm prepared." He pushed back his chair and stood. "We have to find a way to
get up to Machu Picchu before sunrise tomorrow."

"There are a group of old buses that travel the circuit from here up
to the summit every half hour for all the tourists. But they don't run that
early in the morning."

"Then we have to get ourselves up there somehow."

Cab thought for a moment. "We could rent a motorcycle." He
walked to the back of the restaurant. "We can try to find one through
the Internet in our room."

Pete glanced out the window and didn't see the Chinese, but he
still thought it was best to avoid them for now. He caught up with Cab
on the walkway.

Back in his room, Cab booted up his laptop. He tried several times
but couldn't get access to the Internet. "Spotty up here."

Pete walked from one side of the room to the other in six steps,
back and forth.

Cab said from over his shoulder, "You've got to remember where
you are. There's not even a crossroads near here, let alone a city of any
size." He straightened away from the screen. "But these hotels should
have a connection. Now what?"

"Let's go down to the lobby and ask."

When they found a man behind the lobby desk, Cab asked him in
Spanish about the Internet. The clerk explained that since the power
had gone out, the hotel's system was slow getting back on line.

"When will you have a connection?" Cab asked.

The clerk shrugged. "Soon. This is highly unusual, but we think the
power plant on the far side of the mountain must have interrupted electric service." He smiled to show four gold-edged teeth. "Do not worry.
We will accommodate your every need."

Cab sighed and turned around to face the floor-to-ceiling window
that looked out onto the street. Several poles crossed the window at
angles for decoration. "Come on. It's not a big place; we'll walk around
till we find a rental place."

On their way across the lobby, they met Anita Montana coming inside. "Good breakfast, boys?"

"Anita, we're busy," Pete said. "I don't want to be—"

"You act so gruff, but I know you're a sweetheart underneath it all," Anita said with a full smile.

Pete paused for a moment. What could it hurt? "All right. Come on."

They all left the lobby and stepped out to the street that dropped off to the right. Pete and Cab paused, but there was no sign of the Chinese. They walked downhill, looking for a rental office. Restaurants lined the sides of the street that was so narrow, only pedestrians could walk along it. Each restaurant had a menu handwritten on a board in front.

The shops were small and squeezed against each other. The three turned several corners and walked up or down depending on which direction the street ran. Those going toward the rivers ran downhill. Pharmacies offered botanical cures for the aches and pains of hiking up to Machu Picchu. Dozens of massage parlors offered their own cure for the same sore muscles. They found a trekking store loaded with hiking gear, tents, and boots. Pete thought to buy a few flashlights and plenty of extra batteries, just in case.

Clouds of gnats swarmed them, so small they were almost invisible. But when they bit, without any pain, they left red dots on the arms and legs. They passed a group of a half dozen Peruvian nuns, all dressed in black and white and all about five feet tall. Anita asked them if they knew where a rental shop was located. They pointed up a steep incline.

When Pete was able to get a glimpse of the mountains surrounding the city, he was astounded. For as far as he could see, they stacked up into the distance as if they were sitting on each other's laps, all of them various shades of green because the jungle grew up the sides of each one. The group turned onto the main thoroughfare, Avenida Pachacútec.

Ten minutes later they still hadn't found the shop, but Pete could feel and hear the coming rain. The steep slopes of the mountains turned to gray as the clouds lowered. The air cooled, and he could hear a deep rumble from somewhere up the valley. Cab left to find the rental shop. Pete and Anita ducked under the shelter of a canopy that stuck out from a used bookstore.

The rumbling sound surrounded them, and torrential rain fell. It bounced hard off the granite steps in the street, and after a few minutes, the water flowed over the same steps in multiple waterfalls. No one ventured out into the streets.

Pete hadn't been in a tropical storm of this power since he'd been in Southeast Asia. He'd forgotten how much water could fall in such a short time. All sound was drowned by the roar of the rain. It fell so heavily it looked like the streets were full of smoke, and the buildings blurred in the distance.

In fifteen minutes, it stopped and a feeble sun appeared above the mountains. The air smelled clean and cool. The wide fronds of palm trees glistened bright green and bent under the weight of the water still clinging to their leaves.

They ventured out from under the canopy, turned another corner in the short block, and crossed over the train tracks on the rickety wooden bridge Pete had used last night. At the bottom of the hill they found a motorcycle rental office. Anita spoke Spanish with the owner and nodded several times before coming back to Pete. "We can pick it up later this afternoon." Three bikes leaned on kickstands in front of the shop. The owner recommended the Yamaha XT250.

"Very versatile for street or back trails," he advised. The body of the motorcycle rode high above the wheels for extra clearance in case the driver hit potholes or slippery gravel, or fell off the edge of a trail.

"What did you mean by 'we'?" Pete asked her.

"Well, you don't know your way up to Machu Picchu, do you?"

"Not exactly, but I've hired a guide."

"Who? Wilson? I'm better."

"I'll stick with him."

Anita shook her head to clear hair from around her face. "Pete, you may as well admit that I could be a great help to you. Especially now, when we're so close."

He was amused by her self-confidence but didn't let it show. "Oh? You remind me of my daughter."

"Are you close to her?"

"Uh, not exactly. But she's the only family I have left."

"I have a large, extended family. It's very important to us, and we value family. Maybe you should be the same. Americans always move so fast, how can they get to know anyone in their family?"

"You've got a point."

"You must spend time with your daughter. Try to understand how to—"

"I don't need your help about that." Pete turned to pay the shop owner for the motorcycle. He thought Cab could ride on the back, and Pete texted him about the rental.

"Okay, okay. Sorry." She stepped next to him and told the clerk, "I'll pay for my own."

They both left a deposit and stepped through the door down into the street. Pete looked around but didn't see the Chinese. It was the word "understand" that made him upset, because he realized that was exactly the problem. He didn't understand Karen's mother, didn't understand Karen, and hadn't understood Judd either.

After the rain, other people ventured out to walk the town also. Groups of hikers passed Pete and Anita. The hikers wore heavy, over-the-ankle boots, baggy shorts, and red handkerchiefs sculpted to their heads. Most looked hot, with sweat covering their arms and faces. Many also carried huge backpacks that could have tipped them backward if they faced a strong wind.

Several of the streets converged on a small plaza surrounded by ornate buildings three stories high. A fountain splashed water in the center. Standing with both legs spread above the fountain was an enormous statue of an Incan king. He wore a gold crown, and his chest was covered with sacred feathers. He looked up at the mountain rising immense and imposing at the far end of the town—and holding Machu Picchu, hidden at the top.

Pete let his eyes follow the steep side of the mountain. Dense vegetation wrapped around the cylindrical mountain. It looked impossible to scale, which made him appreciate the effort Hiram Bingham must have gone through to summit the peak.

"This is a statute of Pachacutec," Anita said.

"Who?"

"The ruler who united all of the various tribes to create the Incan empire. Archeologists think he's the one responsible for building Machu Picchu."

Water burbled in the fountain, and Pete could hear the muted conversations from groups of tourists in the plaza. The buildings reminded him of a cross between Swiss chalets and the flat-roofed huts of Katmandu in Nepal. On the far side of the plaza, Gringo Bill's Boutique Hotel invited them to stay the night.

In spite of the fact they were surrounded by an impenetrable rain forest, the feel of the town reminded Pete they were also in the mountains. A block away from the plaza, the Rio Vilcanota trickled between immense boulders, bleached white from the sun and carved into fantastic shapes. They walked to the edge and looked down.

"Those are ginger plants." She pointed to other bushes upstream. The wild beauty of the jungle impressed Pete. He could see how humans had managed to cut out a small triangle between the rivers for the city, but it was obvious that Nature was simply waiting until it could reclaim what it had owned from the beginning.

A cold breeze blew up from the river, and Anita shivered. "I think we should get back to the hotel."

"Okay. Maybe I can get an Internet connection by now."

Groups of school children darted by. The kids were all dressed in American-style clothing. The boys wore baseball caps with NFL team names on the front, and the girls wore tight jeans with running shoes that matched the colors of their t-shirts. To Pete, they all looked Indian: dark skin, long noses, and beautiful, shiny black hair.

After a few minutes' rest, he followed Anita higher. He noticed that the colors were still intense—the cobalt sky, white clouds, and orange tiles of new roofs. At the next corner, a small shop offered private tours of Machu Picchu. As Pete and Anita approached it, he saw the group of Chinese men. Xiong Lo walked in the middle. Coming up the steep incline, they had their heads bowed while they trudged uphill.

Pete felt his body tense. The street was narrow, and he felt confident that if he had to fight, he could win. Besides, the Glock 43 rested in a holster in the small of his back. But it was smarter to avoid them. Pete nudged Anita into the tour shop. It was tiny, with no place to hide.

185

When Pete glanced out the window, the first of the Chinese had reached the shop.

Pete smiled at the owner behind a narrow counter and pulled Anita by the hand. He ducked around the edge, pushed aside a curtain hanging in a door, and found what he'd hoped to see: a short hallway that led to a door in the back. They stepped through it and found themselves in an alley. It was obvious this side of the shops was not intended for tourists. Garbage sat on the sidewalk in ripped-open bags, partially constructed buildings sat vacant, and a broken chair thrown away by someone cluttered their path.

"Let's pick up the motorcycle now. I don't want to run into those guys again and not be able to get our transportation," Pete said.

Anita agreed, and they zig-zagged along the back alleys to reach the shop, rented helmets, and rode up the street to El Mapi Hotel. They parked and locked the bikes. Anita left after getting Pete to agree to a later contact.

In the lobby, Pete learned the Internet was working again. It was late afternoon, and in spite of his hunger, Pete hurried to the room. Cab met him there. Pete tried to reach Mateo in Quito, and he responded immediately. He'd figured out the code on Judd's flash drive. Mateo's message continued:

Have you heard of the 'stuxnet' virus?

Pete responded.

No.

In 2010 a virus invaded small computers designed to run engines in large facilities. The small computers are called PLCs. They maintain operation of the engines. The hack attached itself to the PLCs and, for a long time, just watched them.

Pete keyed in a question.

Where did this happen?

That's scary part. Hack invaded PLCs in nuclear plant in Iran. Specifically, they infected the frequency converters—small engines

—in nuclear centrifuges. PLCs changed normal frequencies of engines to make centrifuges run faster and faster, which wrecked them and shut down nuclear facility.

Couldn't the scientists detect the virus?

No, because hack was designed to play back data that looked normal. Ever see film *Speed* with Keanu Reeves/Sandra Bullock? To fool villain, they looped a video of the interior of the bus to make it look normal. That's what stuxnet virus did to fool people trying fix frequency converters.

Pete shook his head.

I don't understand, and what does this have to do with Judd's CD?

Judd's code does same thing. Fools analysts by looping normal operations.

He's interested in a nuclear facility?

No. He's hacking electric power plants.

Pete fell back from the computer. He felt like he was looking down at the yawning abyss of the Grand Canyon. Had Judd caused the electric power failures in Aguas Calientes and the train?

How could Judd break through security at electric company?

Three possible ways. Crack encryption codes—close to impossible. Socially engineered hack through social media. Hacker pretends lost a password, gets temporary one, follows it through social media until gets access to employee of electric company. Most companies have security against this now. Third way is to attack the most vulnerable part—the network and the humans who communicate on it.

How would Judd get into the network?

Most common way is to drop several CDs around offices of the electric company. Official logo is printed on the CD. Hacker hopes a curious employee picks up CD, inserts in company computer, and opens the CD. Works because people think CDs and thumb drives only contain data. Wrong. Can harbor a nasty virus. Now hacker sneaks inside the security perimeter and virus can move from one computer to another in network. The employee opened it for hacker.

I can't believe it.

Statistics show there's a 100% chance that some employee will open a CD, especially if a word like *salaries* is also printed on cover. Keeps people like me with jobs.

Pete knew that was how Judd had broken in. Mateo continued:

These small computers, the PLCs, are in millions of plants and facilities in world. They maintain low-level operation of various engines and functions to save larger computers' time and capacity.

Do you know what Judd's trying to do in power plants?

Not sure, but can tell you effects. He hacked into PLCs of Peruvian electric plants. It does not look like virus is designed to stop any engines there.

What the hell is he doing?

Electric plant PLCs networked to facilities all over and control engines in those other facilities. Common so other facilities do not replicate same work. Judd hacked engines that control locking mechanisms in hundreds of facilities.

How about basic power?

Could be affected also.

Why locking?

???

Any idea what Judd's virus has to do with Machu Picchu?

???

What else—

The screen turned gray and went blank. At the same time, the lights in their room flickered, dimmed, and went out. Blackness fell around Pete for the second time.

Chapter Twenty-Eight

September 21, late Wednesday afternoon

"Now what?" Cab whispered into the black space between them.

"How the hell should I know?"

"You don't have to yell at me."

"Sorry. Nothing works in this damn country."

Cab shuffled toward him until his outstretched fingers bumped Pete's shoulder. "You mean we're in deep shit."

"I'm beginning to think so."

The darkness was impenetrable. Total lack of light. Pete said, "Think about it: Judd is shutting down an electric power plant. He was always audacious, but this is crazier than anything else he's ever pulled." Pete reached for the flashlight he'd bought earlier. He flicked it on and waited.

"Well, the message made it look like he's just shutting down some locks around here."

"I'd guess he's the one shutting all the power off. Did he screw up, or is this something he intended?"

"What does it have to do with Machu Picchu?"

"Tomorrow at seven twenty-one."

"We should be up there before sunrise."

"Why so early?"

"The spring equinox actually starts at sunrise. The path of the sun's light is critical to the religious importance of the day. By noon, it will stand directly above the Intihuatana stone so that it casts no shadow. For a moment, the Incas believed they had 'tied' the sun to the hitching post and thereby controlled it. But the time prior to that is also very significant and can point out different sacred spots in Machu Picchu."

"And Agent Castillo is probably here by now. Along with the Chinese gangsters. Maybe I can work with him to keep the others away."

"This is a lot bigger than I ever imagined when you hired me."

"You want out?"

Cab let a burst of air out of his lungs. "Hell no! It's a lot more exciting that dusting off the artifacts in the museum."

"I'll still need your help, especially when we get up there."

Pete sat on the side of the bed. He could hear Wilson's shoes scrape across the floor in the opposite direction. The lights in the room started to glow dull yellow. They remained dim, but at least there was some light in the room.

"Back-up generator?" Pete asked. He shut off the flashlight.

Cab nodded and went to the window. He peered out into the darkness and said from over his shoulder, "The entire city is still out except for two other hotels. Must have gas-powered generators."

"One good thing about the blackout: we can probably slip out of town tomorrow morning without anyone else knowing we've left and beat them to the top." Pete stood to pace while he thought. "We'll roll the bike down the hill and only start it at the bottom. Do you know the way to get up there?"

"Yes. The main road leads past the bus stop and dips down beside the river. It becomes gravel and then makes a sharp left turn over the river. From there, it switches back and forth almost twenty times as it climbs straight up the side of the mountain. It's narrow, with jungle on both sides."

Pete raised both hands and dropped them along his sides. "Great. We'll be wobbling along on a motorcycle in the dark on a gravel road with hairpin turns." He turned to face Cab. "And I suppose one side of the road drops all the way to the Urubamba River thousands of feet below?"

"There are a few trees and vines growing beside the road to break our freefall. Of course, the weight of the motorcycle may be a problem—" He laughed until the look from Pete silenced him. "Okay. I will drive."

"No—"

"Yes. I've been up there before. I remember the way."

Pete came to him quickly. "This isn't a story in one of your history books. This is real, and it's dangerous in all aspects. I've been in situations like this before, but I'm trained. You're not."

"You'd be surprised what I can do if necessary. But if you insist—"

Pete spun around and stomped to the corner of the room. Why was he going? Certainly anger at Judd, deep anger and resentment for the betrayal. But Pete was also a professional. He'd come down here to finish an investigation job. He looked up at the ceiling and said, "How early should we leave?"

Cab studied his watch for a moment. "At least an hour early. I'd say we should be moving on the bike before six o'clock."

"Good. We'll prepare as best we can tonight."

"I'm starving. I wonder if the kitchen in the hotel is back on power." Cab walked into the bathroom and shut the door.

Someone knocked on the door. Pete froze. He reached behind him to feel the holstered Glock, walked to the door, and peered through the peephole. It was Agent Silvio Castillo. Pete opened the door.

Castillo came through quickly. "Are you alone?"

Pete introduced Cab Wilson when he came out from the bathroom.

"You will not give up, huh?" Castillo said.

"This has become more than investigating Judd Crowe; it's about getting justice now."

Castillo's face clouded.

"Never mind. It's a long story that doesn't concern you."

"Those people at the electric company meant business about getting you charged. They have immense influence with the governor general. I can hold them off for a while, but even I have to submit to the jurisdiction of the state."

Pete didn't answer. He hoped to have finished everything and be out of Peru before they caught up with him.

"So, tell me what you've learned." Castillo sat heavily on the bed.

"I don't know exactly how he's doing it or why, but Judd is hacking into the electric company right now."

"Which explains the power outages?"

"I think so."

"What does that have to do with Machu Picchu?"

Pete shrugged. "Haven't figured that out yet."

"When are you going up there?"

"We've arranged transportation two days from now," Pete lied.

"We'll go together. I can provide the necessary armed assistance we may need."

"Of course."

"Have you heard from Oswald Lempke?"

"No. I've been too busy. Why do you want to know?" Pete asked.

Castillo stood and paced to the far side of the room. In the dim light, his hat looked bigger than usual. "We've had him under surveillance, but his secretary said he left to go back to the States." He stopped moving and came close to Pete. "I know you're trained, and you're a damn good investigator. But this is a different world down here, Mr. Chandler. It's changing rapidly. The Chinese influence and criminality are rampant, for instance. You must be more careful than ever."

Pete snorted. "Your people think I'm a foreign spy or worse."

Castillo remained still, but his shaded eyes moved around the room. "If I give you some information we've learned, will you cooperate with me?"

"Depends." It was the best Pete could offer. He hoped Castillo would take it. He did.

Castillo took a deep breath. "We are certain he is shutting off the electric power. That's probably to prevent tourists—or anyone else—from getting up to Machu Picchu tomorrow. The security system has a series of locks. For instance, the front gates have steel doors that are locked by computers to keep people out."

"Why would Judd want to lock himself out?"

Castillo stood and looked up at Pete. "You've got it backwards. He wants to lock himself in."

The revelation struck Pete as hard as the rain that had fallen earlier. But he still couldn't understand what Judd's plan was. "What—?"

"It sounds crazy, but we're certain that Crowe is after the fabled Inca treasure." Castillo's words drifted off into the dusty corners of the room until everyone sensed the still silence and the weight of what he'd said fell on them all.

"Treasure?" Pete asked. "Is that story really true?"

Castillo didn't say another word. He adjusted his Panama hat on his head and walked to the door. "We will keep in contact." A thin smile squirreled across his lips. "But I am going to leave with you tomorrow morning." He ducked out of the door.

Pete reacted immediately. "Let's look at the flash drive again." He led Cab to the desk, brought the laptop to life, and inserted the flash drive. It opened, and he scrolled down the list. They read:

13.583300

72.5313900

Pete squinted at the screen. "That's latitude and longitude measurements, except they're expressed in decimal degrees. More accurate. I should've seen that immediately."

"Here. Look at this." Cab handed his phone to Pete. He had Googled the numbers onto a map. It centered near the middle of Machu Picchu.

"Dammit," Pete said. "In front of us all the time. And I bet these other numbers on the flash drive also refer to the location. Look at this: 452 feet, elevation degrade." He stepped back from the desk. "But I still wonder if the Inca treasure is a myth or true."

"We know for certain that Manco Inca took the empire's riches into the valley ahead of the Spanish," Wilson said. "They searched all over but never found it. Therefore, where did it go?" His voice dropped. "There were a few explorers in the nineteenth century who managed to get through the jungles of the Sacred Valley. They weren't archeologists. Instead, they wanted to cash in on the potential mountaintop El Dorado. There was a French painter and diplomat posted to Peru during this time. His diaries recount stories that 'immense treasures were buried among the ruins when the last survivors of the race of the sun retired to this savage asylum.'"

"I think we saw his name on Judd's flash drive."

"Léonce Angrand."

"Yeah, that's him. If there's a treasure up there, is it very valuable?" Pete asked.

Cab's eyes opened wide and he explained, "You have to remember, this was the same empire that a few years earlier had filled a large room with gold and silver to pay the ransom for Atahualpa before the Spanish executed him. That was only a small portion of the treasure. Archeologists have estimated its value today at millions of dollars—that's on legitimate markets. If some of the rare pieces of gold artwork are dispersed through the black market to private, secret collectors, it could be priceless."

"Billions?" Pete said.

"More—priceless. Think about what we display at the La Casa Concha museum. That is a hint at the entire scale of the possible riches. Worse yet, if he steals the artifacts, they would be lost to the world and to the indigenous Indian people who have rightful ownership of them."

"Okay, but how would he extract all that? From what you describe, the treasure could weigh tons. Then he'd have to sneak it down the mountain without anyone seeing him. It's hard enough to get up there," Pete said.

Cab shrugged. "That answer I don't have."

Pete had to sit down to contemplate the information. Finally, Pete spoke. "And what about Xiong Lo? They're after the same thing. They were probably investing in Judd's private company to help finance the search for the treasure—until Judd double-crossed them."

"What happened to Judd?"

"They probably tried to kill Judd, and that's when he faked his death to throw off the Chinese," Pete said. "And sent me a postcard."

"What?"

"Nothing." Pete waved him off.

"I think we should use Agent Castillo's help," Cab said. "It's well known how dangerous the Chinese are, and if they catch you, they'll kill you before you can blink. They'll toss your body over the edge and down into the jungle like a dead dog." Cab blinked. "Come to think of it, they'll kill me too. Maybe you should let Castillo take care of everything."

It was tempting, but Pete didn't trust Castillo entirely. He'd seen too much corruption all over the world to believe Castillo would do what was legal and right. He'd probably take the treasure himself. After all, Pete still hadn't forgotten Castillo's efforts to accuse him of being a spy and threats to arrest him on fake charges—in spite of the agent's recent change of attitude.

Pete's shoulders dropped. "I've come so far to get to the bottom of this, I don't want to stop when I'm this close." Besides, Pete wanted to face the son-of-a-bitch for what he'd done in Afghanistan.

"What if we let Castillo take charge—while we're up there and you can still face your friend."

"He's not a friend." Pete bit off the words. If the others were going to be there in force, it might be easier anyway. Pete and Cab could hide and wait for the takedown. At that point, Pete could step in and confront Judd.

Wilson looked at his wristwatch. "All right. It's settled. The 'magic' time is seven twenty-one. Not only is tomorrow the spring equinox, but the constellation patterns you asked me about earlier will be lined up right over Machu Picchu. It would have been one of the holiest times of the year for the Incas."

"Which would be the perfect time for them to bury the empire's treasure," Pete added. "That would assure the sun god, Inti, would bless the hiding of it. At noon the sun would've stood directly above the Intihuatana stone. Captured by the Incas for a brief moment, at least, of sacred help."

Cab looked at him, surprised. "Inti, the sun god? How do you remember all that?"

Pete grinned. "I've been listening to you." He heard a whirring sound from somewhere deep in the hotel. Around him, the lamps glowed brighter until they shone with full light again.

Chapter Twenty-Nine

September 22, Thursday before sunrise

Although they intended to leave before six o'clock, Pete and Cab had been awake since five. The dressed quickly in the darkest clothing they'd brought and found their flashlights, Pete's walking stick, and a few oranges to eat later if they had time. Pete strapped his holster around his waist and settled the Glock 43 in the small of his back.

"Bring your smartphone," Cab said. "It's possible we may get a signal at the top of the mountain."

Neither one said anything more, keeping their thoughts private. They bobbed around each other as they finished packing. Pete put on his hiking boots that had traveled with him all over the world. They were lightweight and waterproof, thanks to the latest boot technology. They were a little hot, but he might need their stability, depending on how rugged the steps were in Machu Picchu. He remembered the key to the Yamaha motorcycle and stuffed it into his front pocket.

He looked at Wilson, noticed his eyes, and found them bright with fear. Pete could read it easily because he'd seen it so often in other people in dangerous places.

Without mentioning his own fear, Pete stuffed the mag light in his pocket and hefted a pack across his back. "Ready?" When Cab nodded, Pete led them out the door into the hallway. It was five-twenty.

They took the stairs to a back exit that emptied them on the ground above the river. Even it was silent in the darkness. The front side of the hotel was attractive and in good repair. The back side, like that of its neighbors, was trashed. Some of the rooms on the floors weren't finished and looked like open boxes. Pieces of sheetrock and plywood littered the back yard between shards of broken glass. A garbage can without a lid stood at a precipice above the river.

Pete and Cab flicked on their flashlights and worked their way through a tear in the chain link fence to come out on the side of the hotel. The motorcycle leaned against the wall, its lock still securing it to a pole.

Pete unfastened it and, gripping both handlebars, rolled it out to the street. A glow from the hotel lobby colored everything dull yellow but couldn't penetrate far into the black space beyond. As Pete and Cab turned down the hill, they heard roosters crowing from the far side of the town and the *shish* of rubber tires rolling over the cobblestones.

They listened for the waking sounds of people and animals and possible danger. Cab whispered, "We need to get through the main plaza in order to reach a gravel road. It runs along the river, which we'll cross to start up the mountain."

"You know the way?"

"Of course." Walking slowly, as if he were blind, Wilson stepped ahead of Pete. "Do you know what we're looking for up there?"

Pete hissed, "I told you: I don't know."

"Don't get mad; I'm only asking."

They continued down the hill as they angled toward the main street, Avenida Pachacútec. Pete could smell the humidity coming from the jungle around them as it woke up. He stopped walking and pulled up his sleeve to read his watch. He flicked the flashlight once. "Good. I think we've beat them all. I bet they won't get there until nine o'clock." They turned onto Pachacútec that would lead to the main plaza and the road out of town.

"What is our plan?" Cab asked.

"You're going to help us find a place to hide and 'watch the show.' After they catch Judd, we can come out. If it's necessary, I'll intervene. I can't wait to face the son-of-a-bitch."

"You sure they'll catch this guy?" Cab said. "From what you've told me, he's eluded everyone for a long time."

Pete looked at him. "He'll be up there. I know him, and I can feel it." He leaned on the handlebars, and the Yamaha rolled forward.

About two blocks ahead, they spied something white and round glowing faintly in the distance. It was still too dark to make it out, but the object bobbed up and down.

"Must be the ghost of Pachacutec," Cab joked to break the tension.

As they came closer, they recognized a Panama hat. Two other white hats bobbed in the background behind Castillo. "I don't want him to know we're leaving this early," Pete said. He knew that the motorcycle would slow down their ability to evade the officers. Turning the handle-bars sharply, Pete leaned it against a trash can and darkened lamp pole. He pointed it uphill. Anyone trying to go down to the gravel road would leave the bike pointed in that direction. Therefore, he hoped Castillo would ignore the bike. Pete didn't have time to lock it up, so he draped the chain over the front fork and left it.

Signaling to Wilson, Pete ducked into an alley beside the trash can. If for any reason Castillo became suspicious and took the motorcycle, Pete would be marooned in town, unable to reach Machu Picchu in time.

Hiding in the dark recess of the alley, Pete watched Castillo and two other officers climb up the incline. They moved slowly and stopped directly beside the bike. Castillo glanced back and nodded his head at the other two. "Keep up; this is an important mission." On the side of his leg, a holster with a Sig Sauer hung in a big bulge.

"What are our orders, sir?"

Castillo said, "We move to the site and secure the area against any-one trying to trespass up there."

"When are we leaving?"

"Before sunrise."

Pete could feel time leaking away as they waited for the men to continue up the road. One of the officers lit a cigarette, and Pete could smell acrid smoke drift into the alley. They all waited until the officer crushed the butt out on the damp street. Finally, the detectives trudged uphill. After five minutes, Pete couldn't wait anymore. With a wave of his hand, he signaled Cab to follow him.

Pete turned out of the alley and froze. The officers had stopped again only twenty feet away. They stood looking uphill. Without a sound, Pete lifted the chain off the bike and set it on the ground. He worked it around in a tight circle on the street until it pointed downhill. Pete strad-dled the machine and motioned for Cab to climb on behind. When they were settled, he jammed the starter button, the bike roared to life, he pressed his right foot against the gear shift, it clicked, and Pete twisted the throttle under his right hand. With a jerk that almost flung Wilson off the back, Pete shot down the hill.

"Hey!" Agent Castillo shouted. His body twisted around so quickly his hat flew off.

Pete gained speed. When he reached the small plaza he yelled over his shoulder to Cab, "Which way?"

He pointed to the left. Since no one was out this early, they shot across the vacant plaza and popped out to a paved road that tucked under the rickety wooden bridge they'd crossed from the train station the first night.

Cab shouted into his ear, "Turn right and go past the bus stop."

Pete obeyed, leaned the Yamaha over on its side, and gave it more power. Once it straightened up, they shot past a gray-green bus sleeping along the curb.

The road still descended as it ran parallel to the river. The vegetation that grew along the river and had looked so beautiful yesterday now hung over in ghostly images bleached of all color except gray. Pete felt like he was racing through a tunnel since the only illumination was a cone of light from the headlamp. Everything else—to the sides, above them, and below on the road—was black.

To his left, behind him, Pete heard the roar of another motorcycle. It couldn't be Castillo; he wouldn't have had the time to get going. Pete turned his head. The rider was shrouded in the blackness behind the halo of the bike's headlamp.

Pete gunned his machine and tried to outrun the other person. He kept up with Pete, then pulled alongside. Pete glanced over to see Anita Montana waving at him. He slid to a stop as she did also.

"What the hell are you doing?" he shouted at her.

"Followed you two. I guessed at the time." She looked behind her. "You left one hell of a commotion back there. We better get moving, fast."

Pete didn't like the interference, but there was nothing he could do, and he wanted to get moving also. Both bikes roared, and they raced ahead.

The pavement gave out, and they bumped onto a gravel surface. Pete felt the front wheel skid, so he backed off on the gas until he felt confident about handling the bike. At least the road was wider at this point than the city streets. They roared through clouds of bugs that threatened to clog their eyes and mouths.

"Slow down," Cab shouted. "Take a left here."

Pete throttled down and saw a sign advertising a campground below the road at the river's edge. An empty guard shack stood at the corner of a bridge. Pete leaned left and drove the motorcycle over the bridge. The rumble of the cycle over the bridge echoed underneath them to mingle with the crash of water over boulders.

Across the bridge, he saw a sign on the right side that read *Machu Picchu Museum. No Cars Allowed.* The gravel road took a sharp turn to the left again. He stopped and let the roar of the engine diminish as he listened for any pursuit. He turned his head but didn't hear Castillo coming up from behind. Pete unthreaded his leg from over the bike and held it while Cab also dismounted.

"Where do we go?" Pete asked.

"It's up there." Cab pointed to the left. "This is the road with all the hairpin turns that the buses use to get the tourists to the top. Be careful; it's treacherous even in the daylight."

Anita had come up beside them. She idled her bike and waited.

Pete looked at his watch in the light of the bike's lamp. "I don't care; we have to go—now!" He mounted again, waited for Cab to get on, and twisted the throttle. The rear tire dug into gravel and wobbled until Pete straightened out, and he followed the one-lane gravel road uphill.

Within fifty feet, the vegetation closed in on them. In the faint light to the sides, Pete could see fantastic shapes surrounding them: vines with elephant-ear-sized leaves, primordial trees that soared out of sight into the blackness above. Palm trees, which had always seemed so benign to Pete, now weaved their trunks up through the jungle canopy and re-minded him of cobras swaying before Indian pipers.

When the motorcycle drifted to the left side of the road, the vegetation thinned, and beyond that was nothing. The mountain must have dropped off in a sheer precipice.

Then they came to the first turn. Pete took it wide, leaning to the inside, but the bike began to slip out from underneath them. The tires scraped across the gravel, and Pete tried to maneuver the Yamaha. It kept sliding until Pete braced them with his right leg, hopping along with his foot. He backed off on the throttle, corrected the angle into the turn, and gained control again. Around the corner, the road rose even steeper.

Pete gave the bike more gas and it whined in protest, but they were able to still gain speed.

Back and forth they traversed the steep side of the mountain. Uphill to the right, around a hairpin turn, gravel pinging against the raised fenders, and then straightening out, climbing to the left. After four turns, Pete could feel the altitude change. It was cooler, harder to breathe, and even in the dark, he could sense the enormous chasm beside them. He stopped for a minute. Pete strained to see into the darkness below them. The faint smell of rotting vegetation carried on a soft breeze that flushed against his face.

He was about to take off again when he saw two faint yellow lights blinking through the jungle below. Sometimes they'd disappear but show again at a different angle. It must be Castillo making the tight turns in the road. Pete was shocked that the lights were almost directly below him. There was no slope to the side of the mountain; it rose straight up.

"Come on," he yelled in Cab's ear and gunned the engine. It roared, and they shot forward.

Soon Pete had learned how to bank the bike into the turns, when to give it more gas, and when to straighten up. As they climbed higher, the engine groaned louder. He couldn't get as much speed, and it coughed in the thin air. Pete hoped Castillo and the captain would have the same problem.

The road narrowed even more, forcing Pete to drive in the middle. He saw an occasional set of stone steps that led from the road into the jungle. What was their purpose? Who would want to try to penetrate the rain forest at this height?

In ten minutes, he curved around yet another turn when his body jerked backward. The gravel had washed out, leaving a deep hole in the ground like an upside-down satellite dish. Pete tried to swerve around it, but there wasn't enough room to maneuver. They dropped into the depression at top speed. He fought the bike. Stomping on the brakes only caused the back end to slide out from underneath. They spilled off the motorcycle and onto the gravel, scraping along their sides. The bike spun out ahead of them while its wheels churned uselessly into the dust.

Anita skidded into the same washout but managed to keep control. She stopped at the far side and dismounted.

Pete crawled onto his knees, stood up, and felt for broken bones. He didn't notice anything more serious than torn clothing and skin. He reached for Cab to help him stand. He, too, had escaped any serious injury. The Yamaha had idled down to a low rumble.

"You okay?" he asked. When Wilson nodded, Pete went to the motorcycle and lifted it. One handlebar was bent, but it still ran. Without a word, they climbed on and kept going.

In a half hour, Cab pointed ahead around Pete's shoulder. Cab must have meant they had almost arrived. Pete looked to the side. Above the jungle, he could make out the peaks of mountains in a gray light that rose above them into the sky. He was shocked to see that many were at the same level as they had achieved.

After two more hairpin turns, Pete slowed the bike. The road spread before them in the first flat space since the bridge far below. He stopped and dismounted. To the left he could make out a one-story stone building with a peaked roof over the entrance.

"The Sanctuary Hotel," Cab said. "Very expensive. I bet the guests are very upset because they do not have any electric power. It is completely isolated up here, and they depend on daily shipments of supplies by truck."

No one stirred in the hotel, and of course, it was totally dark.

Pete pushed the Yamaha forward as quickly as they could walk. He breathed hard until he stopped to rest for a moment. The engine burbled, and the headlamp shone across a wide parking lot. To the left the mountain rose steeply behind the hotel, and to the right it dropped off into blackness. They could only go back down the road or straight ahead into the ruins.

"The buses turn around here," Cab said. He laughed once. "Usually, this area is packed with those green buses and thousands of tourists standing in long lines waiting to get into Machu Picchu."

Anita had arrived and, following their lead, walked beside them. She remained quiet. Her hair was frizzy and damp.

They all moved forward, and Pete saw a raised platform with a metal tent over it. Circular tables were surrounded by chairs tilted against the sides. Must be a restaurant. To the left, a narrow set of concrete steps led up a flight to another platform. He swung the bike's lamp to illuminate the rock wall that crawled up behind the platform. It was covered with tangled vines and moss that looked black in the light. A few posters offered maps of Machu Picchu. Another sign read *Baños a la derecha*—for most tourists a necessity before venturing out to the expanse of the ruins.

Pete leaned the bike on its kickstand and shut off the engine. It pinged a few times and died. The damp jungle around them seemed to breathe in long, deep sighs. Or was it the wind up here? But Pete had never heard any wind sound like this. From their backpacks they removed the flashlights and flicked them on.

He listened and heard the faint chirps of birds. Otherwise, it was silent. Silence like he'd never experienced since he'd been in the deserts of the Middle East. The flashlight's feeble beams seemed laughable. The darkness ate them up as completely and casually as a leopard would devour a bite of flesh. He felt small.

"Up there," Cab directed.

They started up the concrete staircase and reached the next platform. It stretched to the right, and they followed the flashlight's lead across the concrete expanse. They walked carefully because it was wet and slick.

"The official entrance used to be straight ahead," Wilson said.

Although the temperature was cool, the humidity was so high that sweat broke out over Pete's face. They reached another set of concrete steps that were bracketed by iron posts on either side. Limp ropes hung from one post to the next. It was narrow, and he couldn't imagine thousands of tourists squeezing through this "eye of the needle" to get inside.

Cab stopped to catch his breath and scanned his flashlight ahead. At the top of the steps a small opening held three silver turnstiles. Between them were black squares like entrances to a tomb. A green roof covered the area. "Maybe it's open," he said and led Pete up the final steps.

They crawled over the turnstile on the right when they noticed a dark brown metal wall still ahead. It blocked the entrance between two stands of stone blocks. When they reached it, Pete gave the metal a kick. It didn't even echo from behind. Solid and immovable.

"This is new," Cab said. "This must be what your friend locked."

Pete dropped to his knees and played the flashlight across the ground. He could see a metal track fitted into the stone floor. The door rested in the track. It probably ran on powerful electric motors that could roll the door shut at night, lock it, and open for the customers by day. Could they climb around the entrance somehow?

Anita walked to the left until she ran into a vertical stone wall. It was smooth-faced and covered with slimy moss. When Cab shone his light upward, the wall continued as far as the beam carried. No way up there.

Pete worked his way to the right, past the edge of the door and the stone column that framed it. He lifted his flashlight, and the light disappeared into blackness. He used the aluminum walking stick to tap ahead on the stone until he bumped into a split-rail fence. Beyond that, as far as his light shone, both up and down, was blackness. He couldn't see anything, but he could sense a sheer edge to the stone—straight down for who knew how far.

They both turned around. "Okay, now what?" Pete said.

They climbed back over the turnstile and sat on the steps between the iron posts. He couldn't see it in the dark, but it seemed to Pete that a mist had surrounded them. He could feel moisture caress his skin. It felt good to sit, as his right thigh still hurt from the spill they'd taken on the road.

Anita sat next to them, breathing hard. "We can't be beaten at this point."

The gray layer in the sky above the mountaintops had turned to blue-gray, and the snow on the peaks looked like ashes. Sunrise was coming.

"There must be another way into these ruins. They're huge," Pete insisted.

"Ninety-five percent of the perimeter falls off in rock faces that drop straight down, thousands of feet, to the Urubamba River. After all, that's why the Incas built it here. It's impregnable. Oh, there are series of terraces that hang over the edges, but they're impossible to reach except if you come down from the ruins," Cab told them.

Pete dropped his head in his open palms.

Cab jabbed him in the side. "Down there," he yelled.

Pete looked in the direction he pointed. He could see it also. The twin beams of a car lanced through the vegetation, turning back and forth as if they were searching for prey. In a few minutes, the beams shone on the drooping trees at the far end of the parking lot, opposite from where they all sat.

Pete jumped up and hefted the backpack across his shoulders. "We've got to move," he shouted.

Anita turned in a circle, her head thrown back. "There! Up there. I think we can link to the Inca trail and get up to the Sun Gate."

"How far is that?" He looked high above at the ridge of mountains. In the blue-gray light, he could see a notch in the ridge. "Up there?" he yelled.

Anita's eyes shifted between the two men. "It's our only chance."

"Can we get in?" Pete said.

"Yes. There's no closed door up there. When tourists hike the Inca Trail, that's where they end just before entering the ruins. I'm sure it's open—if we can make it."

"What's that mean?" Pete said.

Anita didn't answer but hurried forward toward the corner of the Sanctuary Hotel and Spa. Pete followed her, his flashlight beam jerking across the ground.

"I don't want any problems with you," Pete shouted at Anita.

"You're not my boss."

He was angry but, at the same time, felt protective toward her. Pete would have to take on her safety also.

Wilson reached the wall of foliage first. He pushed aside some thick bushes and probed the darkness ahead with his light. "I think there's a service path somewhere back here. There are no roads up there, so repair men must climb to reach it." He penetrated the dark green mass and, within a second, disappeared.

Pete followed. Wet vines resembling gauzy veils and leaves slapped him as he skirted through the hole in the jungle. On the far side, he found a slick mud path that angled upward. It was narrower than his shoulders, but from the beam of his light, it looked like it continued ahead. He thought it shouldn't be too hard so long as he didn't slip. He heard the slap of Anita's boots on the path ahead of him. The tunnel of vegetation felt claustrophobic, but at least it led upward.

Pete moved forward in a crouch until he caught up with Cab. Pete heard him take a deep breath, and his legs churned when he started to climb. He reached the same stone steps. They angled to the right and left and were set at different heights. Narrow and slippery, at least they gave Pete something solid to step on. He kept climbing up.

Within ten minutes, sweat drenched his clothing. He breathed hard and just plodded forward. When he finally looked up, he saw the vegetation had thinned, and in the lavender light of the coming dawn, he was shocked at how steeply the mountain fell away at his side. It was lucky he hadn't been able to see it before the trek upward. It was more dangerous than he'd imagined.

They climbed up the twisting trail. On his right side, ancient blocks, carved by the Incas, rubbed against his shoulder. Occasionally, he had to step over roots of trees that had grown between the steps. Some of the steps were missing, and Pete had to sidestep across a muddy bridge between them. Then the trail narrowed to less than his body's width. He placed his feet carefully while trying to keep moving. The trail surface contained carved stones that had shifted their positions over time or were missing, so nothing was flat.

He watched Anita's legs bunch with each step she took. A dark patch of sweat blossomed across her back. Her flashlight bobbed up and down across the stones. Then she disappeared around a sharp corner.

Pete followed slowly. To the left, the trail dropped off into nothingness, and he felt a cold wind blow up from below. He shuddered as his mind drifted off the edge of the cliff until he reined in his thoughts. Although he couldn't get a grip on the stone wall to his right, he still ran his hand along it as if it was a safety feature. It felt greasy with dampness. When Pete made it around the corner, he saw Anita. She had stopped, turned, and was waiting for him. "How are you?" he called to her.

She paused to take several deep breaths. "Okay. How much farther?"

"It can't be far. Wait there; I'll help you."

"We've been going straight up the side of the mountain. Even a llama couldn't do this."

She smiled in a strained fashion. Pete reached her side, wrapped his arm around her waist, and lifted her through each step upward.

After a half hour, Pete lost track of time, his lungs burned, and his legs felt like rubber. Every time he looked up, he saw yet another green wall stretch above him, yet another group of stone steps ever rising. His military training had taught him that in order to get through a tough situation like this, he had to shut down his mind and simply trudge forward.

When he looked up later, he saw the top of the sky had changed to a light blue, and the green sides of the mountains shone with a brightness that only existed in the thin air of this altitude. He paused to take in the sight. In spite of his fatigue, Pete was impressed with the scenery. For as far as he could see, jungle-covered mountains rose straight out of the deep valleys. There was no sign of civilization anywhere. No roads, no power lines, no shopping malls, and no vacation homes built at the peaks of the mountains in order to market a room with a view.

The panorama was stunning. He could see the Andes, jungles, and even the highlands. It was obvious to him why the Incas had chosen this site as a holy place in their universe.

A shroud of pearl-colored mist filled the dark valleys, hiding the river far below. The wind twisted the clouds so that they rose into the air to dance like ancient ghosts.

Pete heard Anita shout above him. He looked up and saw her at the edge of a square pile of old stones. They were mottled with moss, and some had cracks in them. Pete felt his energy surge, and he plodded up the final flight of worn steps. He turned into a small courtyard of white stone. It linked to a second identical courtyard to the right. In between, a stairway disappeared between two square stone pillars. Cab was standing on the far side, gazing out over an empty space in front of him.

When Pete looked through the portal, he didn't see anything beyond it except gray-blue sky. No more green walls, steps, jungle, or anything above him. They had made it to the highest portal into Machu Picchu—the Sun Gate.

Chapter Thirty

September 22, Thursday, Sunrise

Oswald Lempke found the abandoned motorcycles at the tourist center before the locked gates. He had come up in a Jeep, followed by two more that contained a small force of armed men. He'd hired a private security firm to help him head off the inevitable. After all the work and risk, he wasn't going to lose everything now—no matter who he had to confront.

His team poked flashlights into every crevice, looking for Chandler and whoever was with him—probably the damned reporter. As a rule, Lempke never liked to expose the bank to the press. Even if she was up here, he would prevent any news from getting out.

"Sir, we can't find anyone here," the contracted team leader said. His forehead glistened with sweat.

"Well, unless they fell off the mountain, Chandler's up here. I want him found," Lempke said.

As he'd suspected, Crowe had locked the gates to prevent access. Lempke was prepared for that. He waved over the demolition expert. "Blow that sucker," Lempke ordered. "Get the damn C-4."

The expert ran back to the second Jeep, removed a small box, and came back to the steel doors of the site. He kneeled before the corner and opened the box. Inside, five cylinders wrapped in gold paper lay on their sides. He removed them. The material packed inside looked like yellow wax, and the man fitted them into a solid plastic tray designed to hold them upright. These contained 91% nitroamine, guaranteed to blow even the most stubborn of materials. At the bottom of the plastic tray were three small holes into which the expert slipped detonating caps. From these, he ran thin wires back to the Jeep.

Everyone retreated to kneel behind the vehicles. The expert triggered an electric charge from the Jeep, which created an extreme shockwave that fired the detonators. In turn, that exploded the C-4.

A white flash and thunderous explosion shook the ground the men stood on. They had plugged their ears to protect from the shock wave of the blast. Lempke could feel the wave of heat blow over him, even though he was sheltered behind the vehicle.

When the expert gave the "all clear" sign, the men surged forward. They ducked through the smoke with flashlights crisscrossing each other. Lempke followed them. It took a while to climb over the pieces of rock, steel, and shrapnel that covered the tourist platform, but when the men reached the locked door, it was hanging half off the hinges, swinging open.

Chapter Thirty-One

September 22, Thursday, Sunrise

An explosion from far below urged Pete to step through the open gate. He took a deep breath, and all the fatigue dropped away. He forgot the sweat, the mud caked on his boots and smeared across his hands, and he didn't notice the altitude effects that crimped his breathing. In the narrow portal, Anita pressed her body along his, and he heard her sigh as they both looked down through the blue dawn.

Huge vertical fingers of green mountains stood around Machu Picchu like a protective hand, cupping the ruins on the only flat space for as far as Pete could see. Hundreds of stone houses were piled around and on top of each other. Some were clumped together in odd configurations for purposes lost to antiquity. Surrounding these, bright green lawns of grass rolled off to disappear over the edges.

Pete thought he was looking at a giant's jewelry box—full of cubbyholes, small boxes and secret compartments, and lined with a layer of green felt. He spotted the giant's thumb, the mountain on the far side, that looked like it cradled the jewelry box.

Pete had to lean against one of the stone pillars. After all the photos he'd seen over the years, all the effort it had taken to get here, and the high stakes that they faced, he hesitated. He was surprised by the spiritual feeling—from the ancient Incas' religions to the modern-day *misticos* with their crystals—the power of the place and the monument was overwhelming. Maybe the Incas were correct when they'd declared this site the home of the gods.

There was a rind of orange on the horizon above the surrounding mountains, and a particularly big peak to the east loomed out of the darkness. They switched off the flashlights and started to work their way down another stone trail into the ruins.

"This was built by Pachacutec as a royal road that pilgrims could follow to enter the holy city," Cab said. He glanced back at the Sun Gate. "That was the front door."

"You mean the Incas didn't use a road like the one we came up?"

"No. Everyone had to hike what we now call the 'Inca Trail.'"

Pete was reminded of the fatigue he felt and marveled at the physical ability of those people. It was also obvious why the Spanish had never made it up here with horses and armor and cannons.

As they got closer to the ruins, Pete was surprised. It had looked small from up at the Gate. Now he realized it stretched out over an immense area. He knew that archeologists estimated about 6,000 people had lived here at the height of the empire.

Wilson stopped for a moment and pointed at a stone culvert sunk into the ground next to the trail. "This was an aqueduct that supplied the city with drinking water for sixteen fountains."

His constant history lessons annoyed Pete. There wasn't any time left. "We can't get caught in the open here when the sun comes up."

"I know. Can't help it." He apologized and started down the stairway. Some steps were broken and some were missing. Nothing was level except the plaza below. In ten minutes, he stopped again and grabbed Pete's arm. "Look. Over there next to that tower of rocks."

Pete strained through the gloom to see it. "I don't see—"

"There, in the middle is the tower we saw in the model at the museum in Cusco. That's called the Torreon. I think several people are moving around below it. And there's some kind of a van beyond them."

He still couldn't make out anything that small. "Probably Judd." He hurried down the stairway. As the light brightened, he noticed the colors of everything take on a new intensity in the thin air: the green shine of the grass fields, the stones, the yellow gravel spread over the courtyards of Machu Picchu, and the soil in the terraced farms that clung to the edges of the city like envelopes stuffed with brown foam.

They reached a small stone house with a thatched straw roof. Hiding behind it, Pete looked down again. He saw the classic picture of Machu Picchu photographed in travel guides and TV programs. Anita wanted to move on, but he was riveted in place. For so long, he'd imagined this view. Now he saw it with his own eyes.

"Come on," she urged him.

They skirted around the corner of the house and picked their way down through the wide stone staircases. Along the way were platforms of rock that could be used to set up a tripod and camera. In the dusk below, Pete could finally make out the Torreon—the sun temple—and the observatory, the Temple with Three Windows, and a clot of people standing below the Torreon. It was still too dark to identify who they were, but Pete was certain Judd was among them.

They all worked their way lower. The light had brightened to the point they had to crouch behind the numerous stone walls. Alleys and steps led in all directions. It would be easy to get lost here without some light.

Cab whispered, "I think we can hide above the Torreon. See those walls?"

Pete followed his outstretched arm. Like a maze, the spaces between the walls zigged back and forth. About one hundred feet behind the Sun Temple, he spotted a low wall. It would give them cover while still allowing them to peer over it. They crabbed their way toward it, trying to keep quiet in spite of the loose gravel. They had to reach it before the sun brightened and exposed their position.

By 7:10, they had almost reached their hiding spot, but the first rays began to glow around a peak to the east. "Cerro San Gabriel," Anita said. "Come on! Hurry."

The first beams streaked out from the left side of the mountain. Pete and Anita tried to run while crouched over. It was difficult, and their feet scraped the path, the sound echoing along the walls. They took a turn to the right, went down five uneven steps, turned to the right again, and skirted around a corner to the left. "Almost there," Anita hissed.

The sun continued to rise above the top of San Gabriel. It glowed like a halo around the darkened peak.

They slid on their butts into a space behind the low wall and flopped onto their backs. They both breathed heavily but smiled at each other at their success. Cab came crashing in right behind them. By 7:20 the beam of sunlight had traveled toward the flanks of Machu Huayna, lighting it up. It shone bright green, and clouds trailed from the peak like large dirigibles still tethered to their night fastenings. The light turned and rolled toward them, moving with authority because nothing could stop it now—as it had done for centuries.

The air warmed, and Pete took a moment to sip from his water bottle. He noticed the swarm of insects that dipped toward them from out of the darkness. The cloud hovered as if looking for the best place to attack.

"Mosquitos," Anita said. "You won't feel the bites, but if you aren't covered, you'll see the results later in dozens of bloody spots."

Although he was sweating, Pete rolled down his sleeves for protection. Coming from Minnesota, he knew the power of mosquitos well.

Cab turned around and inched his head above the stone wall. "Watch the window in the Torreon. Since it's the equinox, the light should shine directly through there. That's what the Incas designed this for. It marked one of the holiest times—and places—for them."

Pete lifted his head and found the window, still shrouded in gray light. By 7:20 the sun burst completely from above San Gabriel. It seemed to hover for a moment, as if pausing before the full force of the light would reassure humans, once again, of new birth in this holy spot.

A wave of warmth spread through Pete's chest. He took deep breaths. Something was overwhelming him. He blinked to maintain clear sight and realized the spiritual aspect of the sensation. For a moment, it all came together for him. His inability to understand people, to become close to them, lacked a spiritual dimension. He'd missed that for all these years.

He found Anita studying his face. "You okay, Pete?"

"Yeah, yeah. I'm really okay."

He turned back to the Torreon and squinted while watching. A faint square of light appeared on the stone inside the curved wall. Pete sucked in his breath. Cab had been right; the historical record had been right; Judd's calculations had been right. He stared as the rectangle brightened until all four sides of the window appeared directly on the wall.

Within a few minutes, the outline of the window sharpened, with no shadow. When Pete commented on that to Cab, he said, "It's an ancient special effect. The Incas angled the frame of the window to concentrate the light there. We don't know what importance the square of light held exactly, but—"

"Down there." Pete almost shouted. "Look, down there beyond the Torreon." His eyes traced the beam of light backwards, from the window across the jagged tops of the ruins to the flat space spread below. In the perfectly straight line from the sun to the window, the clot of people they'd seen earlier moved into action. Even after the sun rose higher and the special effect through the window disappeared, the people remained along the former line of the sun across the ground.

The large panel truck rumbled forward. A sign on the side read *Pesca del Mar*, and it pulled a machine behind it. The machine had three metal legs with wide feet at the ends. A structure that looked like a praying mantis rose above the legs to curve back toward the ground, and a small seat perched behind that. The legs were orange, but the structure was black, with a bucket that resembled a mouth at the end.

The van stopped, circled, and backed the machine into place, precisely along the line where the sunbeam had fallen.

The men shouted to each other. One measured the distance from the Torreon to the group. Two others approached the machine. They distended the legs to balance it on the ground, and one of them mounted the seat. He kept jabbing his finger toward a spot on the ground. A small gas engine fired, and Pete could hear it chugging.

As the light grew, Pete could see what he'd come for—Judd Crowe. Judd squatted above a spot on the green field. He stretched a white cord in a trapezoid shape around pegs stuck into the ground. When he finished, he stood and nodded at the machine operator. The engine growled with a deeper voice as the arm of the structure rose. The bucket opened like a hungry animal's mouth, and the operator inched it down to the surface.

"Judd!" Pete yelled and stood up. He couldn't help himself. All the effort and time and danger to find Judd overwhelmed Pete.

Anita and Cab tugged at his pants leg. "Down. Get down," Cab ordered.

"I'm going to get that son-of-a-bitch."

"Yes, but not now."

"I want to slug him in the face after what he's gotten away with."

"Later. Get down."

While Pete shouted, a man from below had looked up. He appeared to be searching to determine where the voice had come from.

"They're probably armed," Anita warned. "Get down."

"If I don't stop him, who will?" Pete folded his legs and sat down.

"Castillo. Remember, he's got officers with him," Cab said.

Pete looked at him. "But where is he? Judd will have the treasure and be gone by the time Castillo gets here. It'll be too late." Pete started to stand again. Anita pulled him down.

Pete's phone buzzed. "What the hell?" He pulled it from his side pocket, swiped the face, and saw he had a text from his daughter, Karen. "Must be able to get a connection up here." He opened the text and read: *no more time left dad. What is answer? Need your help more than ever k.* Pete felt his stomach rumble, but for the first time, he felt her presence. Reluctantly, he clicked off the phone.

From far behind them, they heard men shouting. Pete looked up toward the Sun Gate and saw Agent Castillo and two men following him. They picked their way down the steps on the trail like they were knee replacement patients. At that rate, they'd be too late.

Pete stood and decided: he had to stop Judd before anyone else got there. This was personal for Pete. "Come on," he yelled to Wilson. "Castillo won't make it." He swung his legs over the stone wall and skirted around buildings to climb down the long stairwell that ran alongside a high wall.

Cab and Anita followed along the stone steps behind him. "Stop, Pete. Wait for help," Anita yelled.

Pete ran and leaped from one step to the next. He felt the sun burn into his skin, unfiltered in the high altitude. He almost tripped, grabbed for the wall, balanced, and kept going down. "Judd! Don't move, you son-of-a-bitch." He reached a terrace of short grass, picked up speed, and jumped over the edge onto another set of steps. This site was better than a Stairmaster for exercise. The walking stick he still carried, looped around his wrist, banged against the side of his thigh.

Judd looked up and followed Pete's progress. Judd didn't move as the men around him continued to dig. Some were on their knees with small shovels. One man began lifting wooden boxes from the back end of the panel van.

In a few minutes, Pete reached the dig site. He stopped a few inches from Judd. "Do you know what the hell you've done?"

"Hey, Leftenant. Thought we'd meet eventually. That's the point —I know exactly what I'm doing. For hundreds of years, people have searched for the Inca treasure, but none of them put it all together like I did." Judd's face glowed in the bright sun.

Anita rushed up to Pete's side. She was breathing hard. Cab followed.

Pete yelled, "You asshole. Why did you send me the card? Do you have any idea all the shit I've gone through?"

"Sorry, boss. At first, I was in deep trouble and thought only someone I could trust—like you—could help. Why the card? It's the only form of communication that can't be hacked. After all, we worked together to get out of that shit in Afghanistan."

Pete's face flushed hot at the mention of Afghanistan. "But then you disappeared and faked your death."

"Had to. Those Chinese gangsters don't like to be double-crossed."

"How'd you manage to fake it and your cremation in Quito?"

Judd smirked. "Easy, if you've got enough money. I paid off the fake cops and the guy at the mortuary. That's the point—if I've got enough money, I can do anything. This little dig will give me everything I need."

From high up on the trail he'd just passed, Pete heard the scrape of stones as Castillo and his men came closer. Pete saw one of them trip and tumble over two steps. The group stopped for the man.

"I don't care. You have to finally pay for your crimes. No more cover-up or lying—I made the biggest mistake of my life with you in the Middle East. I'm here to make you face justice for that. Besides all this crap, you're guilty of murder."

Judd took a step back as if he knew Pete could carry out the threat. "You're standing on top of one of the greatest lost treasures in the history of the world. And I found it. The constellations lined up exactly for the measurements, and the light beam identified the edge of the burial site. The Incas believed all these were holy, so it only made sense they'd choose a location that coordinated with all these cosmic events to hide their greatest possession. I was able to break the Inca Code and find this spot."

"But what about the electric company? The hack on their computers?" Anita said.

Judd looked at Anita, and his face screwed up. "Who's this?"

Pete started to say a journalist. He hesitated and said instead, "A friend." He felt her hand on his arm.

"Whatever. I had to lock down the site to keep everyone out of here. I practiced shutting down the electricity a few times to make sure my calculations and software worked." He grinned. "They did."

"How will you get the treasure out of here?"

"Two of the largest drones I could rent in the country are going to be here in a few minutes."

From off to the right, Pete glimpsed a group of men running toward them. One was Oswald Lempke.

Pete stepped closer to Judd. "Why? Why the hell did you do it?"

"Hey, Leftenant, you know me from way back when we were getting our asses shot at in the Middle East. I swore if I ever got out of that, I'd make sure I got rich and never had to do anything I didn't want to do. Besides, this was the greatest challenge of my life." He bounced twice on his toes. Behind him, the machine, a DR towable backhoe, chewed into the soft ground, biting at chunks of earth to lift them up.

Pete felt all the frustration and anger boil within him. He lashed out at Judd with a front snap kick, an *ap chagi*, that was designed to knock him down without killing.

The men at the dig saw it, dropped everything, and reached for Pete. They pinned his arms to his sides and wrestled him to the ground. Two others reached for Anita before she could squirm out of their grasp. Another one grabbed Wilson and threw him ahead with Pete.

Judd stood up slowly, rubbing the side of his chest. "You can still fight. I was hoping you'd understand and maybe even join me. But it's obvious that's not the case. I even sent you a text, warning you to get out. Too bad. It's nothing personal, Leftenant." Judd nodded at the men and turned back to the dig.

One of the men twisted Pete's arm up behind his back in a painful crunch. A second man patted down the sides of Pete's body until they found the holster. They removed the Glock and threw it off to the side. Then they forced him to stumble toward the edge of the terrace. He thought of the walking stick, still looped around his wrist. But with his arms pinned, he couldn't reach it to use as a weapon. Pete stiffened his legs and dug his heels into the ground. It didn't work, and he inched closer to the edge. Within two feet of it, Pete felt nauseous. The drop went straight down for thousands of feet, past granite and a few branches of hardy trees. A cool wind blew up from the valley and wrapped around Pete's legs.

Anita stood next to him, Wilson on the other side. He refused to go over without a fight—he owed it to them to try and save anyone he could.

Behind him, he heard shouts. The sound of the engine died.

Judd called out, "About time. I didn't mean to—"

Two pistol shots echoed back to Pete from the stone walls behind the dig site. The men on either side of him dropped their grip and turned to run away from the dig. Pete ran back to the site. Oswald Lempke stood there with a gun in his hand. Judd Crowe sprawled over the corner of the fresh hole in the ground. Bright red blood stained the dirt beneath him.

"You?" Pete said.

"I had to get rid of him."

"Get rid of him?"

"Simple. I want it all for myself, and I didn't want to share with him."

"You knew what he was doing?"

"Oh, yes. We were the original partners in his company, although I was the silent one. I let him do all the heavy work. Once I was convinced he had found the treasure, I decided to move in and get rid of him. After all, he had betrayed me by shutting down the power and locks in order to keep me out. I had to blow the entrance door to get in with my men. It was either Judd Crowe getting the treasure or me. He had too many liabilities." Lempke smiled briefly. "After all, you and everyone else were looking for him."

Pete stumbled backward and almost tripped over a stone jutting out of the ground. Bright sun burned into his head, and he felt faint. He gasped for breath. "But, but—"

"I'm sorry, Pete. I had to maintain the charade. You have to admit that I gave you several warnings to leave and go back to Minnesota. But you wouldn't take my advice."

"I couldn't leave."

"As I hoped you would." Lempke glanced up the hill and saw that Castillo and his men had resumed their march down the steps. "We don't have time for any more talk." He waved the gun toward the edge.

"Over there." Two of his men muscled Anita beside Pete again, and the group stumbled toward the precipice. Cab was next to them. Oz followed.

Pete felt like he'd been punched in the chest. His mind clouded, and he couldn't think. He knew he should fight, use his training to overwhelm the men, but he couldn't act. So many people had betrayed him. He'd trusted Oswald Lempke—even against his better judgment—only to have him turn. Part of his brain urged him to fight for his life, but he couldn't.

Until he thought of Anita and Cab. He might go over the edge, but not them.

He realized the walking stick still hung around his wrist. The men were so confident of their power, they'd forgotten to disarm him of that. His brain clicked in again. *Fight.* But a walking stick? Against two armed thugs? How ridiculous.

They all reached the edge and stopped. Once again, vertigo overwhelmed Pete, and he swayed back and forth. He felt Anita molded along his side. She was crying. Pete thought of the color of her hair and her nascent ambition that was soon to be extinguished before it bloomed into success. He thought of how much Anita reminded him of Karen.

Pete said, "How is this going to end, Oz?"

"You can jump, we can push you both, or I suppose I can mercifully shoot both of you."

"I have a choice?"

"Yes. It's nothing personal, Pete. Besides, I can get rid of a snoopy reporter at the same time. Always hated you people." Oz directed his words at Anita.

She twisted from the grasp of the man holding her and spun around. "Go to hell!"

"No, you will."

Pete turned also. "I'll make the choice." His thoughts sped up. Could he stall long enough for Castillo to get here? No, Pete would have to act now. He grasped the handle of the walking stick hanging behind his leg. "My only request is that when you shoot, you get close enough so you don't miss."

A noise from the left interrupted them. Pete looked in the distance to see a second group of men charging toward them. They were all Asian. They must have come through the gate that Lempke's charges had blown open earlier.

A dark look passed over Lempke's face. He jerked his head, ordering two men to peel off to face the new threat. That left only one man with him. "I promise not to miss." Lempke took three steps toward them and raised the gun.

Pete whipped the metal stick from behind his leg and slammed it into Lempke's wrist. He screamed, and the gun jumped out of his hand. It tumbled over the edge in a glinting of silver as it fell out of sight. Startled, the man next to Pete paused long enough for Pete to raise his right leg and execute some snap kicks. These were designed to kill. The leading edge of Pete's foot smashed into the man's chest above his heart, and he crumpled into a heap on the ground. Pete swung to the other side to face Lempke. With a fury Pete kicked, missed, and watched him dart to the side.

Pete spun around and crouched with his legs bent in preparation for another strike.

Lempke stood with his back to the edge and held out both hands in front. "You can't blame me. Think of the riches sitting right there. I'll share them with you. Millions of dollars, Pete. Maybe billions!" His face dripped with sweat, and his thin hair was plastered over his forehead.

"I don't know who I'm more angry with—you or Judd. No way." Pete tightened the muscles in his back in preparation for a final kick to send the son-of-a-bitch over the edge. But he hesitated. Then Pete decided to wait for Castillo. Pete's body twitched as he relaxed the taut muscles.

Lempke must have thought he was about to be hit, because he flinched, stumbled backward, and pitched over the side. His arms cartwheeled, unable to get a grip in the thin air. His body sagged in the middle like an uncooked loaf of bread as it plummeted down, while his pale skin contrasted against the green jungle below. He didn't even scream.

Pete's stomach lurched as if he'd gone over himself. He sighed with sadness at the end of the man who was now a tumbling body that grew small against the immensity of the rain forest.

Anita screamed from behind him.

Pete whirled around and found himself facing yet another enemy. Xiong Lo stepped from between three armed Asian men. Pete had prepared for this moment. He half-expected them to look like Ninja warriors, but instead they looked like pale versions of Peruvians covered in colorful striped blankets. They whipped the ends around their shoulders to reveal the Type 95 automatic rifles they all carried. Pete knew the weapon. Chinese made, it used a small caliber bullet of 5.2 millimeters designed to mushroom upon impact with a human body. Pete, Cab, and Anita would be dead before their bodies hit the ground.

Lo smiled with yellow teeth as he came closer. "So, you finally found Mr. Crowe. Good work; you led us right to him. We have that to thank you for. Our investors will also be grateful for us to finally get a return on our assets." He glanced back at the dig site, turned, and smiled. "Our biggest return yet."

"Let her go," Pete demanded. "I'm the one who came down here and caused you trouble."

Lo turned his eyes toward the edge of the city and squinted into the bright sun. "Such a beautiful place," he sighed. "As holy to these ancient people as the Forbidden City is meaningful to our people." He paused for a moment. "I have no more time to waste on you two. We must hurry." He spun around and hurried toward the dig site, followed by one of the men.

The two remaining men crowded toward the three. Pete dared to raise his eyes to travel across the jagged walls of Machu Picchu, up the uneven steps, and spotted Castillo coming closer. Pete had to delay in any way he could, because he knew if they walked to the edge a third time, their luck wouldn't hold.

These men were more careful than Lempke's thugs and stayed out of striking range. Pete had dropped the walking stick in the earlier fight.

"Judd's calculations are wrong," Cab shouted to Lo's back. "I'm an archeologist. I know he's close, but he's wrong. Don't you want to get *all* of the treasure?"

Pete glanced at him but couldn't read anything in the shadows below his furrowed eyebrows.

"I know what I'm talking about," Cab yelled.

Lo stopped. His short ponytail bobbed as if were a curved finger tapping on Lo's neck while he considered the temptation of Wilson's words.

Pete reached for Anita's hand beside his. She grabbed him with her damp palm.

Lo turned around but didn't come back to them. "What do you mean?"

"The measurements don't take into account the history of the Incas. They would never bury everything in the same spot, just like they didn't plant only one crop. They diversified in all their activities. It doesn't make sense they would abandon that practice when it came to their most important possessions."

Lo squinted again and started toward them. "You come with me. Chandler, you and the woman stay to go over right now."

Pete watched Lo push Wilson in the back toward the site. The two armed men closed in on Pete. At first he thought they'd march them to the edge, but then Pete realized they wouldn't even waste the time. They'd simply shoot both of them on the spot, then dump them over. They remained too far out of range for Pete to reach with even his best assaultive kick. He saw the black banana clip that curved down from each rifle when they raised their weapons to point at him.

Chapter Thirty-Two

September 22, Thursday morning

Damp air swirled around Pete, carrying the smell of jasmine from the jungles below. The sun reflected off the polished walls of the temple. He shifted his eyes away to try and find Cab. He was lost somewhere on the immense field of grass.

Most people thought, when faced with a loaded gun and someone about to shoot you, the thing to watch was their eyes. From his military training, Pete knew to watch the trigger finger. When it twitched, you had a millisecond to duck—if you could. He looked at one trigger finger after another. They remained poised without moving.

He heard shouting from behind them, coming from the dig. He sensed movement but couldn't make out what had happened. The gunmen in front of him dropped the barrels of the automatics slightly. Could that mean he'd be spared? He shifted his sight to their faces and saw them both look up into the sky behind Pete. Then he heard the whirring sound.

One man dropped his gun to the ground as he raised his arm to shield his body. From behind Pete, a large object swooped down and almost hit the man. Pete ducked to the right and rolled onto his side across the rocky outcrop. He looked up to see a drone hovering just above them.

It was an immense quadcopter with four spinning propellers that were mounted horizontally around a central engine. They looked like four red bicycle wheels attached to each other. Inside the wheels, the blades spun so fast they were invisible. The drone rose and dipped as if it were drunk. Pete realized it was out of control but somehow still airborne. It almost slammed into the gunman on the right. He squatted and duck-walked backward to avoid getting hit. His partner split off in the other direction. In their fear, they dropped the automatic weapons.

Pete was outside the area covered by the drone, so he could regain his feet and assess what was happening. Judd had said two drones were coming to transport the treasure. They must have been called in by Judd's dig team, and this was the first one. By itself, it was harmless, but since it was out of control, it flew erratically and seesawed back and forth over the area.

That gave Pete an idea. He ran to the last spot Judd's men had been and found one of the remote controllers on the ground—probably abandoned by them in their haste to get away. Pete scooped it up and positioned it between his hands. He hoped it was the correct one programmed to fly this drone.

He'd never piloted a drone, but his time playing a few video games with Tim gave Pete some confidence. The remote was a square black box with two toggle sticks on either side and two sliding switches in the middle. The toggles probably controlled vertical and horizontal movements—what pilots called the ailerons, elevators, and rudders. There was a button at the bottom labeled "Blind Panic Return Home."

He turned around to face the quadcopter. It still wobbled over the edge of the cliff. Pete touched the right toggle stick, and the drone immediately leaped upward. When he pressed it in the other direction, the drone dropped quickly. *Okay. Just a little lighter touch.* The left toggle moved the drone toward him.

Pete could see the quadcopter didn't have any weaponry on it, but it carried a large webbed sack underneath that probably contained some kind of a net for retrieval of the Incan objects. Could he use the drone as a weapon?

He knew he had seconds to make this work, if it was going to work at all. He could hear the shouting again and sensed the Chinese coming closer to him. Pete pushed the button on the right forward, and the drone shot across the field. Must be a throttle. Even if he couldn't fly it accurately, his idea might work. Pete backed off on the button.

He spun around to find the Chinese lumped in a tight group at the edge of the dig. Lo gripped Cab by the arm as he pointed to areas on the ground. One of the men had spotted Pete. He got down on one knee to make himself a smaller target and set the remote on the flat rock before him. With both hands on a joystick, he imagined he was playing Tim's video game.

Pete still wasn't very good at it, but at least he could get the drone to generally fly where he wanted. It wobbled and dipped erratically, but Pete managed to get it moving in one direction—back from over the edge of the cliff. He reversed the sticks' direction and caught his breath as the drone charged toward the dig. He pushed on the throttle button, saw the quadcopter leap forward, and tried to direct it toward the group at the dig. At the first pass, the drone flew too high and the Chinese didn't move. One of the gunmen looked up at the passing drone, laughed, and started to march toward Pete. He must have figured out Pete's plan, because he squatted as he came forward.

The drone swooped around in a wide loop, wasting time, and Pete remembered to use more of the left joystick. He lined it up as best he could, gave it more throttle, and this time, cued the left stick. The drone plummeted like a hawk that had seen a mouse on the ground and attacked the group. At the last minute, Lo ducked and barely avoided getting hit. One man stumbled backward and fell into the hole behind him left by Judd's workmen.

Still, the gunman angled toward Pete.

After the drone lifted up and took another loop into the air, Pete directed it back like a boomerang. He managed to control it with a tighter turn and set it on a course to intersect with the people on the ground.

Before the drone reached them, a second gunman broke off and started toward Pete. There was nowhere for him to escape. Behind Pete the cliff dropped off and to either side. He could only run alongside the cliff, as the two gunmen had cut off any route that would allow him to go toward the ruins.

Even though he was kneeling, Pete felt his body go slack. His muscles seemed weak and unable to move. Only his hands still functioned as he worked the joysticks. It seemed to take forever for the drone to bank to the left, drop sharply, and skim just above the Chinese. They ducked and scattered.

But the gunmen were unaffected since they had left the group. The first one dropped to his knee. He propped his elbow on his upraised knee to steady the weapon for the shot. Pete thought he could see the black hole in the barrel and even down the barrel to the brass bullet waiting to come out. He heard the crack of the gunshot.

The rock formation in front of Pete was not big, but it gave him a little cover. Ignoring the drone, he flattened himself behind the Inca handiwork, and it saved his life—for now. The bullet crashed into the rock, exploded bits of it into the air, and left a cloud of dust hanging before Pete's face.

In films, the bad guys always fired dozens of bullets from their automatic rifles. In real life, Pete knew that practice was inaccurate and seldom worked. Instead, the gunman took his time sighting again, probably taking a deep breath and letting it out slowly as he fired again. The bullet must have gone high, because nothing struck the rock or Pete.

Pete discovered that he could remain down behind the cover, which protected him from the angle of the shooter. At the same time, he could still operate the drone. He was getting better with practice. He brought the drone around quickly, lined up his own shot, and dropped it at the Chinese.

This time the drone struck one of the men, knocked him over, and caused the others to run back to the ruins to seek shelter among the protective stone structures. If it wasn't for the two gunmen, Pete would be able to escape.

He wondered where Anita was and if she was safe. When Pete peeked over the rock in front of him, he saw the second gunman had advanced closer—and at an angle that exposed Pete to a new line of fire. Pete was completely exposed to this man. He lay on the ground in the classic prone position, propped both elbows on the ground, and sighted directly on Pete.

If Pete shifted to the other side to avoid the coming shot, he'd be exposed to the first shooter. He felt naked and held only a plastic box in his hands for his defense.

He must take out the shooter. Pete toggled the sticks, watched the drone obey the commands, and jammed the throttle as far forward as it would go.

The quadcopter jumped ahead, streaking out of the sky toward the ground. Pete dared to lift his head for a better look, adjusted the sticks slightly, and at the last minute, the drone slammed into the back of the second shooter. It bounced off him and wobbled into the sky again. Pete hoped the blow hadn't disabled it.

The shooter's head was flat on the ground, and his weapon lay motionless beside him.

Pete brought the drone back from over the cliff to return toward the first shooter. He lined up the shot, confident it would work again. But before Pete could direct the quadcopter down on the shooter, he jumped up and ran away toward the entrance of the ruins. Pete shouted out loud and found his voice was only a hoarse squeak.

He crawled onto weak legs and surveyed the ground in front of him. The Chinese had dispersed. Pete could see three of them crawling up the steps of the wall around the temple. Two others headed for the entrance. Where were Lo and Wilson and Anita?

Pete held onto the remote control as he ran toward the dig. He reached it in a few minutes, looked around, and saw a crumpled form at the bottom of the hole. Cab. Lo had disappeared.

Pete stumbled down the incline, reached Wilson, and rolled him over. He was covered in dirt, his clothes torn, but his eyes fluttered open. When Cab saw Pete, his smile broadened to stretch across his blackened face. "More fun than the museum ever was." Tears leaked over his cheeks to mix with the dust on them.

"You're okay," he assured him.

Wilson nodded. "Where's the woman?"

He heard shouting and the clumping of shoes on stone. Pete helped Cab stand and climb out of the hole. From up on the rock walls, Agent Castillo jumped down the steps toward them. He was followed by a team of men with drawn weapons.

Not again, Pete thought. *Now what?*

"Stop right there," Castillo ordered.

They stopped. Pete felt totally drained. He couldn't fight anymore.

Anita popped up from behind one of the rocks near the dig. She ran to Pete's side. Without thinking, he reached for her hand and held it tightly.

"You're under my jurisdiction from now on," Castillo said. He stopped in front of them, out of breath.

Pete said, "We had to get up here before Judd Crowe got away. I tried to explain it to you, but you wouldn't listen."

Castillo paused and frowned. He thought for a moment. "What do you mean?"

"Let us explain," Anita said. She separated from Pete.

Between Pete and Anita, they were able to tell the entire story. They told him what had happened on the field with Lempke and the Chinese.

As they continued, Castillo started to nod. "I saw that. Clever idea to use the drone to—"

"Where is it?" Pete spun around. He searched across the rolling green grass. There, out by a low stone wall, the quadcopter teetered on its side, red wheels glistening in the sun, propellers whirling slowly as if they were tired from all the work.

Castillo's voice brought Pete back to the group. "Under all these circumstances, I may choose to be lenient with the three of you—provided you give me a full and detailed statement of everything you know."

They agreed.

"If you help me to assemble the evidence to prosecute these criminals, I will recommend that you be released from confinement."

"Confinement?" Pete croaked and looked at Anita to see her face blanch white.

Chapter Thirty-Three

Confinement, luckily, was brief and consisted of riding in Agent Castillo's Mercedes down into Aguas Calientes. Pete and Cab sipped thick Peruvian coffee in the conference room of Castillo's hotel while a smartphone sat between them, recording their long statements. Anita sat off to the side. She was mad that Castillo had not let her make contact with her editor.

It took several hours. Pete didn't think he could sit up much longer without some rest. They finished and asked Castillo if they could go.

He pursed his lips like he was thinking carefully. He had taken his own notes in the leather notebook with Mona Lisa on the cover. With a smacking sound, he opened his mouth. "It is a very close question. If I didn't have the authority I do, you would be going to a Peruvian court now, and probably to prison." He waved his arm across the table. "But I will be generous. After all, this evidence is so powerful, I am confident my agency will succeed in not only prosecuting these people, but may even recover some of the missing funds. It is unfortunate that the actors involved, Crowe and Lempke, are dead."

The mention of their names jolted through Pete's body. He hadn't expected the reaction.

Anita slumped in the chair. She roused herself and said, "We appreciate your kindness. But we have given you everything we promised from the beginning, right?"

"Well, I suppose you have."

"And I will only run the story after you have pursued the suspects and money."

"That would be appropriate."

"There is no reason to keep us here any longer." She sat up and bored her eyes into Castillo's.

He pushed the notebook away from him. It sat, opened to a yellow page, on the polished wooden table. "I am certain I have enough evidence —primarily obtained through my own efforts. Your information is helpful. And yes, I can authorize your release."

Pete could see Anita suppress a smile when she glanced at him. He stood first, anxious to get as far away as possible from all of this. Cab sighed and stood up.

Within two days they had driven back to Cusco, flown to Lima, and caught a late flight to Quito. He'd said good-bye and thanked J. Cabot Wilson, who couldn't stop smiling at the adventure he'd just completed. Pete checked into the NH Royal Quito Hotel, where he collapsed into bed for ten hours of much-needed sleep. In the morning, he received an e-mail from his ex-wife, Barbara, and a text from Karen.

Crunch time, the text warned.

Pete didn't respond to Barbara's e-mail, but he thought about Karen. Really, she was the only family left that meant anything to him. He thought about Anita and her extended, interlocked family, so common in Latin America. He'd learned from her about the value of that network. In some ways, Americans were so anxious to leave home, pursue careers in distant cities, and forget aunts and uncles because people were too busy to remember. Pete had vowed to be different from his father. Now was the time to do that. Crunch time.

He texted back to Karen: *I'll loan the money to you and Tim. I can transfer it right now, but you must agree to a repayment schedule that I'll include.*

He hit the send button and sat back at the desk in the hotel room. It was still a gift, but at least he'd put it on a more professional level and treated her like an adult with adult responsibilities in running a business. More importantly, he would preserve their relationship. He looked forward to sitting on the upper deck at the stern on the boat when he got back to Minnesota, talking with Karen and Tim.

The memory of Oswald Lempke and Judd Crowe stabbed him again. The shock of their betrayal was still raw. He had to get over it somehow. Perhaps focusing on Karen, Tim, and their efforts would help heal the pain. In a crude way, Pete had accomplished what he'd come to do: Judd Crowe had been brought to justice.

As if to interrupt his thoughts, Anita texted him. *Can you meet me in the cloisters of the church of St. Francis in a half hour?* He agreed.

In twenty minutes, he'd taken a cab and stepped into the long hallway that surrounded the beautiful gardens behind the church. Palm trees soared into the air to explode in drooping branches like spent fireworks.

Trimmed bushes sparkled in the midday sun, and the air smelled fresh, clean.

Pete looked out at the peaceful setting from underneath the arches of the loggia. The hall was wide, and between huge paintings that hung from the walls, a few wooden benches offered a rest for the penitent and the pensive. He saw Anita sitting on the second one.

When she spotted him, she jumped up and came toward him. Her white smile contrasted with her dark skin. She wore slacks and a thin alpaca sweater. Black hair hung down to her shoulders and cupped each side of her face. Pete noticed again how attractive she was.

Anita came to him and reached up with both arms to hug him closely. He could smell her sandalwood perfume and felt the warmth of her face against his. "Nice to see you in a safe place," he told her.

"Funny what a shower and a little sleep will do for a girl. Are you hungry?"

He shook his head.

A monk dressed in a black cassock shuffled forward as he passed beside them. His head was bent in concentration.

"When are you going to run the story?" Pete asked.

"My editor wants to go right now. Print and TV both."

"Castillo?"

"They're not afraid of him. I've given them the details; now it's up to CNN Latinoamerica to take over. I've done my job."

"And they appreciate your work?"

She grinned. "Of course. In a short time, I'll be posted to Miami."

The thought of her being in the US stirred Pete for a moment. He discarded the thought. "I'm sure you'll do a great job."

"Yes. It's scary to think that I'll finally face a bigger world."

"Is that the end?"

"I don't know yet." She looked up at him while her eyes searched his face. "Do you ever get to Miami?"

Pete took a breath. "Not too often."

She pulled back from his arms and stood back a foot as if to get some perspective. "I've come to like you, Mr. Chandler."

He shrugged. He didn't like the way this was going. "Good luck to you."

"Can you stay in Quito and work for the bank here for a while? At least until I move to Miami?"

Maybe he could, but he also wanted to be back with Karen and his boat. "I don't think so." He fudged the truth.

Her eyes dropped.

"Anita, I respect you in many ways. And I could be happy here, but my family . . . You taught me the value of that. I can't abandon my daughter again."

Anita took a deep breath. Her chest rose against the sweater. She reached into her purse, pulled out a card, and handed it to Pete. It was heavy stock with a rough texture. "It's the address and official e-mail of the office in Coral Gables. Maybe you can visit." She swung her head toward the gardens and stood still. From over her shoulder, she said, "You're always welcome."

"Is that because I provide a good story wherever I go?"

She nodded and turned back to him. "You do seem to find trouble. Walk me out." She reached for his hand. They moved along the hall toward the floor-to-ceiling wooden doors of the church. They were worn with age to a deep black color. One side stood open, and the sun peeked in to create a triangle of light on the stone floor. Anita led him through it.

Without another word, she dropped his hand and left quickly. Pete watched her shoulders dip from side to side as she walked away. Shiny hair bounced across her back in rhythm to her stride. Her shoes were red and fell silently on the worn stones of the ancient courtyard.

The next evening, Pete sat in the narrow seat on the flight that would take him to Miami and then on to Minneapolis. People squeezed through the aisles and hefted carry-ons into the overhead bins. He closed his eyes to the chaos.

So many women lost in his past. When would he stop and stay with one? The closest he had come was Julie, the congresswoman, but she'd left him on her own terms that were permanent when she committed suicide. Pete's family was in Minneapolis, and he wanted to be there.

He turned to look out the window at the fading light of day. Something Oswald Lempke had told him rattled around in his head. He turned over his memory, trying to recall what it was, when it came to him. Lempke had told Pete about his mother and how Pete had lived with her in San Francisco for a few years as a child. What was that about, and was his mother still alive? It gave him hope of finding more family.

With the sun dropping below the western mountains, Pete saw the shadow of the plane on the tarmac. It stretched out until it looked like it would reach the volcano, smoldering Antisana, on the far side. Pearl-colored smoke twisted up from the cone. The vapors looked like dancing ghosts that disappeared into the dark blue sky.

If you enjoyed this story, please go to Colin Nelson's website at www.colinnelson.com to sample his other work.

CPSIA information can be obtained
at www.ICGtesting.com
Printed in the USA
LVOW12s0846160418

573622LV00003B/231/P